Emily Kerr has been scribbling since she learnt how to write. She is based in Yorkshire.

She can generally be found with her nose in a book, or hunched up over her laptop typing away, though she has been known to venture outside every so often to take part in various running-based activities.

Her novel *Take a Chance on Greece* won the Jane Wenham-Jones Romantic Comedy award at the Romantic Novelists' Association Awards in 2023.

www.emilykerrwrites.com

instagram.com/emilykerrwrites
facebook.com/emilykerrwrites

Also by Emily Kerr

Duvet Day

Meet Me Under the Northern Lights

Take a Chance on Greece

Her Fixer Upper

The Typo

READ BETWEEN THE LINES

EMILY KERR

One More Chapter
a division of HarperCollins*Publishers* Ltd
1 London Bridge Street
London SE1 9GF
www.harpercollins.co.uk
HarperCollins*Publishers*
Macken House, 39/40 Mayor Street Upper,
Dublin 1, D01 C9W8
This paperback edition 2025

1

First published in Great Britain in ebook format
by HarperCollins*Publishers* 2025
Copyright © Emily Kerr 2025
Emily Kerr asserts the moral right to be identified
as the author of this work
A catalogue record of this book is available from the British Library
ISBN: 978-0-00-865347-7

This novel is entirely a work of fiction. The names, characters and incidents portrayed in it are the work of the author's imagination. Any resemblance to actual persons, living or dead, events or localities is entirely coincidental.

Printed and bound in the UK using 100% Renewable Electricity
by CPI Group (UK) Ltd

All rights reserved. No part of this publication may be reproduced, stored in a retrieval system, or transmitted, in any form or by any means, electronic, mechanical, photocopying, recording or otherwise, without the prior permission of the publishers.
Without limiting the author's and publisher's exclusive rights, any unauthorised use of this publication to train generative artificial intelligence (AI) technologies is expressly prohibited. HarperCollins also exercise their rights under Article 4(3) of the Digital Single Market Directive 2019/790 and expressly reserve this publication from the text and data mining exception.

To librarians, champions of books and the heart of a good community

Chapter One

'Good morning, beautiful. I wanted to leave a quick message to wish you a happy day. I fell asleep thinking about you last night and woke with your name on my lips. I can't wait until you are with me in more than just my dreams. Sending love your way.'

I played the voice note, savouring the way Brian's rich, deep tone made me feel all tingly and desirable. No previous boyfriend had ever called me beautiful, and their first thoughts on a morning had been either more coarsely expressed or merely caffeine-related. I pulled myself up. It was way too soon to be referring to Brian as my boyfriend, even in my head. As for the 'beautiful' thing, well, given that we were yet to meet in person, it was probably best not to let myself get carried away by that either. But there wasn't any harm in listening to the message again, right?

'Blimey, Kat, is that Hot Brian?' My colleague Moira burst into the break room at full volume, making the most of not having to speak in the librarian-quiet voice we were encouraged to use when on duty in the reading rooms. She took the phone out of my hand and tapped the screen so the voice note started from the beginning again. 'Maybe I should try online dating. I love that gravelly sexy thing he's got going on there. It's giving me serious Alan Rickman vibes, although I appreciate that's probably more a my generation reference than yours.'

'It's okay, I know who he is. He was Professor Snape, and didn't he play Colonel Brandon in that nineties adaptation of *Sense and Sensibility*? The original and the best, if you ask me. He came across as gorgeous and thoroughly decent. And his voice was yummy, just like Brian's.'

'I was thinking more of his role in *Die Hard*,' said Moira with a grin. 'I should have known there's not an Austen adaptation you haven't seen. Colonel Brandon in that film oozes sex appeal, *and* behaves like a gentleman, what more do you want in a man? It sounds like you've finally got yourself a keeper, which means we need to come up with a stronger nickname for him.' Moira flung herself down onto the sofa next to me, but her voice remained at the same volume. I smothered a grin at my friend's exuberance. 'Hot Brian's a bit generic,' she continued. 'It always works better if there's some alliteration in there, don't you think? But B for Brian doesn't really give many options. What's his surname?'

'James. Brian James.' I realised I'd subconsciously mirrored the way James Bond famously introduces himself. It seemed appropriate. Brian had sent me a picture of himself in full black tie and he definitely could give 007 a run for his money.

Moira frowned. 'Hmm, I'm still not getting inspired. It's very'—she paused—'ordinary.'

'It's solid. Dependable. And "a rose by any other name" and all that. Shakespeare knew what he was talking about,' I said, feeling the need to defend Brian, even though I'd admittedly experienced a few pangs about it myself in my more superficial moments. Brian James as a moniker wasn't quite up there with proper hero names like two of my personal favourites, Fitzwilliam Darcy and Edward Rochester, but as my sister Caro was always telling me, this was real life, not the rarefied world of fiction.

'And remind me again, what does Mr Brian James do?'

'He's a soldier. An officer, if we're being really precise.'

Moira fanned herself. 'I don't know how I forgot that. *An Officer and a Gentleman*, I hope. I hereby christen him the Sexy Soldier. Sexy Soldier, Lovely Librarian.' She wolf-whistled. 'I'm sure we've got that book in the romance section somewhere. One of those ones with the rippling biceps on the cover. I mean, there's other stuff on there too, but that's where one's eyes tend to be drawn.'

I laughed. 'Brian is sexy, it's true. He hasn't quite got the rippling biceps look, but he's not far off. In fact, he's way out of my league. I've no idea what he sees in me. I keep thinking he's going to message me and say he's made a horrible mistake, or worse, stop contacting me altogether.'

Moira folded her arms and frowned at me. 'Now listen here, young lady. That's enough of that talk. Women suffer enough with other people putting them down, without doing it to themselves. You are what I believe is known as a real catch. You're lovely inside and out. It's time you started believing that. *He's* lucky to be chatting with *you*.'

I felt my cheeks grow hot. The reality was that I felt lucky Brian seemed so invested in our budding relationship. I was too used to being the 'filler girl' – good enough to date, but not good enough to consider anything long-term with. I cleared my throat and mumbled my thanks.

'Once more, with feeling.' Moira was clearly not going to let this go.

'Thank you, Moira,' I said sheepishly.

'Hmm, I guess that'll have to do for now. Now remind me, how do I look at his profile pictures again? I could do with a bit of eye candy to brighten up the day.'

'You can't give me the feminist spiel one minute, then start objectifying men the next,' I teased. 'Besides, they're for my eyes only.'

'Oh, they're *those* kind of pictures, are they?'

My cheeks grew even hotter. 'Absolutely not. Brian is one of the good guys. He would never dream of sending a dick pic.'

Moira chuckled. 'Your face. It's just too easy to wind you up. Go on, let me have a peek.'

Her exaggeratedly pleading expression was so ridiculous that I relented and showed her the latest snap of Brian. He was in full work mode, calmly directing the distribution of aid parcels in a village recently hit by an earthquake. When I'd asked him about it, he'd been adorably reticent, clearly worried that he'd come across as virtue signalling or showing off to score dating points, but that had only made me fall for him even harder. Who wouldn't love a man who used his strength to help the vulnerable? And yes, I admit, he looked damn fine doing it too: powerful stance, strong jawline and kind eyes, all wrapped up in one.

'Quite the Hollywood hero. And does the Sexy Soldier have a friend? Just keeping my options open, you know.' Moira waggled her eyebrows suggestively.

'I'll ask him when we meet up,' I said, knowing full well that Moira had recently celebrated her thirtieth wedding anniversary to the man she'd been with since her first year at university, and was as likely to join the dating apps as I was to start a bonfire using books as fuel.

'And when exactly is that joyous occasion going to occur? You've been chatting for a couple of months now, haven't you?' she pressed. 'I know half the fun is in the anticipation, but you've got to get to the really good stuff before long. I'll spare you the "in my day" speech, but suffice to say, the hubby and I did not hang around.'

I sighed. 'Mr Moira wasn't answerable to the whims of the military. Brian's on deployment for another month, but I'm trying to look on the bright side. The anticipation is making things more exciting, and at least this way we get to build a proper connection with each other. He'll be back in Oxford before I know it.'

It had been a big disappointment to find out early in our conversations that Brian was on an extended overseas deployment. The main reason I'd joined this particular app, SO Ox, was that it promised to help people in my home city find their Significant Other through a mixture of virtual interaction and in-person events. That, and the fact that all members were carefully screened before they were allowed to join, which significantly reduced the chances of encountering the time wasters and ghosters who'd so disappointed me on my previous tentative foray into online dating. While my sister might tease me about my enduring love of the 'happily ever after', so common in the books I adored, I refused to believe that it was impossible to find in real life too.

'I know Brian will be worth the wait,' I added. 'I have a very good feeling about where we're heading. Besides, there's something even more romantic about getting to know a person through emails and voice notes. I'm sure Jane Austen would have been into it if she lived nowadays.' I glanced up at the clock and took a final gulp from my now-cold mug of tea. 'Right, I'm going to love you and leave you. The front desk calls, and it's nearly time for the lunch rush. You know what Mondays are like.'

'Go forth, recommend those books, and solve those people's problems. I'll be back once I've had my biccies,' said Moira, saluting me as I exited the room.

That was another thing that had drawn me to Brian when we'd first started exchanging messages. Instead of going down the librarian stereotype route, the way so many sleazy guys had done on the previous app I'd tried, asking if I wore glasses (I prefer contacts) and whether I kept my hair back in a tight bun which they could take out (always sounds like the recipe for a headache), he'd immediately told me about his favourite books (self-improvement ones, definite green flag) and asked me about mine (even bigger green flag). I normally worried about coming across as too much of a book-ish buff, but with Brian I'd been confident from the beginning that I could be my authentic self, just like he was with me.

I quickly surveyed the library floor as I walked back to the front desk, waving to a couple of regulars, and making a brief superficial assessment of those I didn't recognise. As expected, there was a growing queue, and the comfy sofas which were placed near the entrance were also full. Mondays were always the busiest day of the week. Problems escalated on Sundays when we, along with most other services, shut down, leaving those in difficult circumstances even more desperate for help as a new week started. What many didn't appreciate was that librarians are social workers, counsellors, and problem-solvers, all tied up in one. Where else could people come and sit in the warm for hours for free, borrow books and access the internet without charge, or even just use the loo without having to buy something? The books were what had drawn me to the profession nearly five years ago now, but the people we supported were the ones who kept me from pursuing a potentially more lucrative career. From the harassed families who couldn't navigate the complexities of the child tax credit system to pensioners who were being left behind because they didn't have smart phones, we helped them all, filling out forms, mopping up tears, listening, caring, and simply being there for people. There was so much more to my job than stacking shelves and putting books in alphabetical order. Although I did a fair bit of that too.

'Hello, welcome to Oxford Community Library. I'm Kat, how can I help?'

The next few hours passed in a blur of navigating job applications, arguing with the council about why it wasn't right to exclude Gavin and his beloved dog Robin from the homeless hostel, and recommending the spiciest of reads for library favourite Doris, who outwardly looked like she'd be the type to disapprove of an unmarried couple even holding hands.

'I do love a bit of demon action,' said Doris, after she'd finally settled on her choice. She slipped the well-thumbed volume into the sleeve she'd crocheted with innocuous-looking flowers and bumble bees. 'These reads help me save on the heating bills.' She let out a throaty chuckle which made me smile in response.

'I can imagine,' I replied. 'How many followers do you have for your bookstagram account now?'

'Oh, I don't really keep tab. Maybe something approaching ten thousand?'

'That's amazing, Doris. That's way more than this library has on its socials. I need to ask you for some tips.'

'Always happy to help.' Doris lowered her voice. 'Actually, I was wondering if I could ask your advice about something, pet?'

'Of course, what's on your mind?'

She glanced around to make sure nobody was listening. 'The thing is, I keep getting all these direct messages from people claiming to work in the publishing trade. They're offering me advance copies and proofs, but I don't want to be handing out my home address to any old so-and-so, even if it is flattering that they think a review from me is worth having. I've done my due diligence, and they look like they're legitimate, but they're always saying on the news that you can't be too careful, and well, you know what happened before...' Her voice tailed off.

I nodded, experiencing the familiar ache of sadness and anger that I got whenever I thought about the reduced circumstances Doris now lived in, after an unscrupulous financial advisor she used to date persuaded her to go against her normally savvy judgement and invest her pension in a scheme which had promised high returns and delivered precisely nothing. She always appeared cheery, but she'd once confided in me that she feared she'd never recover from the damage the incident had inflicted on her self-esteem.

'That's very sensible; you're doing the right thing.' I reached across the counter and squeezed her hand, wishing once again that I could fix things for her. 'But getting an advance copy of your favourite author's next book is not to be sniffed at. Tell you what, why don't you give them the library address? We'll happily take delivery of the books here, and if any dodgy types try asking for information about you, I promise we'll protect your privacy to the last.'

'I don't doubt it, Kat pet. Thank you for the offer, I'll have a think about it.' She straightened up and I recognised her armour of positivity going back on. 'My to-be-read pile is already fairly hefty as it is. My son keeps muttering about needing to get the floor strengthened if I bring any more books home. Hence hiding my borrowings with the craftwork.'

'Oh I...'

'You thought I didn't want people to see what I was reading?' There was a glint of amusement in her eyes as she spoke. 'I'm long past the age of caring what strangers think about me. If they want to get sniffy about other folk's reading material, that's up to them. They're the ones who are missing out on some brilliant tales.'

'You're absolutely right. I wish more had your attitude.' While I never judged reading choices, I knew I was definitely guilty of caring too much about other people's opinions of me. I vowed to try to follow Doris's example.

'Mind you, it does amuse me the contortions folk get themselves into when they're trying to read over my shoulder on the bus. One of them nearly fell into the aisle on the way here.' She chuckled. 'Tremendously unsubtle. I ended up writing down the name of the book and the author on a piece of paper and handing it over. The man pretended he didn't know what I was referring to, but I noticed him tucking the note into his breast pocket as I got off at my stop. You'll probably see him in here before long. I made a point of telling him that the library could get hold of any book.' She checked the contents of her rucksack. 'Right, I'll probably be back tomorrow, pet. The Wi-Fi here is so much better than at mine, and I enjoy the company. I need to make the most of it before you lot grow sick of the sight of me and ban me for my own good.'

'We wouldn't dream of it. It wouldn't be Oxford Community Library without you. And I promise I'll chase up that inter-library request. I'm sorry it's taking so long.

I'm told the system hasn't quite recovered from that attempted cyber-attack the other week.'

'That's very kind. I hear it's you we've got to thank for making sure the effects weren't any worse.'

I pulled a face. 'You give me greater credit than I'm due. The IT bods were the ones who drew up the drawbridge and stopped the hackers getting any further. Quite why anyone would want to attack a library, I do not know.'

'Ah, but you were the one who flagged the dodgy phishing email in the first place,' said Moira, joining the conversation. 'She's very switched on, is our Kat.'

'That she is,' said Doris. 'See you later, ladies.'

We waved her off, marvelling at how she managed to keep upright while carrying her heavily laden rucksack full of books.

'Good old Doris, it's always great to see her,' I said. 'I wonder if she'd be up for teaching one of the seniors' social media sessions? She clearly knows way more than we do.'

'Undoubtedly, and they'd probably be far more likely to do what she tells them,' said Moira with feeling. 'Give me the little ones' story time any day. Toddlers might act like tiny drunks, but they're still easier to control than the bunch of retired academics from the social media group, who like to turn everything into a philosophical discussion. If I have to debate what Socrates would have thought of TikTok one more time, I shall throw their phones out of the window.'

'Well, it is Oxford,' I said.

'And don't we bloody know it. Right, do you want to do the reshelving rounds? I can hold the fort here,' said Moira, looking around the emptying foyer. 'I think we're over the worst of the rush now, and you'll want to get your legs moving after manning the desk for so long, while I've swanned about looking decorative.'

I playfully nudged my hip against hers. 'It's what you do best. Sure, I'll get to work. If it's anything like last Monday's round though, I'll need an emergency nap before I go to class tonight.'

Moira pulled a face. 'Or you could just go straight home and chill out for a change,' she suggested. 'That suffragette history class of yours sounds a lot more energetic than advertised.'

I laughed. 'I was a bit worried when I first turned up and the tutor told us the full curriculum, but I'm learning all kinds of skills, and you never know when they might come in handy. Right, I'd better get on with it. Give me a shout if the after-school crowd start swarming.'

I sorted the returned books on the trolley, quickly checking them over for any damage that needed repairing. I tried to restrain myself from reading the blurbs, but inevitably succumbed and ended up setting aside a few volumes to borrow. I told myself that having a good knowledge of the books we had in stock was a key part of my role as I set off pushing the trolley between the shelves.

'Either you or that trolley is in need of some serious WD40. I thought libraries were meant to be quiet places.'

I glanced across to the source of the criticism. The guy was taking up an entire table between the business books stacks, papers strewn everywhere, leaning his chair back on two legs like an overgrown teenager, while resting a sturdy pair of boots on another seat. I shuddered when I noticed bits of soil and goodness knows what else already accumulating on the upholstery beneath his soles.

I fixed him with my best stern librarian expression. It wasn't often that I brought the big guns out, but he looked too robust and sure of himself to be classed as one of the waifs and strays who needed delicate handling, and I didn't like the insult implied in his comment both to myself *and* the institution.

'The trolley may need a little bit of TLC, but she's got a lot of life left in her, and we prefer to direct our budget towards other areas.'

'And how about you? Similar to the trolley?' He grinned in what I'm sure he thought was a charming manner.

I tried to ignore his teasing, but his presumptuous cheekiness got the better of me.

'We do try to keep a peaceful atmosphere in here, but if you want a completely silent environment, I suggest you try one of the university libraries. Although I don't think they've managed to eliminate the noise of rustling pages, which might prove exasperating to you. Or you can always head upstairs to our designated quiet reading room, although again, it's probably best to expect some form of general ambient sound in there, people daring to breathe and the like.'

'General ambient sound,' he echoed back to me. 'So, what you're telling me is that there's nowhere for a bloke to enjoy a bit of peace and quiet in this city? I thought librarians were famously good at shushing.'

'Would it work, if I tried it on you?' I couldn't resist retorting. I never normally talked back to patrons, especially new ones, but he'd started it and was looking irritatingly amused by the exchange. 'We prefer to make this library a welcoming environment for everyone. For everyone who behaves themselves, that is. Speaking of which, would you mind kindly removing your hooves from the furniture? Someone else might like to sit there today, and I'm sure they won't appreciate having to sully their clothes with whatever disgustingness you've obviously been wading through.'

'Hooves, you say'—he paused and glanced at my name badge—'Kat ... Fisher? Are you implying you see something devilish in me?' His eyes sparkled in that grating way good-looking men sometimes have when they know they're attractive and, therefore, can get away with stuff others wouldn't.

I cursed my slip of the tongue. I'd obviously spent too long talking romantasy with Doris.

'Hooves, clodhoppers, whatever you'd like to call your oversized boots, which should be firmly on the ground rather than messing up my furniture. Unless there's a medical reason for your feet to be elevated, of course?'

He shook his head.

'In which case, kindly remove them from the chair.'

He looked like he wanted to say something in response, but my increasingly stern expression obviously made him think better of it, and he did as he was told.

'Thank you. No! Don't do that, you'll make it worse,' I said in a slightly louder whisper, jolting him as he was pouring water onto a tissue. No doubt he intended to scrub at the muddy marks on the seat, but some of the water missed its target and ended up on his lap instead.

'Great, now look at the state of me,' he said with a sigh.

I smothered a smile. 'At least it didn't get on your papers, or worse, the library's books. I'm sure if you sit quietly in the corner here, no one will see it. Or you could go and make use of the hand dryers in the cloakroom, but be warned, they're noisy, and you'll have to make your way across the library. Of course, we're a judgement-free zone here, so don't worry about everyone staring at you.'

'Judgement-free zone? I hadn't noticed,' he muttered, turning his back and shuffling his chair tight under the table so the unfortunately positioned damp patch was out of view.

As I walked away, pushing the trolley, I swear I heard him mimicking the sound of the squeak under his breath, but when I looked back, he seemed to be deeply absorbed in his paperwork.

I had to warn the rest of the staff to keep an eye on him.

By closing time, I was aching all over and debating following Moira's advice to head home and curl up with a book, rather than go to class, even though it would be the last one before the Easter break.

'Fifteen thousand steps today,' called the woman herself as she locked the front door. 'That's nearly a personal record. Let me add it to the sweepstake chart. I *will* win that chocolate.'

The step chart had been introduced by management as an allegedly fun way of promoting our health and wellbeing. Inevitably it had turned somewhat competitive, and the weekly prize of copious amounts of chocolate provided by the previous week's winner rather undid the good intentions.

'Nice work,' I said. 'Let me take a look at mine.'

'You should invest in a smart watch, like the rest of us,' said Moira. 'And you'll have the added bonus of messages from the Sexy Soldier popping up on your wrist.'

I pulled my phone out of my pocket, but all thoughts of checking my step count went out of my mind in an instant.

'Speaking of... Brian's sent another message.' I felt my insides glow just seeing his name on the screen. He was always so attentive and thoughtful, even though the nature of his job made it difficult for him to be in touch as often as he said he wanted to be.

'When? What's he said? Tell me everything,' Moira said, bustling over to peek at my screen.

'Give me a chance to read it myself,' I chided gently. 'It was sent an hour ago. I must've missed it. You can't hear anything over that squeaky trolley. Remind me to have a look at it; it was attracting complaints earlier.' I couldn't help glancing towards the business section where the chairs were still askew thanks to their earlier occupant.

'Never mind work. What has the Sexy Soldier got to say for himself?'

'You're right.' Why was I letting the annoying guy with the clumpy boots distract me from Brian?

I quickly swiped the message open, read it, then read it again, just to make sure I hadn't got the wrong end of the stick.

'Oh my goodness. Brian's coming home to Oxford. At last.'

My pulse instantly quickened in anticipation as my imagination ran wild with thoughts about what it would be like to finally see him, smell him, touch him…

'And?' pressed Moira, bringing me back to reality.

'And he wants to take me to The Ivy for dinner as soon as he gets back.'

'The Ivy? Fancy. The man has good taste. Although we knew that already, because he's fallen for you.'

'You flatterer, you. His unit's being brought home earlier than expected and he's now due back this Friday.'

'Better and better.' Moira began humming *Let's Get It On* under her breath.

The butterflies started fluttering in my stomach. The moment I'd been dreaming about for weeks was soon to become reality.

'What on earth am I going to wear?'

Chapter Two

I normally didn't bother leaving the library during my lunch break, preferring to eat in the back room, in case I was needed. But with the imminent arrival of Brian, I decided to make an exception. The Oxford Community Library would need to manage for an hour without me while I made an emergency foray to the shops. After staring into the abyss, otherwise known as my wardrobe, and coming up with zero inspiration, I'd spent the last few evenings doing some panic internet shopping. My bank account was taking a beating, especially as I'd forked out extra for fast delivery, but none of the clothes I'd purchased had felt right.

Somehow it had got to Friday, and I still hadn't found the perfect outfit for our first date, hence the last-minute dash to the shops. At least my workplace was handily situated in a side street just behind the Ashmolean Museum and only minutes from a wealth of retail options. After extracting a promise from Moira to summon me back if it all kicked off, I hurried out of the library, crossed the road near the Randolph Hotel and dived into the chaos that was Cornmarket Street. It seemed like half the world and his wife were out and about this lunchtime, making the most of the spring sunshine to enjoy some retail therapy. They all looked much more relaxed than I'm sure I did. The only thing worse than having no date clothes was wearing ones purchased in a panic. The fear was real.

Weaving my way through the crowds, I paused briefly in front of a shoe shop window, before sternly telling myself I shouldn't get distracted by metallic pink Mary Janes with contrast pearl-effect buckles, especially when I didn't have an outfit to match them with yet. Of course, I knew that it shouldn't really matter what I wore to meet Brian for the first time, and that, if our relationship was meant to be – like I assumed it was – I could turn up in sackcloth and ashes and it wouldn't make a jot of difference. But as a matter of personal pride, I wanted to look my best and, more importantly, I knew a good outfit would give me a much-needed confidence boost. It wasn't that I was completely wracked with anxiety about our first date, although there was definitely a jangling sensation of nervousness alongside the dreamy anticipation, but it felt like there was a lot riding on it. We'd been exchanging messages back and forth for a while now, sharing confidences, and opening up to each other in a way I'd never experienced before. It felt like we were developing something truly special. Try as I might not to get carried away, the eternally optimistic voice of hope at the back of my mind kept repeating that Brian could very well be The One, and that many years in the future, the pair of us would look back at this momentous first date and reminisce happily about how it had changed our lives forever. I did not want us to look back and remember how I'd turned up looking like the result of an explosion in a fashion factory.

The decision fatigue hit me properly on the third floor of a department store, weighed down by armfuls of clothes, none of which I liked. There were just so many outfits to choose from, and I didn't have a clue where to pitch my dress level. I didn't want to look like I'd gone to excessive amounts of effort, but equally I couldn't exactly turn up at a fancy restaurant in my current work attire of smart(ish) jeans and Converse, could I? They'd probably take one look at me and refuse entry, then I'd have to ask them to summon Brian over to vouch for me. I really didn't want his first sight of me to be as I was being escorted from the premises by the maître d'.

I wandered aimlessly between the racks of brightly coloured jumpsuits and flouncy dresses, trying, and failing, to picture myself in any of them. The models in the pictures on the walls looked effortlessly chic, the clothing complementing their confident, happy-go-lucky demeanour, whereas I was afraid that these outfits would wear me, rather than the other way round.

'Can I help you?' asked an eager assistant, homing in on my general air of agitation.

In normal circumstances, I would have smiled and beat a hasty retreat, but today I reluctantly acknowledged that I needed all the help I could get and nodded in a slightly dazed way.

'What's the occasion?' she asked kindly.

'It's a first date. But it's a different kind of first date because we've been talking for two months so we're potentially a bit further on than the phrase "first date" would suggest. He's in the military so he's been out of the country for ages, but now he's coming back at last, so it's kind of a big deal. But I don't want him to think that I think it's a big deal.' I spoke so fast that I'm sure some of my words merged into each other. 'Sorry, I bet you wish you hadn't asked.'

She laughed. 'Don't worry, I get where you're coming from. You want to look cool and in control, gorgeous, but without seeming like you're trying too hard. In other words, the Holy Grail of fits.'

My heart sank. Was she trying to let me down gently by pointing out that I needed a miracle? Clearly, I was asking too much. But her next words gave me some hope.

'I got you. I reckon I have the perfect option.'

She bustled around the racks, picking out a sunny yellow tea dress with a delicate white polka dot pattern, and a denim jacket to go with it.

'You can dress it up with heels, or go for more of a smart-casual look with the Converse you're already wearing. They're great, really on trend. Either option, you're guaranteed to hit the right tone.'

'Even for somewhere quite fancy?' I asked.

'Undoubtedly. It's boho chic.'

She sounded so confident, that I found myself believing her. I allowed myself to be shown into the changing room, cringing at the number of mirrors and how bright the lighting was. There was nowhere to hide. I reluctantly removed my shoes, peeled off my jeans and top, pulled the dress on and nervously examined my reflection from all angles. The yellow fabric was a much bolder colour than I'd normally go for, but something about it made me smile.

I experimentally gathered my hair up into a loose bun at the nape of my neck, but then let it free again, remembering the librarian stereotype I so hated. I'd stick with my usual approach of giving it a good brush before I went out and hoping for the best. I'd need to take a little more time with the make-up, of course. Perhaps Moira could help me with my eyeliner, so I didn't mess it up. She was always so elegant with her perfect flicks of kohl extending from her lids.

I turned slowly on the spot and then a little more quickly, enjoying the feel of the silky fabric floating around my legs, then pulled on the jacket and put my shoes back on to get the full effect. Somehow my well-worn Converse looked a lot smarter paired with a dress. And, most importantly, I wouldn't spend the evening worrying about getting blisters or turning my ankle, both distinct possibilities if I went down the heels route.

Maybe, just maybe I could pull this off. But was I getting swept up in the shop assistant's enthusiasm? I needed a second opinion.

Moira answered my FaceTime call on the first ring, almost as if she'd been expecting me.

'How goes it?'

'Good, I think. I reckon I've found the perfect get-up, and I need to see if you agree. Or rather, the assistant found it for me. I've not dared to check the price tags yet, so potentially this call is a bit premature. I really should have considered that before trying the stuff on. Keep your fingers crossed.'

I reached down the back of my neck with my right hand, keeping hold of the phone with my left, and then contorted myself so I could read the tag in the mirror behind me. Maybe a high price was the reason why the assistant was so keen for me to go for this dress.

'Phew, unless my backwards reading skills have failed me, I won't have to eat beans on toast for the rest of the year. Well, as long as I actually do my returns,' I mumbled, correcting myself. 'Probably the less said about them the better. I'm rapidly becoming the postman's least favourite address to deliver to.'

'Stop moving off topic,' said Moira. 'Can we get to the point, please, young Kat? We've established the outfit is within budget, excellent news, hooray and all that, but so far I've seen nothing of it, just a close-up of your face as you pull weird expressions. I'm not complaining, mind, but it's not achieving the object of the call, is it? Stop with your delaying tactics and let me see the thing.'

'Fine, I'll show you now. Excuse the dodgy camera work. And promise you'll give me your honest opinion.'

'When have I ever not?' she demanded.

She had a point there. Moira was blunt almost to a fault, but it was always from a place of kindness. If Moira said I looked okay, then I knew I could believe her. I moved the phone further away and tried manoeuvring it so she could see my full-length reflection. I clearly needed to work on my mirror selfie skills.

'Hold it to the right, you're blocking the key cleavage area,' was her first comment.

I reluctantly did as I was told, feeling even more self-conscious.

'Nice. I can see why the assistant picked it out. That colour shows off your complexion perfectly, and it reflects those honey undertones in your hair.'

Honey undertones? Moira was definitely in a generous mood. I'd never heard my mousy hair described in such a flattering way. I felt myself stand slightly taller, then realised that was probably why she'd said it.

'Polka dots are always a winner,' she continued, 'and you can't go wrong with a denim jacket, date or no date. Practical and perfectly pitched. You look lovely, Kat. Sexy Soldier will be thanking his lucky stars when you turn up looking like that. Outfit very much approved,' she concluded. 'Don't you agree, girls?'

Etta, our student librarian, suddenly popped up on screen, giving an enthusiastic thumbs-up.

'It really suits you, pet,' added Doris, startling me with a close-up view of her tonsils as she seized control of the phone and held it near the end of her nose for a better look at me. 'It's giving definite main character vibes.'

'Thanks, Doris, that's very kind of you.'

'More importantly, how do you feel?' Moira asked in the background. 'Is the whole ensemble secure? That's the real test. You'll want to give your attention to much more important stuff than worrying about clothing riding up or falling down. Or at least, not at the dinner stage.'

I tried to ignore Etta's snigger as I considered Moira's question.

'Everything feels fine, there's no risk of any inadvertent flashing, even if there's a breeze. It's very comfortable, but not in a boring way. I like the way the skirt swooshes,' I said. 'And the colour is really pretty and cheerful. But are you sure it's not too "look at me"? It's a bit bolder than I'd normally go for.'

'And what exactly is wrong with giving off "look at me" energy?' said Doris. 'You're a gorgeous woman going on a date. You shouldn't feel the need to shrink back and hide away. A little bit of self-confidence wouldn't go amiss, if you ask me. The heroines in my books don't get their happily ever after by fading into the background, isn't that right, Moira?'

'Abso-bloody-lutely. They pick up their swords and go after the rippling bicep men. And you could, and should do the same,' said Moira, grabbing the phone back.

I was briefly treated to a shaky view of the library and noticed immediately that the man with the muddy boots was back taking up half of the business section again, head apparently deep in a dusty volume. I really hoped he hadn't been eavesdropping on the conversation. He'd be bound to make some snarky comment about my outfit paranoia, when I got back, given my criticism of his footwear earlier in the week.

I lowered my voice, just in case, although it was probably far too late.

'Okay, you've talked me into it, but I think it's probably for the best to leave the sword behind on this occasion. I'm not sure the good folk at The Ivy would be very happy about me turning up with one. Thanks for the pep talk, I don't know what I'd do without my library ladies.'

'Don't you dare hurry back,' said Moira. 'Everything's under control, and it would do you the world of good to take a proper break for once in a while. Lord knows the library owes you one.'

As the clothes shopping had taken less time than I'd feared it would, I decided to stop by the make-up counter on my way out of the store. I'd normally avoid it at all costs, intimidated by the pristine perfection of the staff behind it, but the brave, bold, clothes-shopping Kat could do whatever she put her mind to, right? Moira could still help me out with a few touch-ups at the end of the day, but I might as well take the opportunity to see what the professionals could do for me.

There was obviously a very effective staff grapevine in the shop because the guy behind the counter seemed to know exactly what my situation was and just what I needed, both from the make-up perspective and the confidence-boosting sense.

'I still want to look like me,' was my opening gambit, slightly concerned that he might be about to style my eyebrows in the same dramatic way he wore his own. I mean, he looked fabulous, but as with most things, I preferred a more subtle approach. There was no way I could carry off such a strong brow.

'You've got it. Relax, enjoy the experience.'

I submitted to fifteen minutes of blending and primping, and found I did just that. It was actually quite nice to be the one being taken care of for a change. I was feeling distinctly Cinderella-like, except it was my own credit card taking responsibility for my transformation, rather than a benevolent fairy godmother.

'Okay, you can look now,' the make-up artist said eventually, passing across a small hand mirror.

I stifled the nerve-induced reflex to deviate into another fairy tale and recite 'Mirror, mirror on the wall', and looked critically at my reflection.

'Oh,' I said, surprised at who I saw staring back at me. I did still look like Kat, but a Kat who was well-rested and bright-eyed, groomed, but not within an inch of my life, basically me but on a really, really good day.

'Wow, thank you,' I said, admiring the subtle smoky eyeshadow. The one time I'd tried something similar for work, I'd spent the day fielding questions from concerned library users about my apparent black eyes. Maybe if I came back another day, the make-up artist would give me a tutorial on how to recreate the look myself. 'You're seriously talented. You've worked miracles in no time at all.'

'There was nothing to it. You've got good bone structure, and that's half the battle.' He smiled back. I was sure it was what he said to all the people who sat in his chair, but it was still nice to have it directed at me, even if it wasn't true.

I emerged from the shop weighed down with products the make-up artist had recommended, but feeling lighter in myself as thrilling anticipation took over from the nerves.

Inevitably, the first person I encountered on my return to

work was the muddy boots guy, although today at least the trendy leather loafers he was wearing looked reasonably clean.

'I thought Fridays were generally dress-down days,' he said, immediately clocking the swish branding on my shopping bags. Or maybe it was the makeover he was commenting on.

'Fridays are actually "don't bother the staff" days. In fact, some people could do with following that rule every day of the week,' I responded defensively.

He held his arms up in mock surrender. 'Only making conversation. Enjoy your evening when it comes.'

That mischievous glint was back in his eyes. Clearly, he had overheard my conversation with Moira and the gang. I decided it was better to ignore him. He was obviously trying to get a rise out of me, and the best way to respond to that was to walk away.

I carefully hung up my new dress and jacket in the break room, and then resumed my position at the front desk. Even though it was my turn to do the trolley round again, Etta insisted on taking over.

'We don't want you getting a sweat on and worrying about your make-up coming off,' was all she had to say on the matter.

I whiled away the next couple of hours by making polite conversation with the library visitors, trying, and failing, not to get carried away with my daydreams of how the evening would go. How would Brian and I greet each other? A kiss on the cheek at the very minimum, I thought. Would I have to stand on my tiptoes to reach? His profile had said he was over six foot, and he looked tall in all the pictures, but you never knew for sure until you met a person. Maybe I should have gone for the heels after all? But then I'd have been worried about stumbling and making a fool of myself. No, the Converse were the right choice. And surely, when I finally met Brian, all thoughts about my personal appearance would go out of my head in the joy of being in his presence. How would it feel to be so close to him at last? Would he slip his arm around my waist as we left the restaurant? What might happen after we'd shared a meal? My stomach gave a funny little flip of anticipation.

I'm ashamed to admit that I wasn't giving my full attention to the job, but I hoped that my normally diligent and dedicated service would balance things out. The news of my impending date must have spread around the rest of the library because I was on the receiving end of a lot of indulgent smiles, and visitors were far more patient than usual when I asked them to repeat their questions, which I had to, frequently.

With just an hour until closing, my phone pinged.

'Brian's messaged to say he's landed safely. We're in the same country at last,' I swooned, holding the phone to my chest, transferring my desire to be close to him to the device which had connected us in the first place.

'He's going to be cutting it a bit fine to get here, isn't he? What time did he say he'd booked the table for?' asked Moira, ever practical.

'Eight o'clock. He was flying into London, so I'm sure he'll make it with bags of time,' I replied confidently. 'You know what the military are like. Everything will run with precision.'

'Well then, as you're practically vibrating with excitement, why don't you go and change into your glad rags? I can keep an eye on things here while you do. It's so quiet I've already let Etta go home.'

'Are you sure? I'm not going to abandon you before closing, but it would be nice to get myself sorted. It won't take me long to change, but I think I'll feel more relaxed if I've got a bit longer to get used to wearing the new dress,' I replied gratefully.

'Off you pop. If we get a move on while we're locking up, we can go for a quick drink before your date. That'll definitely make you feel more relaxed.'

'Maybe,' I said, vowing to stick to the soft drinks. From experience, Moira always bought doubles when she roped me into having a so-called quick drink. It was more accurate to say that the 'quick' aspect was how fast the booze went to my head.

I emerged from the break room twenty minutes later feeling like a woman transformed. My pretty dress swished as I walked, my make-up was on point, and the extra squirt of the expensive perfume I reserved only for the most special of occasions, meant that I was surrounded by a delicately fragrant floral cloud. The world looked like a brighter, better place. Even spotting that irritating guy in the business section with his feet back up on a chair couldn't put a dent in my good mood.

Three steps from the front desk, my phone buzzed again

and I came crashing down to reality as I read the baffling message.

> *Hello beautiful, I'm so sorry, but I'm having cash flow issues and I'm stranded in London. I wouldn't ask in normal circumstances, but I'm desperate to see you. Could you arrange a bank transfer to cover my ticket back to Oxford, and a few essentials I need to buy after being out of the country for so long? I can't wait to hold you in my arms at last. Brian xoxo*

Chapter Three

I stared at the text, trying to make sense of it. April Fool's Day was last week, so it couldn't be some kind of strange joke. The message seemed so out of character, and such a weird request. What had happened to cause Brian to be stuck in London without funds? Surely the army wouldn't bring their soldiers back to the UK and then leave them with no means of getting home? It seemed totally illogical. Suddenly my pre-date nerves morphed into something much more uncomfortable. He couldn't be ... I mean ... I hadn't been ... had I? I instantly fought back at the questions, trying to ignore the disloyal thoughts which were swirling around. This was Brian I was wondering about. Brian who'd sent me cute voice notes from the start, who'd always seemed so keen, so open.

Well, open to a degree, the warning voice reminded me, incidents which I'd previously dismissed flooding into my head. Despite many promises that we could FaceTime, somehow it had never happened. The excuses had always seemed so reasonable and plausible – bad signal, a sudden change of orders, prioritising internet time for the lower ranks – all things that had seemed to be a normal part of army life, things that were ultimately beyond his control, despite his best efforts. He'd never gone into details about exactly where he was deployed, but again that hadn't seemed out of the ordinary. I didn't know anyone in the armed forces, so of course I had a lot to learn about the way things worked. But now I thought about it, surely only special forces soldiers were so particular about not revealing their whereabouts? And Brian had always made out he worked as a regular officer. To be honest, if he'd told me he was a member of special forces, that would have set the alarm bells ringing much earlier.

I hated that I was thinking this way, but the more I examined our interactions, the more concerned I grew. I tried to argue with the warning voice. Maybe this was just another manifestation of the insecurity which was always present at the back of my mind, niggling away at me, telling me that I wasn't worthy of being loved. Why shouldn't an attractive man like Brian fall for me? He'd explained his sudden need for funds. And it wasn't like he was asking for a huge amount of money. He was probably exhausted after travelling, and at the end of his tether. Wasn't it natural for him to reach out to someone he cared for, someone he trusted to help him? Was I such a selfish person that I couldn't assist the man who might turn out to be my soulmate?

But why wouldn't he approach his friends or family first? And what if asking for a relatively small sum was a test to see how gullible and easy to manipulate I was, the voice of reason countered, louder still. What if I transferred the money, then he encountered another 'problem' which would require more funds, and prevent him from arriving at our dinner date? If one of our library patrons had come to the front desk asking my advice on an identical situation, wouldn't I have immediately intervened and advised them not to give the scammer a penny?

Okay, I'd acknowledged the elephant tramping noisily around the room. Scammer. The very word made me feel hot with shame. Was that what Brian was? Had I been played from the start? Or was I paranoid and overthinking the situation? I needed an impartial opinion.

'Moira, would you take a look at this?' I asked, hurrying over to where she was reshelving books in the business section. I still wanted to believe that I was wrong, to have Moira look at the message, laugh at my suspicions, and send me happily on my way to enjoy my first date.

'What's the matter? Have you had bad news?' she said the second she saw my face.

'Maybe,' I said, still hesitantly. 'Probably. But I'm really, really hoping I'm wrong.'

The chair which the annoying guy was sitting on creaked.

I lowered my voice, hoping that it would make it harder for him to eavesdrop.

'What do you make of this message? Do you think...' I hesitated to say it, not wanting to plant ideas in Moira's head. 'Do you think he's a fraudster?' The words came out a lot more bluntly than I'd intended.

Moira started reading the message out loud.

I hissed at her to be quiet, but it was too late. Muddy Boots wasn't even bothering to hide his interest and was sitting up straight watching me carefully. I deliberately turned so he was out of my line of sight.

'I'm being ridiculous, aren't I? I've been single for too long and I'm totally overreacting to something completely normal, aren't I?' I said, ashamed at the note of desperation in my voice.

'Oh Kat,' said Moira. The sympathetic tone was nearly my undoing. I hugged my arms to myself, wishing that I wasn't standing there in a ridiculously bright yellow dress, with my glammed-up face, posh perfume, and all ... for what? To be made a fool of. I felt so silly. Why was I even surprised? Of course it had been too good to be true that a gorgeous guy like Brian would even take a second glance at someone like me. I swallowed hard, fiercely ordering my eyes to stop watering. If I cried over this, I'd appear even more pathetic.

To my shame, I tried one last plea.

'Brian isn't a romance fraudster, is he? Is he?'

Muddy Boots stood up and sighed.

'The red flags are so big I'm amazed you've not been knocked over by the strength of them blowing in the breeze. I guarantee the guy's not even called Brian to start with. He'll be using an alias to avoid getting caught.'

Way to make me feel even more stupid.

'Right, and what exactly qualifies you to make such a confident statement?' I bit back, turning my rage and devastation towards him. I would never, ever speak to a library user in such a rude tone in normal circumstances, but everything I thought I knew had been turned upside down and I felt utterly mortified that I'd allowed myself to be taken in. Having it pointed out by a complete stranger was the final straw.

He smiled and held out his hand to introduce himself. I scowled back, refusing to shake it. How dare he be so insouciant at such a time? Was he enjoying seeing me being made a fool of?

'I'm Leo Taylor and I'm a police officer.' He cleared his throat. 'I was a police officer.' Even in the midst of my emotional turmoil, I couldn't fail to notice the shadow which passed over his face as he corrected himself.

'You *were* a police officer?' It was cruel of me to emphasise the past tense, and I regretted it almost instantly, but I remained silent. If I made a fuss about it, it would make it into a bigger deal. Besides, he wasn't exactly going out of his way to be sensitive to me, despite my obvious distress.

'Yes, in CID. That's the Criminal Investigation Department. It means I was a detective. I dealt with a fair few romance fraud cases, and that message is a textbook example of one. Let me guess how it went.' He rocked back on his heels and started checking things off on his fingers. 'He's been building up your trust over the last few weeks, all the time seeming to be really keen, but somehow he's never been able to meet? And now he's stuck in a terrible situation, and only you can help him? I'll tell you what happens next in this scenario. You transfer a train fare to his bank out of the goodness of your heart, and before you know it, your account has been drained and lover boy has run off to target his next victim. Or worse, he sticks around, always with an almost plausible sob story, and you become his human cash machine. You take out loans, sell your possessions, always eager to help this man who has the worst luck but who says he loves you so very much, and when he's squeezed you dry, finally he'll move on to his next victim, leaving you alone, in debt and feeling like a fool.'

I already felt like a fool, and far-too-full-of-himself ex-police officer Leo Taylor was making me feel so much worse. It was such an effort to fight the sob building at the back of my throat that my nose started running. I sniffed, desperately wishing I had a tissue handy. Was I doomed to lose all dignity in front of this man? I hated what he was saying, and I hated the fact that he was probably right even more.

He reached into the pocket of his jeans, pulled out a packet of tissues and offered me one. I really didn't want to accept anything from him, but the only other option was snot dripping on the floor. Reluctantly I took it and blew my nose vigorously, mopping up a couple of traitorous tears that were slipping down my face. The tissue came away with smears of dark mascara on it. Great. The last thing I needed was to go full-on panda.

'Thanks,' I said half-heartedly, then tried to claw back some poise. 'And there's no need to mansplain the concept of CID to me, or how fraudsters manipulate people. I do live in the real world. I'm not a complete idiot. Despite appearances to contrary,' I added under my breath. It was just that whenever I'd thought of romance scammers, I'd pictured the way their victims were portrayed in the media, as defenceless, lonely people, desperate for connection at any cost, their vulnerabilities blinding them to what was so obvious to everyone else. Not a person like me. Or maybe I was still deluding myself. Maybe I wasn't so different from that stereotypical picture of a victim.

'Whatever you say,' said Leo. 'I just would have thought, with a name like yours, you'd have been more aware than most of the possibility of scammers, Ms Kat Fisher, isn't it? I remember your surname from your badge.'

He knew full well that was my name. Had he been waiting for an opportunity to stick the knife in? If I'd been cross before, now I was properly seething. I'd chosen to be called Kat rather than Katherine at primary school because of my complete devotion to the caretaker's pet, a bundle of fluffy kindness who'd always had an incredible knack for knowing when a shy small child like myself was in need of some feline love and friendship. Of course, by the time I hit senior school, there was more awareness among my peers of the concept of catfishing thanks to the MTV show, but it was too late to change my nickname, and to be honest, it felt strange to be called anything else. I'd endured years of comments, from gentle teasing to the downright nasty. To have that kind of cruelty shoved back in my face again when I was already so low was the final straw.

'Right, that's it. You need to leave the library.'

Moira nudged my elbow, but I ignored her gentle warning. I stared Leo down and gestured angrily at the door, in case he hadn't got the message.

He spread his palms as if trying to appease me.

'But it's not closing time quite yet. I meant no offence, I promise you. I was only trying to make a joke to lighten things up.'

'You think what I'm going through is a joke? How dare you? You insensitive, insufferable...' I lost the power of speech as another angry sob threatened to erupt. I took a deep, shuddery breath and attempted to muster what was left of my self-respect. 'It's not closing time, but patrons are reminded that the library reserves the right to ask them to leave if their behaviour is deemed to be disruptive or problematic to others,' I quoted from the terms and conditions which every prospective member was required to agree to. 'I think that describes your behaviour exactly, so I'm throwing you out. Please leave. Right now.'

Ex-copper, ongoing nuisance, Mr Leo Taylor looked surprised by the vehemence of my tone. Perhaps he didn't expect such a show of strength from a woman who wore frivolous yellow polka dot dresses and allowed herself to be duped by a sweet-talking man online.

'Look, I'm sorry, I really didn't mean to upset you with the catfisher comment,' he said. 'I obviously hit a sore spot. As I said, I was trying to lighten a difficult situation, but I clearly went about it the wrong way. I can only apologise.'

'Any idiot could probably guess that I've been tormented by catfisher jibes for years. And sadly, I'm sure you won't be the last to try such an unimaginative approach to having a go at me.' His look of sympathy and sorrow riled me still further. I could have kicked myself for letting the words out of my mouth. Time to save face. If I could.

'The only thing that is difficult about this situation is your refusal to exit the building,' I said, cursing the continued wobble in my voice. 'Are you going to make me summon security?'

I was completely blagging it now. The Oxford Community Library's budget didn't stretch to having security staff. It was down to Moira and me and the rest of the librarians, and frankly, most of us were of the firm opinion that the pen is mightier than the sword. If things got bad, we were expected to zip round the corner and throw ourselves on the mercy of the Ashmolean Museum's security team, or if it was really, really bad, the protocol was to lock ourselves in the break room and wait for the police to arrive. Thankfully, it had never got to that point. Most of the challenging situations we'd faced had been defused by a cup of tea and a sympathetic ear. I was definitely not in the mood to offer either of those options to this particular man, although I could do with them myself.

'Okay, okay, I'll go quietly.' He started packing up his things, slowly and methodically.

'A little bit of speed wouldn't go amiss,' I said, tapping my foot on the floor as he took an unnecessary amount of time to save a document and shut down his laptop.

'Come on, Kat,' said Moira quietly. She was being a supportive friend by not openly challenging what we both knew was totally unreasonable behaviour on my part, but I recognised the subtle caution not to push the situation any further.

Leo hesitated as he packed away his final notebook.

'You shouldn't feel ashamed, you do know that, don't

you?' he said. 'These people prey on kindness. Don't beat yourself up about it.'

'I'm quite capable of managing my own emotions, thank you very much,' I said, an ill-timed tear making a liar of me.

He shrugged. 'Sure. Have a good weekend, both of you.'

He walked out of the library with an easy stride.

'I hope he doesn't come back,' I said.

'I'm certain, if you apologise when he does return, you'll get over your embarrassment,' said Moira.

'That's not what...' The sentence trailed off. I knew exactly what she meant.

I plucked helplessly at the yellow dress. 'Do you mind if I go and take this off? I can't bear to wear it any longer. I feel so stupid. Who did I think I was kidding, making myself a laughingstock with a silly polka dot dress and prancing around with a starry expression? Why did I even take the tags off? Do you think the shop will still take it back without them?'

'Oh, come here, love,' said Moira, and before I knew it, I was wrapped in a bony bear hug. Moira was never very touchy-feely, so this was a big deal, and I think that was what finished me off.

'Why am I such an idiot?' I blubbed. 'I can't believe I fell for it. It was so obvious from the start. Why on earth would a sexy soldier be interested in someone as ordinary as me? That kind of thing only happens to characters in books. Of course he was trying to scam me. I'd even turn out to be a disappointment to him on the financial front, especially now I've wasted so much money getting ready for a fake date.'

Moira gave a final squeeze then held me at arm's length.

'I'm not quite sure where to begin with unpacking all that. I don't think you're in the right frame of mind to believe me if I start extolling your many virtues, so I'm not even going to bother. As to returning that beautiful dress, absolutely not. I forbid you to do it. What's more, you're going to leave it on and we're going to go out and have a lovely meal, exactly as you were planning. Well, maybe not exactly like it,' she corrected herself.

I told myself to get it together and not fall to pieces again at her act of kindness.

'Nothing like it. Thank goodness. You're the kind of dinner companion I could only dream of. Unlike a certain somebody who deserves a fate which I probably shouldn't be vocalising within the hallowed halls of the library.'

Moira laughed. 'Atta girl, that's more like it. Your fighting spirit will be back before you know it. Right, let's lock up and get going. Pub grub?'

'The perfect salve for a broken heart,' I responded bleakly.

'Your heart isn't broken, love, is it?' she asked. 'I do hope not.'

I took my time answering, thinking about the dreams that had been dashed, the foolish hopes which I'd allowed to cloud my better judgement.

'Perhaps it's better to say wounded,' I said eventually, trying to pull myself together for my friend's sake. 'Definitely badly bruised, although my self-esteem has probably been the worst hit. I'll get over it eventually, I guess. And food will definitely help.' I forced myself to attempt a watery smile, although I'm sure it came out more like a grimace. 'Tonight, I'm going to eat all of my chips, probably half of your portion too, and I'm going to have extra ice cream with my dessert.'

'Good woman. Give me a few minutes to check nobody's hiding in the stacks and trying to camp in here overnight, then we'll get going. You go and touch up your face and give yourself another squirt of that lovely perfume, that'll make you feel brighter. Everything looks better after chips.'

We ended up in The Turf, an ancient higgledy-piggledy pub hidden down a narrow alleyway behind the majestic stonework of Hertford College. Unsurprisingly, given that it was a Friday night, it was packed to the rafters with members of both town and gown communities, everyone shouting over one another to be heard. I hesitated on the threshold, not ready to be surrounded by so many happy people while I was nursing wounds which felt very raw. But I didn't want to abandon my friend when she'd been so kind, and what was wallowing alone at home going to achieve? It would only make me feel even more pathetic.

Somehow Moira managed to secure us a tiny table in a relatively quiet corner, and I sucked down the 'medicinal' whisky and lime that she insisted on buying me.

'I think my throat is on fire,' I said, my eyes watering all over again.

'That's the good stuff for you,' said Moira. 'Kill or cure, that's my philosophy.'

I don't know whether it was the whisky, the bustling atmosphere where nobody knew me, or the trauma I'd just endured, but the tension in my shoulders started to ease. By the time the food arrived, I was feeling almost relaxed.

'It's not Brian himself per se that I'm grieving,' I eagerly explained to Moira as I shovelled in my fish and chips, washing them down with a second whisky, which may have been responsible for my talkative mood. 'It's the possibility that he represented. You know, the potential of the whole 'happily ever after', of having a proper partner for once, and not yet another bloke who views me as 'nice, but not nice enough' to settle down with. I mean I'm completely, totally happy single. No honestly, I really, really am,' I said, realising that with each assertion I sounded more and more like I wasn't. 'But it would be lovely to have someone to share the fun with, you know? Someone who gets me, who I don't have to change myself for, who's there for me, always, as I am for him. Like you and Mr Moira.'

'You know it amuses Rami no end that you refer to him as that,' said my companion.

'I hope he doesn't mind,' I said, suddenly worried that I'd been inadvertently causing offence to my favourite couple all these years.

'Oh no, he enjoys it. He says he's proud to be known as Mr Moira. And I promise you that, one day, you'll find someone who will be equally thrilled to be known as Mr Kat.'

'Mr Kat.' I made claw shapes with my hands. 'Miaow, he

sounds like a special one.' I giggled and wondered if two whiskies might actually be my limit.

'He does indeed. And that lucky man is out there somewhere, I promise you. Dessert, and then I think it's time to get you home,' Moira replied with a smile. 'Things will look brighter in the morning.'

Only if I woke up and realised this had all been a bad dream, I thought glumly.

Chapter Four

The world was indeed brighter in the morning, but that was mostly because I'd forgotten to close the curtains when I went to bed last night. I was woken at an unreasonable hour by the sunrise streaming through the big bay windows of the ground-floor studio flat I rented from Moira and Rami at mates' rates. I flinched at the light and pulled a pillow over my head, trying to block out the noise of the birds who seemed to be holding some kind of rave on the fence which separated my meagre patch of scrubland from the road. I could still hear their muffled chirrups as I groaned, the shame and embarrassment of yesterday flooding back to me. Was it acceptable to stay here hiding under my pillow for the rest of my life?

I probably would have spent the whole day like that, if my phone hadn't pinged a couple of hours later with a message from Moira.

MOIRA

> I prescribe Paracetamol, a strong coffee, and a good attitude. Thanks again for agreeing to pick up my shift today.

The text ended with a cheerful-looking emoji blowing a kiss. I had zero recollection of agreeing to the switch. The idea of having a duvet day seemed like a much better one, but I couldn't let her down, especially not after she'd sacrificed her Friday night with Mr Moira to allow me to cry on her shoulder.

Normally the library was my safe haven, but I wasn't particularly keen to return to the scene of my humiliation so soon. What if Mr Leo Taylor, former policeman, current pain in the neck, was visiting again? I knew I owed him an apology for the rude way I'd spoken to him, but I could do with a few days to build myself up to it first. I'd had enough of feeling vulnerable. But I comforted myself with the thought that, as he'd been in the library every day this week, he probably had other plans for the weekend. I just hoped those plans didn't involve laughing at my plight with his clever-clogs mates, who'd undoubtedly never be foolish enough to fall for a romance fraudster.

I double-checked the time, then swore. I would have to forgo the prescribed strong coffee if I didn't get a move on. Hurrying over, I closed the curtains so I could change out of last night's outfit, hoping that no early-morning passer-by had seen me passed out face down on my bed. Normally in a student town it was a safe bet that nobody would be around at this time on the weekend, but the road I lived on was on the way to the university gym and the rowing teams were notorious for being up and about at stupid o'clock for training sessions.

An ultra-speedy cold shower did at least make me feel halfway human again. I dry-swallowed the Paracetamol, then realised I didn't even have time to dry my hair or put my contacts in. After pulling on fresh clothes, and leaving the polka dot yellow dress crumpled up on the bathroom floor where it belonged, I jumped on my bike to get to the library. Helmet hair was bad at the best of times, and wet helmet hair didn't bear thinking about. The warm spring breeze would sort that soon enough, although the result would be equally questionable. But it wasn't like I was trying to impress anyone anymore, and I had more important things on my mind. The cold light of day hadn't lessened the feeling of utter humiliation and hurt, but I was determined not to think of myself as a victim. Instead of wallowing in the denial stage of the grieving process, I was going to make myself fast-forward to the anger stage. And boy, was I angry; although the jury was still out on whether that rage was directed more at Brian, whoever he really was, for his deceptive manipulation, or at myself for being such a fool. Would I ever be able to trust my own judgement again?

Once I'd opened the library and welcomed the first visitors, I plugged my phone in to charge at the front desk and navigated to the terms and conditions page of the SO Ox website. I knew a lot of people didn't bother to read the boring legalese before clicking to accept them, but I was not one of those people. After I had finally acknowledged that it was highly unlikely that my Mr Darcy was going to rock up in the library or the usual places I hung out at outside of work, I'd reluctantly conceded that joining a dating app was the best way forward. I'd gone with a popular one to start with, but found it full of bots and weirdos. Then I did my research, figuring quality was better than quantity, and chose SO Ox instead because everything about it seemed so thorough. The terms and conditions set out a standard of behaviour expected by members, it was an app founded in Oxford, for real people in Oxford, and most importantly, it promised to screen every single person who joined to make sure they were who they said they were. Well, something had seriously gone wrong, then. How had the alleged Brian James, or whatever he was really called, slipped through such an apparently watertight system? I needed to get in touch with customer services immediately and warn them so they could take the necessary action before he could cause more harm.

As I navigated to the 'Contact us' section of the app, a little green dot on my screen lit up to indicate that my match was online.

I miss you. I'm sorry we didn't manage our date last night. Are you okay? xoxo

The message flashed up before I could block him.

'No, I am very much not okay. And neither will you be by the time I've finished with you, Brian bloody James,' I said out loud in lieu of typing it. 'You can take your xoxo and stick it up your—'

'That's the spirit.'

I looked up to find Leo Taylor standing in front of me.

'Oh' was all I managed in response. Why did he have to be here, once again catching me at a vulnerable moment? Didn't he have other things to do on a Saturday? Five-a-side football or something else equally energetic and noisy? He struck me as being exactly the type to be grunting in Christ Church Meadow doing show-off squats or ridiculous one-hand push-ups, while the rest of the world tried to enjoy a peaceful picnic brunch in the park.

'I wanted to check that I'm okay to go back to my usual table. I've not been permanently banned or anything, have I?' he asked. To my sensitive ears, it sounded more like a pass-agg statement from a man used to getting his own way, than a question.

I pretended to be considering my answer. In truth, the decision to ban a patron was way above my pay grade, but a wicked part of me wanted to make him squirm after the 'Kat Fisher, catfisher' comment yesterday.

'I'll try to keep my feet off the furniture,' he added, in a manner which I'm sure he thought was utterly disarming.

I glared at him, wishing I dared tell him where to go. I'd much prefer not having him around to remind me of my momentary loss of control yesterday. But I was self-aware enough to know that he was merely the convenient whipping post for my Brian James-related anger.

'Try isn't good enough. How about you'll promise to keep your feet off the furniture?' I said sternly.

'Yes, ma'am,' he said. His arm twitched as if he was fighting the urge to salute.

I frowned. Was he taking the mickey? Who, in the UK, said 'ma'am' in normal conversation?

'Kat will do just fine,' I said.

'Yes, Kat. Happy to obey.'

'Good. Because I'll be watching you.'

'Lucky me,' he said, deliberately misinterpreting my comment. 'Great chat. I'll be over there again.' He gestured in the direction of the business section.

'We close at four on Saturdays,' I responded, wishing I had a better comeback.

'Duly noted.'

I watched him walk away with that irritatingly easy stride of his, so perfectly sure of himself. Just before he sat down, he turned to look back towards me and I quickly pretended to be checking the clock on the wall. There was no need to inflate his robust-enough ego.

Right, what was it that I'd been doing before Leo Taylor came and distracted me with his demands for attention? Ah, that was it. The complaint to SO Ox. I needed to get a move on. Another message from the Scammer Soldier had pinged up on the screen in the meantime, which made it clear that he hadn't given up on trying to win me over.

> *I'm so sorry about the misunderstanding yesterday, hon. I really want to explain everything to you, but I have to go through a post-mission debrief so unfortunately I'll be out of contact for a couple of days. Take care in the meantime, gorgeous, I'll be thinking about you every second until we can be together at last. Speak soon xoxo.*

He was sticking to the plausible excuse playbook, just as Leo had said he would. I flashed a V sign at the screen. The sheer cheek of the guy to still be trying it on with his excessive use of pet names and flattery. What did he take me for? How had I ever fallen for someone who ladled it on with a trowel like that? It was so obviously dodgy now I'd woken up to reality.

I started typing my complaint email to the app, explaining everything that had happened, asking them to investigate, and take down the fake Brian James profile as a matter of urgency. Given all their advertising banners stressing the importance of users' safety, I was confident that they would take my concern seriously. Sure enough, within minutes of me sending the message, I got an automated response saying that my issue would be looked into immediately and I would be told the results of their investigation within twenty-four hours. I sighed. I suppose twenty-four hours was better than nothing, but I couldn't help fearing what trouble Bogus Brian could cause in that time. I forced myself not to think of it. There wasn't anything else I could do, for now.

The normal work routine helped settle my still nagging anxiety somewhat, although I did find myself avoiding both the crime and the business sections. I processed loans and returns, read a book about a unicorn saving the world to a bunch of extremely enthusiastic under-fives for Saturday

Story Time, which soon dealt with any last lingering remnants of the hangover, and finally tracked down the contact details for a local author to arrange an event. It was good to be surrounded by a different bunch of readers who didn't know what had happened to me. Everyone except one particular individual, of course, whose presence I did my best to ignore even though I caught him watching me on several occasions with that penetrating gaze of his. He was probably terrified I was going to chuck him out again. Served him right.

At lunchtime, I retreated to the break room and curled up with a battered copy of *Gaudy Night* by Dorothy L. Sayers which had been taken out of circulation for repairs. There was nothing like an old favourite to help distract me from reality and boost my mood with some much-needed escapism.

I was reluctantly about to return to library desk duty when the SO Ox app pinged on my phone.

Dear Ms Fisher,
Thank you for raising your concerns about another member of this app. After a thorough investigation, we have concluded that Brian James is a legitimate user. He will however receive a warning notification that his message could have been misinterpreted as a request for money. We take such matters very seriously and are grateful for you drawing it to our attention. As our terms and conditions policy states, we operate a two-strikes-and-out system. Unfortunately, we also have to issue you with

a warning for making a complaint against another user which turned out to be unfounded. We hope you enjoy continuing to use SO Ox. Happy dating!

*Yours sincerely,
The team at SO Ox*

An unfounded complaint? How dare they give me a warning when I was the innocent party in all this? That was a flawed system at work. In fact, it was downright sinister. Who knew what other shady characters could be operating under the protection of the app which seemed to be condoning dodgy behaviour? I was properly livid now. Despite all the information I'd provided them, they still thought that Brian James was a legitimate user. It was unbelievable. The demand for money wasn't a matter of interpretation; it was clearly there in black and white. And how could I enjoy 'happy dating', knowing that the app was potentially a festering hotbed of scammers who continued to get away with it because there was a 'two-strikes' policy? I'd never trust anyone from the app again. The response was so inadequate I would have laughed, if I wasn't so full of rage. And to top it all, they'd claimed to have carried out a 'thorough investigation' – in less than four of the twenty-four hours they'd promised. They'd essentially given Scammer Brian their blessing to carry on with impunity. Even worse, they'd basically given him guidance on how to be more subtle with his scam, making him all the more dangerous.

I knew I'd been lucky. I'd got wise to the scheme before I'd lost anything more than a little bit of dignity. But others might not be so fortunate. What if it had been a retiree like Doris who'd been targeted? She still berated herself for following legitimate but bad financial advice against her better instincts in the pursuit of love. Falling victim to a scammer like this would kill her. What about the other library users, many of whom also scraped by, working all hours to make ends meet, what if they got tricked out of everything they owned because they committed the sin of wanting a bit of companionship? People like the fake Brian James shouldn't be allowed to get away with it, taking love and manipulating it in order to steal and destroy. Something had to be done. They needed to be stopped. Maybe the SO Ox app would have to reconsider their position if I reported Scammer Brian to the police?

But that irksome voice of reason soon piped up again. If the people at the app didn't think there was enough to my complaint to act upon it, the police were hardly going to be any different. They were probably up to their eyes in much more serious incidents. Thankfully, the crime rate in Oxford was significantly lower than the Inspector Morse books made out, but that didn't mean they'd have the time to give more than a cursory glance at my problem.

I looked down at the copy of *Gaudy Night* lying discarded on my lap. The heroine Harriet Vane was a writer who took matters into her own hands to investigate a mystery which was causing pain and suffering to those who were dear to her. Why couldn't I follow her example and carry out my own investigation? I could track down the fraudster, find more substantial evidence of his wrongdoing, then take a cut and dried case to the police. Somebody needed to stop him. Why couldn't it be me?

I returned to the reshelving trolley full of resolve and with a spring in my step. As I walked around the library with my squeaky cart of books, I started to put together a plan of action. Maybe I could find Scammer Brian by evaluating his online footprint, establishing his pattern and tracking down the other sordid corners of the internet where he carried out his nefarious business. That was how they went about it in crime novels, anyway, and it seemed to work for them.

My fingers hovered by a volume called *Hacking for Dummies*. But, judging from the blurb, it seemed to be more geared towards learning how to protect yourself from rogue operatives, rather than helping you work out who was behind it. And if I was being completely honest with myself, did I really have the skillset to suddenly turn computer whizz and decode whatever information might be out there, to discover the real identity of the so-called Brian James? My search abilities were more suited to tracking down rare books and obscure authors. It was all well and good for the amateur detectives of the Golden Age of crime fiction to waltz around getting their man, armed only with logic and a few smart quips, but with the internet, there were so many more places to hide nowadays.

What I really needed was professional help and guidance from somebody who knew what they were doing.

Maybe I could hire a private detective who specialised in this area? Weren't they the modern equivalents of Sherlock Holmes? The crime fiction shelves of the library were full of the adventures of go-getting PIs who never failed to catch their man, even if the police had been floundering for years. I slipped between the stacks in the classics section, and quickly took out my phone to google 'private investigator Oxford.'

A host of options popped up promising complete discretion for private surveillance, corporate work, and the somewhat sinister-sounding 'spouse investigations'. I was astonished by the amount of choice out there, and the range of services they offered. It was pretty concerning to realise there was enough dodgy behaviour going on to warrant such a thriving industry, judging by the slick graphics of their high-end websites. But as I scrolled through the options, none of them mentioned anything about being specialists in sniffing out romance fraudsters. And on closer inspection, they all seemed to be based in London rather than my home city, not to mention the fact that without exception they charged a small fortune.

Okay, so the private detective option was a no-go. I was back to square one, relying on my own ingenuity. But even Harriet Vane had been able to consult gentleman sleuth Lord Peter Wimsey as her investigation had grown more complex. As I put my phone away with a sigh, my gaze fell on Leo Taylor beavering away at whatever it was he was working on in the business section. Despite his promise, his feet had crept back up on the seat opposite. He obviously felt my stare because he looked up and guiltily lowered his trainers to the ground, smiling apologetically at me. I frowned back, an idea starting to form. I dismissed it immediately; I wasn't that desperate. But then I started thinking about that horrible feeling of humiliation, that desperate embarrassment I'd had in the pit of my stomach since realising the truth about my 'relationship' with the man pretending to be Brian James. Nothing could ever be as bad as that. And if swallowing my pride meant I'd save even one other person from going through what I had, then it would be a worthy price to pay. After all, as I regularly told my library users, there was no shame in asking for help.

Leo stood up as I slowly approached him, still debating with myself whether this was the right course of action.

'Look, I'm really sorry,' he said quickly. 'I know I shouldn't have done it. I get so deep in thought that I'm not even aware I'm putting my feet on the chair, that's the honest truth. I can't guarantee I won't do it again, but I promise I'm really, really trying.'

'You certainly are,' I said.

He smiled in acknowledgement of the insult. 'Please don't throw me out again,' he said. 'I've got nowhere else to go really.' I thought I saw a frown briefly cross his face before his features returned to his usual infuriating grin.

'You're skating on thin ice,' I said, mirroring his teasing tone. If my plan was going to work, I needed to get him on side. 'But as you seem to have made yourself so comfortable in here, it would be cruel of me to turf you out now. How about we start again?'

I held my hand out.

He looked surprised, but didn't hesitate to take it. I'd assumed he'd be the type to have a crushing grip, needing to assert his dominance even in something as simple as a handshake, but I was wrong. His grip was firm but in a reassuring way, his palm pleasantly warm against my perpetually cold fingers.

'I'm guessing that peace is declared,' he said.

'Perhaps. Look, can I buy you a coffee after the library closes?' I asked. 'I need to talk to you about something.'

He raised an eyebrow in surprise at my question and looked silently at me for longer than felt comfortable.

'How about G&D's on Little Clarendon Street?' I said. 'My treat. I might even stretch to an ice cream, if you ask nicely. I'd like to pick your brain.'

He put his head on one side, as if trying to work something out.

'How intriguing. Well, as there's ice cream involved,' he said eventually. 'That sounds like an offer I can't refuse.'

I tried to pretend that I wasn't watching Leo for the rest of the afternoon, as my plan percolated at the back of my mind. But I couldn't help wondering how he would take my proposal. The worst thing he could do would be to laugh it off and refuse, but, I told myself, I was now a dab hand at coping with humiliation. It was clear Leo already had a pretty low opinion of me, so I couldn't make things worse.

'How are you doing, pet? And have you got the next one in this series?' Doris's queries drew my attention back to the work I should have been concentrating on.

'I'm down, but not out. I'm still feeling pretty stupid

about the whole thing, but I'll get over it.' I forced a relaxed smile. 'And yes, the new one arrived this morning, as it happens. If you give me a few minutes to put the protective cover on and make sure it's properly registered in the system, it'll be all yours.'

'Marvellous. I know I need to pace myself because I'm going to run out of her books soon. It's a real shame that her writing pace can't keep up with my reading one.'

'You do average a book a day, Doris. It would be an awful lot to ask of an author to keep up with that. But maybe we should lock her in a comfy basement with only a computer in front of her, then she'll have no excuse not to provide you with reading material?' I suggested with a grin.

'That's seriously tempting. Shame I don't have a basement,' said Doris. 'Now are you sure you're alright, pet? We could do with one of my romance heroes avenging you.'

'Sadly, there's a shortage of those types around here.'

'Sometimes heroes are lurking where you least expect them to be,' she replied, laying a soft hand on mine.

It took me quite a while to convince her that I was going to be okay, but I was touched by how much she cared. Once she was safely on her way, my gaze automatically drifted back to the business section, which was now empty.

'Great, now what?' I muttered irritably under my breath. Leo could have just said no to the coffee rather than taking advantage of my distraction to do a runner. He hadn't seemed the type. But then again, I'd thought that Brian James was perfection. Clearly, I needed to work on my ability to read between the lines.

I marched across to reshelve the weighty tomes on business analysis which Leo had naturally left all over the place, then noticed the piece of paper on the table.

'Had to make a couple of calls. See you in G&D's at half four.'

All was not lost.

Chapter Five

I managed to get to the café at twenty-five past four having locked up the library in record-quick time, thanks to Etta's help, but Leo was already there waiting for me at a table in the corner, two steaming mugs of hot chocolate in front of him.

'I know you suggested coffee, but it's the weekend, and I thought a treat to accompany the ice creams might be a good idea, and it always takes a while for the hot chocolate to get to a more drinkable temperature.'

'As you bought the drinks, I'm definitely getting the ice creams,' I said, determined to claw back some sense of control. 'My invitation, my shout. What flavour would you like?'

'I took the liberty of checking out the selection before you arrived and I've decided I'd like to go for 'Twas Mint To Be – the mint chocolate chip,' he clarified. 'It'll be a nice contrast to the drink. Sweet, but with a bite to it.'

'Like me, you mean?' I said with a smile, getting in there first before he delivered the obvious jibe.

'I don't think I'm really in a position to make that judgement yet,' he replied dryly.

'I'd better get in the queue,' I said, deciding it was best to remove myself from the situation before I said anything else stupid.

I hesitated before selecting the same flavour of ice cream for myself, not wanting Leo to think I was copying him, but he was right, it would be the perfect accompaniment to the hot chocolate.

'Delicious,' I said after my first spoonful. 'Did you see the petition book they've got for new flavours? There are all sorts of outlandish suggestions in there, like curry flavour, but I bet they'd find a way of making it work.'

I knew I was talking nonsense, but I needed to fill the silence and, coward that I was, I was trying to delay the moment when I'd have to make my suggestion out loud and have my companion point out how ridiculous it was.

'Undoubtedly,' said Leo. He took a sip of his hot chocolate, then sat back and folded his arms, watching me expectantly. 'Delightful as it is to discuss the pros and cons of various flavours of ice cream, was that really the reason you invited me to join you?'

'I was only trying to make polite conversation,' I retorted, bristling. 'You should try it some time.'

He pursed his lips. 'Don't you think it's somewhat hypocritical for you to be calling me rude? You may have lured me here with the prospect of ice cream, but that doesn't mean I have to stick around. I'm sure the staff could transfer it into a tub to go.'

'Sorry, please don't leave,' I blurted out. 'I'm nervous because I want to ask you something, you see, and it's making me act weird, I know. I'm sorry,' I repeated.

Again, his lips quirked in what might have been a smile. 'And what is the cause of this nervousness? I'm disappointed if it's me. That's not an effect I like to have on women.'

'I'm sure you're used to them all rolling over immediately, like kittens wanting to be stroked,' I said then wished the words back. Where had that come from? I forced my gaze away from his hands and affected sudden fascination with the menu board behind his head, mortified that my attempt at banter had manifested in such an unintended and unfortunately flirtatious statement.

Thankfully, despite the provocation, he was reasonably restrained in his response. 'But this Kat has claws.'

'Apparently so,' I said. 'Okay, okay, let's start again.'

'This is what, the third time we're starting again?'

'If you say so. You've obviously been counting.'

'It amuses me,' he said, picking up a teaspoon and stirring his hot chocolate thoughtfully. 'So, you're nervous about asking me something. Perhaps it would be easier all round if you just came out with whatever is on your mind?'

'I'd like to make a proposal,' I said, in a tone I hoped didn't sound provoking, irritated or flirtatious.

'Goodness, this is all very sudden,' he responded. 'I'd like a princess cut diamond, and nothing less than eighteen carat white gold will do.'

'Oh, shut up. Now I know you're trying to wind me up. And boy, you seem to know an awful lot about engagement rings.'

Leo laughed. 'I had a summer job in a jewellery store when I was at university. What I don't know about budget sparkles isn't worth knowing. It was an early training in human nature. Would you believe that, one week, I sold two identical engagement rings to the same bloke?'

'Maybe he lost the first one, and was devastated because it was the perfect ring, so he had to go back and replace it?' I suggested.

'Sweet,' said Leo. 'Sadly, it was actually because he was a two-timer who'd been delivered an ultimatum by both women in the same week. I've always wondered what happened next.'

'And he bought them the same ring? Did he think he was being fair or something? What a bastard. Hopefully they called him out and sold the rings to fund a nice holiday apiece,' I said.

'Now you're thinking like a survivor. But enough of my holiday job reminiscences. What's on your mind?'

I nodded, bracing myself for bravery. 'Okay, here goes. As you are already aware, I was the vic—' No, I was not going to call myself that. 'Subjected to the unwelcome attentions of a fraudster,' I amended. 'I feel humiliated'—violated was another word which sprang to mind—'but I know I'm lucky to have escaped with my bank account intact, and my dignity too. Well, some of it, at least. But the company behind the app was totally uninterested in investigating the matter properly and they're not even bothering to ban the perpetrator. I know I was lucky, but others might not be, and I can't bear the thought of anyone else going through this. I need to find out who this fraudster is and stop him before he causes serious damage to somebody else.'

'Very laudable. But why aren't official channels, such as, I don't know, the obvious one ... the police, an option?'

I shook my head. 'If the app won't make the effort to investigate properly, I hardly think the police are going to be able to use their limited resources to do so, even if they wanted to.'

'I'd like to be able to dispute that assumption, but sadly, you're probably right. So, you've decided to turn vigilante and sort out the problem yourself.' He laughed. I'd been expecting that response, but it was still galling to experience it for real.

'Not vigilante exactly, but yes, I want to identify this scammer and make sure they face justice.'

'And how exactly are you planning to do this?' Leo asked. To give him credit, he mostly managed to keep the air of disbelief out of his voice. 'Have you thought that Brian James could be a bunch of people rather than one individual? They could be based anywhere in the world. That's a lot of suspects to consider. You're not exactly going to find your man and expose him by using your knowledge of the Dewey Decimal System, no offence.'

'It's funny how when people say, "no offence" they generally mean the exact opposite,' I said. 'And yes, I am very aware of my shortcomings when it comes to carrying out an investigation. That's where you come in.'

'I do, do I? How, and why does this become my problem to deal with?' he asked.

'You told me you used to be a police officer. Or more accurately a CID detective. They're the ones who do the investigating, remember?' I couldn't resist the dig. 'You made a pretty big deal of the fact that you've dealt with loads of these kinds of case. Who would be better suited to help me track down my nemesis and bring him to justice? And it's definitely a him, I've heard his voice.'

The teaspoon returned to the saucer with a clatter.

'Brian has reached nemesis level. Goodness, things have taken a turn for the serious,' said Leo. 'Well, Kat, you don't mind me calling you Kat, do you?'

'It's a bit late to ask now.'

'Well, Ms Kat Fisher, I see several problems ahead. One of which is that I used to be a detective, but I am certainly not one anymore. The only thing I investigate nowadays is the distinctly low jeopardy problem of where my socks disappear to between the washing machine and the drying rack, and I'm afraid to admit that even the answer to that question remains a complete mystery.'

'Surely once a detective, always a detective,' I pushed back. 'You can't have forgotten everything already. I'm not asking you to do the whole investigation. I was envisaging you in more of a consultant role, a sounding board perhaps. This is too important for me to leave it entirely to somebody else. Especially someone I don't really know. No offence.'

Leo acknowledged the reverse jibe with a slight nod of his head.

'Even if I did have some residual detective skills, what

incentive is there for me to use them to help you on a fool's mission? It's all well and good claiming I'd only be a consultant, but give me credit for some humanity. I'm not going to see you getting yourself into trouble and then not feel obliged to help you out of it. And this is the kind of situation where you could get yourself into a lot of trouble.' His voice took on a serious tone. 'I'm not denying that you have good intentions, but do you not think that you're being somewhat naïve in believing that this is a realistic course of action? Scammers are among the lowest of the low, but sadly the odds are very much in their favour when it comes to evading justice, particularly given the circumstances of your incident. And in the highly unlikely scenario that we do track him down, he's not going to be exactly thrilled about it. Have you thought about how he might react, and the potential danger that could put you in?'

For a second or two I faltered. Not that I would admit this out loud, but Leo made a compelling point. In crime fiction, there's always a limit to the jeopardy because the reader knows that, despite whatever challenges the main character faces, they will eventually prevail, and the baddie will be caught. There was no such guarantee in real life. Wouldn't it be safer to chalk this whole thing up to experience, maybe set up a few scam awareness sessions for the library patrons to ease my concern, and move on?

But scam awareness sessions or no, the fraudster who'd targeted me would still be out there, stealing people's money and robbing them of their confidence. Could I look myself in the mirror if I sat back and let that carry on happening? And besides, I was hopeful I wouldn't be tackling the problem without professional guidance. Leo had said 'we' rather than 'you'. Surely that had to be a sign that he was wavering?

'I'm not at all naïve, but you're entitled to your opinion, just as I'm entitled to mine,' I said, hoping I sounded more confident than I felt. 'Just because something is difficult, doesn't mean we should avoid trying, especially when *we* know that it's the right thing to do.'

'Are you really purely motivated by moral outrage at the behaviour of Mr Brian James, or is good old-fashioned desire for revenge behind this little mission of yours?'

I glared at him. 'What's wrong with seeking justice? You do realise that you come across as incredibly patronising when you insist on describing it as a "little mission"?' I was starting to seriously regret my decision to recruit him. But he was the best option I'd come up with, and if his comments were a tad too close to the bone for my liking, at least they demonstrated that he still possessed the detective's insight that I needed him for.

'That was not my intention,' he said, leaning back in his chair and looking at me piercingly. 'But I stand by my original statement that this is not a realistic course of action.'

I felt like shaking the man, but I wrestled my voice into steadiness. 'There are various reasons why I think the search will be more confined than the entire world. I'm happy to share them with you, if you're interested.'

'The thing is, I'm really not,' said Leo, not even pretending to be polite. 'You seem like a perfectly nice person, and I'm sure you think you're doing this from the best of intentions and genuinely believe what you're saying. But I have no desire to get embroiled in another investigation, no matter how worthy you claim it is. There's a reason why I'm not in the police anymore.'

'Oh?'

He shook his head. 'And that reason is frankly none of anyone's business but my own. You're not wheedling it out of me that easily. It makes no sense for me to entangle myself in a scheme which is undoubtedly going to end in tears. Your tears, rather than those of your so-called nemesis Brian James, just to be clear. I'm sorry for you, but that's the way it's going to be. You'd be wise to put the whole sad affair behind you and move on with your life. Join a chess club, meet some nice geeky bloke there and forget all about the nasty scammer who stole your happiness for a while and tried to rob you of your dosh too.'

Unfortunately, Leo's determination to dissuade me from my mission was having the exact opposite effect. The blunter he was, the more convinced I was that Leo was the man for the job. I liked how he cut through the crap and was more concerned with speaking honestly than tiptoeing around with polite, but ultimately useless, avoidance tactics. He didn't use any flowery language, so beloved by Scammer Brian as a means of manipulation. Leo Taylor might have been rude and selfish, but he was also straightforward, and at least I wouldn't have to worry about where I stood with him. If he agreed to be on my team, he would tell me what I needed to hear, not what I wanted to hear. I could do with some honesty for a change.

'It's flattering that you think I'd only have to click my fingers to have the chess boys dropping their pieces and come running. But I've learnt my lesson, and dating is the last thing on my mind.'

In fact, I couldn't imagine ever wanting to put myself in the position of being so vulnerable again. It was much safer to steer clear of all kinds of emotional complications.

'Good for you. This has been delightful, but I'm afraid I really must go now. Good luck. I hope not to see you sobbing in the library again.' He rose and started putting his jacket on.

'I wasn't sobbing, for your information. But don't leave yet. You haven't heard my full pitch. I promise I'll make it worth your while to help me.'

He paused. 'Tell me you're not about to offer some kind of *Pretty Woman* style arrangement. My services cannot be bought.'

I felt my whole face burn. 'Why would you even think that?'

He laughed. 'It is too easy to wind you up.' Sinking back onto the chair, he shrugged the jacket back off his shoulders. 'Go on then, I've got another couple of minutes before I need to be elsewhere. In what way would it benefit me to help you out?'

I took a deep breath and dived in. 'You used to be a policeman, but now you spend nearly every day in the library's business section browsing books about how to write a business plan and become your own boss and the like. As you're in my library during normal working hours, I deduce that you are currently unemployed. And given your choice of reading material, it doesn't take a genius to work out that you are considering starting your own business.'

'You're correct, it doesn't take a genius to work all that out.' He glanced at his watch. 'So far, all correct deductions. Good for you. Maybe you'll do better in this investigation malarky than I originally thought. I'm afraid I don't see how that is in any way relevant, however.'

'But I suspect it's not going to plan,' I continued, as if he hadn't said anything. 'You're reading the books, writing lots of notes, but somehow, you don't know where to start with putting together that business plan. And without a proper business plan, you and I both know that your dreams of becoming your own boss will remain exactly that: dreams. I've seen the papers scattered all over the place, the look of frustration alternating with the middle-distance stare of doom.'

I'd hit a nerve. I watched as a range of expressions crossed Leo's face. He finally settled on bored indifference, which I suspected was masking his real emotion.

'Is this an attempt to do a Sherlock Holmes routine on me?' he asked. 'Because if so, it's not going to work. Sherlock Holmes's unrealistic deductive abilities began the slippery slope of juries believing no case is proven until infinite amounts of unachievable forensic detail are provided. In other words, I'm not a fan.'

'That's a shame. I'm happy to recommend some other series in which the Sherlock Holmes character features with perhaps less of the irritating pedantry on display,' I said, unable to resist allowing myself to be side-tracked. 'Laurie

R. King's books for example. In that series he gets married to a young feminist called Mary Russell who gives as good as she gets.'

'You really are passionate about your job, aren't you? If I promise to read one of Ms King's books, will you leave me alone?'

I shook my head, and waited for him to take the bait.

He sighed and ran a hand messily through his hair. 'Fine, I admit that the business plans are in fact not going to plan. But I don't see how that's of interest to you, or why it should have any influence on my extremely sensible decision not to embroil myself in your scheme.'

'But you really want the business plans to work. After all, you've diligently ploughed your way through even the driest volumes on those shelves. Anyone with less determination would have put them to one side long ago. You're looking for a way forward, but you haven't found it yet. I think I can assist you with that. If you agree to help me, I in turn will help you with your plan.' I put up my hand to stop his inevitable interruption. 'And before you sneer and ask how I'm qualified to do that, I'll have you know that before I switched to training as a librarian, which I realised I was more passionate about, I started out studying for my master's degree in business in this very city, so I do know what I'm talking about. Admittedly practices might have moved on a bit since then, and I haven't had as much real-world experience as some, but I can put together a business plan for you that will have everything that bank managers and potential investors are looking for, plus I have an extra ace up my sleeve.'

I could tell that he was torn between the desire to ask what that might be and reluctance to show me any indication that he might be about to concede defeat.

I remained quiet. Being a librarian, I wasn't afraid of silence in a conversation, and I knew its power very well.

'Go on then, what is the extra ace up your sleeve?' he asked eventually.

'Doris.'

'Doris. The sea goddess from Greek mythology? Or do you mean that harmless-looking little old lady, who I happen to know reads the most extraordinary smut?'

I battled to keep my tone steady as I fought back at him. 'There's so much to unpack there. For a start, nobody ever refers to "little old men" in such a condescending tone of voice, and as for the "smut" aspect, there's nothing wrong with a bit of spice. Also, how would you know they're that kind of book unless you've read them yourself? Or is that another example of you rushing to judge something you know nothing about? Good Greek knowledge though, I'll give you that,' I conceded, realising that it wouldn't do my cause any good if I spent this whole conversation telling him off.

'You're not the only one to have a previous existence,' he responded. 'And yes, it's a fair cop: you've got me on both charges of making assumptions. My bad. I promise to try harder in the future and be much more respectful in my use of language. So, what extraordinary abilities does the petite wise woman Doris have to offer?'

I couldn't help laughing at this incredibly accurate new description of her.

'Doris, as well as being very well read, and an extremely popular bookstagrammer, is also the retired CEO of a Fortune 500 company, who in the latter years of her career, dedicated herself to using her knowledge to support start-ups and provide mentoring to would-be business owners. She mostly devotes her time to her literary pursuits nowadays, but I know for a fact that she'd be happy to give you the benefit of her wealth of knowledge, should her favourite librarian ask. She still has a lot of connections in useful places, you know.'

I omitted to mention that the reason Doris concentrated on her bookstagram nowadays was because the pension debacle had ruined her confidence. It would be a wonderful bonus if being asked to assist Leo with his business plan helped her regain some of it.

I took a triumphant sip of the hot chocolate. It was lukewarm now, but it still tasted delicious. I knew I'd made a powerful argument. Surely Leo would have to agree to my proposal?

There was a long pause while Leo pretended to wrestle with his decision. But I was quietly confident that I had him on my hook.

'Okay, that does sound like an interesting offer,' he said eventually, before checking his watch again. 'But I wasn't lying when I said I have somewhere else I need to be soon. So, you've got precisely one minute to convince me that you have a better plan to track down your fraudster than simply trying to hack into the SO Ox website and find his IP address. In case you weren't aware, that's an utterly futile course of action, and you can have that advice for free.' I must've looked startled, because he grinned. 'You're not the only one who can observe what's going on in the library. And no, I haven't agreed to help you yet.'

But he still hadn't left. That had to be a good sign.

'Okay, so this is how the app works.' I explained the vetting process and the geographical restrictions on becoming a member. 'So, although Scammer Brian clearly isn't a soldier who's been off on deployment, whoever he really is must be an actual person who's able to show genuine proof of being from this area. Which means, it's possible for us to find him and confront him about what he's been up to.'

'There are many, many ways around those kind of superficial security measures, but let's assume that what you say is true. Even if our perpetrator does have some genuine connection to Oxford, that still doesn't get us any closer to discovering his true identity.'

'It's also a boutique app with a limited membership, which narrows the pool of suspects. I might not know what he actually looks like, but I know what he sounds like, thanks to the voice notes he sent me. I have a few ideas for our initial strategy, but I was hoping you could help me work out the finer details,' I admitted.

'And if I still say no?' He tried one final time.

'Oh, I'm not giving up. I may be many things, but I'm certainly not a quitter. I have to do this. It's the right thing to do. I thought you would be the type to understand the importance of the moral obligation. But maybe I was wrong.' I let the silence hang for a minute, before continuing, 'I'll go wading in, and no doubt get myself into all kinds of trouble while you enjoy watching from the safety of the business section, as you continue to battle with your thwarted ambitions.'

Had I laid it on too thick? But he was the first to blink. Success.

Leo sighed. 'Fine. You've got me. Well played. Game, set and match. I concede defeat. I will help you on the terms that you've already specified.'

'That's brilliant, thank you, I really appreciate it,' I said, reaching out to grab his hand in delight before thinking better of it. I tried to cover the move by picking up my hot chocolate mug for another slurp before realising it was already empty.

'Not so fast. Before you get too carried away, I have some terms and conditions of my own.'

I should have known it wouldn't be that easy.

'I'm listening.'

'One, if you want to work with me, you must listen to my advice,' he said.

I nodded, pedantically noting that he'd failed to specify that I had to follow his advice. A rooky error.

'Two, if I say stop, we stop. While you have a touching tendency to believe the best of people, you must admit that it's part of the reason you're in this situation in the first place. I refuse to let you blunder into a whole heap of trouble.'

I pulled a face. Let him play the overprotective alpha male if it made him happy. I'd soon prove to him I wasn't the naïve fool he believed me to be.

'And three.' He paused. 'Actually, I don't think there is a

third. The second guideline should cover all eventualities. Do I have your agreement?'

'Yes.' I gave him my sweetest smile.

'Why does that lack of hesitation make me even more certain that I'm an idiot to be agreeing to this?' he said wearily.

'Let's get to work,' I said, holding my hand out once more to shake his.

'What am I letting myself into?' he said. 'Right, I guess we'd better swap numbers, and I'll be in touch at some point so we can come up with a plan.'

Chapter Six

Of course, I had no intention of waiting around for Leo to deign to call me, especially as I wasn't completely convinced that he was actually going to, given the note of reluctance in his voice when we parted. There was no time to waste. Every hour we dallied, could be another hour the bogus Brian James caused further heartbreak and duped someone out of their life savings. I would never forgive myself if another person suffered because I'd failed to get a move on.

Being a librarian, I decided more research was in order. Knowledge is power, after all. I spent the rest of my weekend wading through local newspaper archives to see if I could detect whether there was a growing trend of scammers targeting people in Oxford. I also listened to as many true crime podcasts as I could find on the subject of romance fraudsters, educating myself about their techniques and learning the methods that law enforcement used to bring them down. It was a demoralising experience, and frightening to see in black and white how the odds were so stacked in the favour of the wrongdoer, but I refused to let myself get downcast about it. I was taking positive action and that was what was important.

Then I turned my attention to teaching myself some of the practical skills I was going to need for our investigation. One of the first things I learnt was how to do a reverse image search of the photos Scammer Brian had sent me, kicking myself for not having protected myself with this basic bit of research before. It took a little bit of digging, but I managed eventually to track down the originals. They belonged to a genuine British army officer who'd received a medal for his brave action in saving a family after an earthquake in the Middle East. Not only had the fake Brian stolen the images, he'd also pinched part of the man's circumstances to form his back story. He must have been rubbing his hands together with glee to come across a scenario so perfect that it looked like it'd been intentionally designed to reel in gullible targets like me.

Once I had a name for the actual individual in the pictures, I set about searching for his social media profiles. Thankfully his DMs were open, so I sent a quick message warning him that his identity had been stolen by a fraudster. A response pinged back within minutes.

Sadly this isn't the first DM I've had about this. Thanks for the heads up though. I've stopped posting pictures online, but there's not a lot I can do about the images that are already out there. The police advised me to point victims in the direction of Action Fraud. My wife and I hope you're okay.

It was a kind message, although the clumsy reference to the fact that he was married was rather embarrassing, like he felt the need to warn me off because I had some kind of aura of desperation about me due to falling for a romance fraudster. I sent what I hoped was a suitably sexless thumbs up emoji in response, but he'd already blocked me.

I briefly considered sending a screenshot of the exchange to the app, but they'd been so dismissive before that I decided it was better to gather more evidence first. It was a small comfort that the police were already aware of the misuse of the photos, but it didn't help me get any closer to the person who'd misappropriated them. I wished the army guy had told me which force was involved in the case so I could approach them, but as he'd closed down any means of communication, that was a dead end.

I was halfway through watching *The Tinder Swindler* on Sunday evening when my phone rang.

'Is that you, Holmes?' said a voice that I hadn't been expecting to hear from so soon. I smiled to myself.

'Knowing that you dislike the man, I'm rather insulted by your choice of nickname for me,' I said. 'Does that make you my Dr Watson, asking obvious questions all the time and catching on a little late?'

'Definitely not. Okay, I'll stick to Kat Fisher.'

'Thanks, Leo Taylor, but as I said before, just Kat will do fine.'

'You weren't the only one growing up being teased

about their name, you know,' he said suddenly. 'I couldn't move in secondary school without people making splashing sounds.'

'Splashing sounds? Oh, you mean like a Leo DiCaprio *Titanic* reference? That's a bit dark, isn't it?'

'That's kids for you. Although, now I look back, maybe it could also have been a reference to the fact that I was on the swimming team.'

'Oh, I get it. You brought out the sob story just so you could show off about being a high school athlete? Why am I not surprised? I'm afraid your school days are long over, Leo. It takes more than that to impress me,' I retorted.

'Good. You should have high standards.'

I wasn't quite sure how to take that, so I responded in the spirit of banter.

'Did you actually say something nice to me? I'm quite overcome with shock. Hold on a minute while I fan myself.'

Leo cleared his throat. 'I obviously need to up my game. Anyway, what was it that you wanted?'

'You're the one who rang me,' I reminded him with a chuckle. 'Maybe I should rethink hiring you as a consultant, if this is the standard of analytical thinking I can expect.'

He laughed. 'Feel free. But be careful with this talk of hiring. If there's too much more of it, I may actually start charging you for my services.'

'That's the sound of me zipping my lips shut and awaiting further news.'

'An astonishing turn of events. The chatty librarian falls silent for a change.'

I was surprised to hear myself described in such terms.

Sure, I was relaxed and talkative with my friends and library regulars who I'd known for ages, but being naturally an introvert, I was normally a bit quieter and more cautious with people I'd only recently met. But Leo seemed to have the knack for overriding my usual cautious reserve and bringing out a bolder side of my personality.

'Anyway, so, the actual reason I rang was that I've come up with a plan of action,' he continued.

'I'm listening,' I said, although in my head went something along the lines of ridiculing him for imagining that I'd been sitting on my backside doing nothing all weekend.

'If you're still serious about getting to the bottom of who's behind this scam, I think the safest way of doing it is to continue your contact with the alleged Mr Brian James online. You haven't responded to his message asking you for money, have you?'

'No. But he'll have seen from his notifications that I've read it.'

'Just say you dropped your phone shortly after reading his message and it took a while to get it fixed, or something like that. It sounds like a plausible reason for leaving a guy on read without sending a response.'

'Aw, Leo, is that the excuse girls normally give you?' I couldn't help myself.

'Ha, ha, very funny.'

'So, I get back in touch, and then what? We pick up where we left off?'

'Exactly,' said Leo. 'Chat with him, flirt with him, continue the conversation as if nothing has happened. If he thinks that he's got you in his grasp again, he might lower his guard and let something slip.'

'That sounds like an awfully big "if" Won't he just lose interest in me and focus on his other targets when it becomes apparent that I'm not going to give him any money? What would be the point in investing any more time in me?'

'You'll need to string him along. Make it seem like you're about to pay out, but there's always some very plausible reason why it doesn't happen. But next time, it definitely will.'

'In other words, I should use his playbook against him, give him a taste of his own medicine. I appreciate the irony in that.' But what I didn't like the sound of was how unlikely it was that we'd actually get anywhere with this approach. 'Do you honestly think this will work? It feels like I'd be leaving too much to chance. Isn't there something more proactive we could do? I've already worked out the source of his stolen pictures. Couldn't we try to build a profile of the real person behind the catfish? The choices he's made must tell us something about him.'

Leo sighed. 'Let me guess, another pearl from one of your detective novels?'

'There's no need to talk down to me.' I bristled, standing up from the sofa in an outrage that wouldn't have been out of place in an Austen novel.

'That was not my intention. It's just there's very little to go on right now, and I'm trying to be realistic. Unless you're happy sharing the contents of the messages you exchanged with your virtual boyfriend, which might give us some insight into what's going on in his mind, this is my best suggestion. And you did agree that you'd listen to my advice.'

I considered my options while I wandered aimlessly around the room. Letting Leo read Brian's messages and, worse, my replies to them would be horribly exposing – the opening banter which had quickly moved into flirtation and then into shared confidences of long-term dreams. It might allow Leo to build a profile of the scammer, but it would also enable him to learn far too much about me.

'Okay, I'll have a go at picking up where I left off with Brian,' I said without enthusiasm, berating myself for taking the cowardly approach.

'Great, I'll leave you to get on with it. Let me know how he responds, and we'll go from there,' said Leo.

'Wait, aren't you going to help me write the messages? If this is the approach you took when you were in the police, then you'll know the best way of phrasing things so that he falls into our trap.'

It must have been obvious from my tone that I didn't believe that this was how he'd carried out fraud investigations when he was in the force.

'You seemed to manage pretty well for yourself before you clocked that he was a scammer. Carry on along those lines. Show an interest in his interests, tell him how much you want him, how much you need him. I don't know, whatever floats your boat. Let's face it, if I start dictating messages to you, he's bound to pick up a change in tone.'

'Not used to romantic talk, are you?'

'I'm a man who speaks as he finds,' he responded. 'And

for goodness' sake, don't let slip any more information about yourself. It'll be a hard line to tread, trying to elicit confidences from him while avoiding them yourself, but you have a way with words; I'm sure you'll make it work. Keep me posted.'

Was that it? The extent of his plan of action? His restrained tactics were underwhelming. I suspected he was motivated by trying to keep me out of trouble, but I needed an actual result. And if it meant losing a bit of dignity, then I would just need to get over it and pay that price.

I sat back on the sofa and steeled myself. 'Maybe it wouldn't do any harm to share one or two messages with you, just the most recent ones to try to hurry things along.'

'Are you sure about that?' asked Leo. He sounded as reluctant as I felt, which was strangely comforting. I tried to reassure myself that it meant he'd be tactful about what he saw.

'You must have had to read loads of private correspondence when you were in the police. I trust that you'll apply the same level of discretion as if you were still in the force?'

'You have my word,' he said.

I made my decision.

'The problem is, the app blocks screenshots, so I guess I'll share my login details with you,' I thought aloud.

'Ah-ah.' Leo made a noise like a buzzer on a TV game show, making me jump. 'Wrong thing to say. There's no way you should share your login details with anyone. It's rule 101 of cyber security.'

'But that's the only way I can share those messages with

you. We're meant to be working as a team, after all. I trust you.'

'And how do you know you can trust me?' he asked. 'I've made a promise to you, but what evidence do you have that it's worth anything? You don't actually know the first thing about me. You've seen me working in the library and that seems to have been enough for you. At every step of the way, you've taken me at my word, but I could be stringing you along, just like your Brian James did. I told you I used to be a police officer, but have you actually checked that's true? How do you know I'm even called Leo Taylor as I claim? I could be working my own angle and be an even worse person than Mr James.'

The more he tried to convince me that I couldn't trust him, perversely the more relaxed I felt about doing just that.

'The very fact that you're warning me not to share my login details with you proves that sharing them is the right thing to do,' I countered. 'If you had dodgy intentions, you'd have been badgering me for them from the start. And would a real criminal spend so long going on about how they could be putting on an act? I don't think so. Besides, I'm a librarian. Of course I've checked your registration details so I know without any doubt that you are who you say you are. And I can access your loan history any time I like.' I attempted a joke.

'That's hardly a proper background check. By sharing your login details, you're handing me the key to assuming your identity.' Leo sounded increasingly frustrated. 'At best, I could flirt outrageously with every user on the app while pretending to be you, and at worst, I could access your bank account and perpetrate my own scam.'

'You could,' I acknowledged. 'But do you actually plan to do any of those things?'

'Well, of course not.'

'Fine, that's good enough for me.'

'Oh,' he said.

I got the impression it had been a while since someone had put their faith in him like this.

'I'll text you my password,' I said. 'Actually…'

I hesitated, regretting that I'd not saved this conversation until I'd changed my password to something more innocuous.

'You've come to your senses. Good,' said Leo.

'No, I'm sending it now.' In for a penny, in for a pound.

There was a pause as he checked his texts followed by a low chuckle at the other end of the line.

'MrDarcy1whereru? Seriously, that's your password?' he said.

'The IT guys at work always say it's safer to use a pass phrase rather than a password.' I tried to defend myself.

'You have got a bad dose of the romance bug,' was his only reply. 'Look, I still feel uncomfortable with this situation, so here's my guarantee. I won't log into the app and read your messages unless we're together, or you've got in touch to direct me towards a particular exchange. And you should feel free to change your password at any point to lock me out.'

'Thank you. I appreciate your thoughtfulness. Perhaps we can look at a selection of the messages together at the library tomorrow during my break. And in the meantime, I guess I'd better get on with my reply. Wish me luck with this first stage of Operation Get Brian.' I frowned. 'I can hear Moira's voice in my head saying we need to come up with a catchier name for our mission. What did you do when you were in the police? How did you choose operation names?'

There was a long pause. 'Operation Get Brian is just fine. Enjoy the rest of your Sunday evening.'

He ended the call before I could respond.

Chapter Seven

I stared at the screen and drew a blank. Writing to Brian had always come easily to me, but now I felt at a loss as to what to put. What if I ended up saying something that sounded completely unnatural, which set alarm bells ringing? I gave myself a mental pep talk. My favourite fictional heroine Harriet Vane would have come up with the perfect response. I would just have to channel her literary and detective abilities, and pretend to myself that everything was normal.

Hey B, I'm so so sorry I've taken an age to reply. My phone died and I was locked out of everything until I got it fixed. It's been soooo frustrating! My one comfort was that at least I knew you were home safe and sound – and earlier than promised, what a bonus. To know you're in the same country as me at last makes me very happy, but I can't believe the army are still keeping us apart! How's the debrief going? Hope it's not as intense as it sounds, and that they let you go on leave as soon as poss. They will let you go on leave, right? I will be counting the minutes until then xx

I returned to watching *The Tinder Swindler* but could no longer concentrate on the intricacies of the programme. It felt so frustrating to be sitting around at home waiting to see if or how Brian might respond. I wanted, no, I needed to be doing more.

I opened up the SO Ox app again and started spooling through its list of upcoming events. If there was one thing I'd learnt from my true crime binge today, it was that, when you were tracking down a criminal, it was important to establish their modus operandi, or MO, as all the shows referred to it. Yes, I knew how the scammer had acted with me so far. But, after all my research, I figured it was unlikely I was his only victim, and I needed to find out if this was his usual technique when he was courting his quarry. If I could uncover a pattern of behaviour, then Leo and I would have more information to go on in our investigation. There was a chance Brian had discovered a way to set up multiple identities on the app, so if we could identify his MO, we might be able to find these other identities and maybe track down fellow victims.

But setting up fake profiles in response and trying to lure him out still felt like leaving too much to chance, even supposing I could work out how to bypass the app's security measures to do it. Besides, behaviour that was good enough for Brian was certainly not good enough for me.

No, what I needed to do was take the investigation into

the real world. If I signed up for one of the in-person events run by the app, I'd be able to speak to actual people, find out if they'd had any weird experiences, and persuade them to report their situation to the app's staff as well. It would be much harder for them to ignore multiple in-person complaints. And maybe Scammer Brian would even be arrogant enough to turn up himself?

But there was no way I wanted to head to any kind of event without backup, which of course meant roping in Leo. The only problem was that, in order to attend the in-person events, he had to be a member of SO Ox, and I anticipated a battle.

The next day, I set my strategy in motion.

'I'll need to start working elsewhere if you're going to insist on distracting me like this,' said Leo, as I dragged the reshelving trolley past his table for the third time that morning. 'That ruddy thing needs putting out of its misery.'

Given that I'd got into work early and spent nearly an hour unscrewing the wheels and reassembling the trolley to try to fix it, I was somewhat disappointed that my DIY efforts to reduce the squeak had gone unnoticed.

'Still wrestling with the business plan?' I asked sympathetically, hoping his grumpy attitude was related to that rather than being solely the result of my presence.

'She's showing an interest in what I'm up to. That must mean she's after something. Okay, what is it that you want?'

he asked, leaning back and linking his fingers behind his head as he surveyed me.

'I'm doing some reshelving. Not everything is about you,' I said, irritated that he'd seen through me so easily.

He shook his head. 'We really must work on your covert investigatory skills if we're still going through with this plan of yours,' he said. 'Your face might as well have a neon sign on it, the way it signals everything you're thinking. Do you require evidence?' He nodded and gestured for me to sit down as he started pointing out my apparently massively obvious errors. I reluctantly pulled up a chair. 'First, there were the darting glances towards me. She's wondering if I've noticed she's there. Then you did the whole gaze shifting nervously between the books on the trolley thing, none of which are for this section – by the way, you should probably think about that for your next foray into surveillance. She's pretending to be getting on with her job as normal, while working out the lay of the land and whether she dares speak to me about what's on her mind. And now, the final tell, the furrow is back between your eyebrows. I know that one particularly well. It means you're royally pissed off with me for calling you out.'

The last comment was accompanied by a movement of his right hand. For a brief moment, I thought Leo was going to reach out and trace the line of the aforementioned furrow. The skin of my forehead prickled, already anticipating his touch.

Leo started laughing.

I tried to force my face into a neutral expression, not wanting to show him he'd got to me, but it only resulted in his smile growing broader still. The man was completely infuriating.

'Is it any wonder that I'm pissed off? I'm a private person. It's disappointing to discover I've apparently been telegraphing my innermost thoughts to all and sundry this whole time,' I said. What else had he been able to glean from me? I didn't want to think too hard about that.

His expression softened. 'You and me both. Look, I wouldn't worry too much. Most people are so wrapped up in themselves that they don't see what's right in front of them. And if they do, most of them don't really care.'

'That's a pretty depressing perspective.'

'Depressing, or realistic? There's a reason self-defence instructors encourage people to cry "fire" rather than "help" when they're in need of assistance. Strangers are more likely to pay attention and provide aid if they think they're at risk too. Otherwise, they'll probably feign ignorance and go on their merry way.'

I shook my head in disbelief. 'That's really sad. I refuse to accept most people's default state is selfishness. And I'm sorry that that's been your experience. Was that why you left the police?' I regretted the question as soon as I'd asked it. It was too soon in our business relationship for that kind of confidence sharing. The shutters came down immediately, all remnants of humour evaporating in a second. For a moment, I thought Leo might be about to get up and leave.

'Sorry,' I said. 'You don't have to tell me anything you don't want to. Put it down to regularly playing the role of the library's resident agony aunt. I've got used to people pouring out their problems to me.'

'I'm certainly not in need of an agony aunt,' he said in a way which made me even more convinced that he was. I kept quiet, wondering what he might say.

'What was it you wanted?' he asked eventually, making it clear that the subject was closed.

Fair enough, if that's how he chose to play it, I wouldn't pry where I wasn't invited. Even if he'd had no qualms about doing the opposite to me.

'I'd like you to join SO Ox.' I came straight out with it. There was no point in trying evasion when Leo was around. At least my suggestion put a smile back on his face, even if it was a cynical one.

'And why would I want to do that? From what you've described, it sounds like a hotbed of crookery and chancers.'

'I don't think everyone on there is dodgy. At least, I really hope they're not. Otherwise, that's fifteen quid a month down the drain.'

'Fifteen quid a month?' he repeated. 'Are all these potential suitors dipped in gold leaf or something? No wonder a scammer decided it would provide him with rich pickings. You do realise there are dozens of apps out there which you can get for free? Or heck, you could do it the old-fashioned way by meeting "IRL", as I believe they call it nowadays.'

'Stop pretending to be an old fuddy duddy. I am well aware that there are theoretically other options. But I'm not very good at the whole picking up flirtation signals in bars thing,' I said, embarrassed to admit it. Not that being flirted with in bars was a regular occurrence. Somehow, I didn't think clumsy flirting was a problem Leo was familiar with.

'I decided to choose a paid-for app because why shouldn't I make an investment in my future happiness?' I continued defensively. 'Besides, I figured the fee would put off the fuckboys and increase the chances that the members would be properly committed to finding a real relationship. Which is what I'm after. Call me a deluded romantic, but I don't mind paying for peace of mind and a better chance at meeting The One.'

'You *are* a deluded romantic. And I can't believe you're still defending the app, despite the presence of the supremely dodgy Brian James on it, and its staff's unwillingness to help you when you reported him.' He shook his head. 'Can you truthfully say it's working out well for you? Please spare me the clichés about one rotten apple and all that.'

I rolled my eyes. 'I'm not going to argue about it with you. We've established that I'm an idiot. Let's move on and get back to the point.'

'You're far from an idiot,' he said. 'Naïve, definitely. Idealistic, sure. And last time I checked, it wasn't a crime to be either of those things, although it certainly can make life difficult for a person. But an idiot? Definitely not.'

For a man who claimed to prize peace and quiet in the library environment, he was being remarkably loud as he delivered his assessment of my character. I noticed a couple of would-be browsers move away from the section.

'It's incredible how you can make something almost nice sound so insulting,' I responded, uncertain how I should feel about his words. 'There's nothing wrong with seeing the good in other people. You should try it some time. Look, if it's the money you're worrying about, of course I'll cover your subscription. I'm the only reason you're joining the app anyway.'

'A generous offer. Librarians must be better paid than I thought they were.'

'The app offers a free trial for the first two weeks, then a reduced fee for the rest of the initial month,' I admitted. 'I'm hoping we'll have things wrapped up well before that's done. And if you fancy staying as a member after that, then of course the payments will be down to you.'

'We can safely rule out that eventuality. I'm not in the market for a relationship.'

'More of a one-night-stand kind of guy, are you?' I said before I could stop myself. A sudden image flashed before my eyes of a bare-chested Leo stretched out in bed, curly hair even more tousled than usual, sheets tangled around his narrow waist. Why had I even made such a comment?

The words hung in the air between us.

'I don't think that's any of your business, is it?' he said, watching me closely.

I shook my hair forward, fruitlessly trying to shield my expression from him, praying that my face hadn't given away what had just been going through my mind.

'That was completely unnecessary, and totally inappropriate. I don't need to know, and I don't know why I asked. I can only say sorry.' I knew I was overdoing it with the apology, but I was horrified that he might have read in my eyes the weird direction of my thoughts.

After an uncomfortable few moments, Leo nodded in a thankfully business-like fashion. 'Let's move on. Have you considered the ethical implications of what you're asking me to do?'

'Meaning?' I pressed.

'Well, you're essentially asking me to join a dating app which brings with it the potential of other people wanting to go on dates with me.'

'That is generally the idea of dating apps,' I said.

'Is it fair to those other people? What if some woman sees my profile, decides she likes the look of me, but then her hopes are dashed because I'm not really available.'

A wave of shame came over me, tinged with a pang of something else I didn't want to examine too closely. 'I'm sorry, I didn't realise you already had a girlfriend. Why didn't you say? Of course, you shouldn't join the app if it's going to cause problems for you guys.'

'That's not what I meant.'

I waited for him to elaborate further, but his expression turned pointedly blank, and I got the impression he'd already shared more than he'd wanted to.

'Then what's the problem?' I asked. 'Unless you're trying to suggest you're so irresistible that as soon as you join the app, hordes of women will be throwing themselves at you and then be utterly devastated because you're not interested.'

I managed to provoke a smile in him.

'Well, when you put it like that, it sounds ridiculous. But I do think we need to tread carefully when it comes to other people's emotions.'

'You're not going to be leading anyone on unless you swipe right on them. And that's precisely why it's so important that we do this. Because other people's emotions are being trampled on by this bastard.'

The word 'bastard' echoed around the suddenly silent library.

'Oops, sorry,' I said, grateful that it was mostly the regulars in today, who I knew wouldn't be bothered by a bit of light swearing from their librarian. However, they would probably look less favourably on the amount of time I'd already spent talking to this one particular patron, considering the queue starting to form at the front desk and only Etta to deal with it.

'Look, I need to get back to work, and I'm sure you've got plenty to keep you occupied too. I know you're reluctant, but I really do think it would help our investigation if you were on the app. Promise me you'll at least think about it. By the way, I'm catching up with Doris later; I'm sure she'll be keen to hear all about your business ambitions.'

'Hmm,' he responded, but I thought I detected a softening of attitude somewhere in there.

'Why don't we sign you up at lunchtime?' I pressed home my advantage. 'You can share my sandwiches, and I'll even write your profile for you, if you like.'

Leo pulled a face. 'I'm perfectly capable of writing my own dating profile, thank you very much. I dread to think what you'd put in it. And I might be unemployed, but I can still sort my own lunch.'

I held my hands up. 'I never suggested you couldn't. I was being polite. Look it up in the dictionary some time.'

He responded with another grumpy 'Hmm.' I suspected he might be a bit hangry.

'Maybe I should transfer some money across to Brian and lure him out that way,' I said.

Both of us knew it wasn't a serious suggestion, but it had the desired effect.

'Fine, I concede defeat in this particular battle. I'll meet you outside at one o'clock. We can go to the University Parks to eat. But I have final veto on the profile. I am not having you make me look like some touchy-feely wimp.'

'There's nothing wimpish about being in touch with your emotions,' I responded, before recognising the glint in his eye. 'You're winding me up again, aren't you?'

'I don't know what you're talking about,' he said gruffly.

'Tell you what, as a show of good faith to make you feel less worried about the whole joining the app thing, I give you permission to read the last five messages from Brian while I'm working. We'll discuss them at lunchtime as well.'

'I do have my own work to do too.'

I patted his shoulder. 'You enjoy your *How to Build a Business in Your Teens* book. You're at least a decade too late to win at that particular game, but I'm sure you'll find some useful tips on how to invest your pocket money.'

'So much for the judgement-free reading zone,' I heard him say, laughter in his voice as I hurried back to help Etta.

Chapter Eight

Leo led the way to the University Parks like he was leading a route march.

'Would you mind slowing down a bit? Not everyone's a giraffe. Some of us have to manage getting through life with a considerably shorter stride. Besides, people take one look at the thunderous expression on your face and dive out of your way, whereas I need to do more weaving in and out of the crowds,' I called after him, slightly breathless with the effort of trying to keep up as he ploughed forward.

He came to a sudden halt, forcing me to take evasive action to avoid slamming into his broad back.

'They do what?' he asked.

'They all move out of your path. It's called male privilege. Obviously, I'm generalising, but society has programmed us humble females to move automatically out of the way, while most men charge ahead not even realising that's what's going on. It adds a lot of unnecessary steps to one's day.'

I braced myself for him to argue back at me.

Leo tilted his head to one side, reflecting on what I'd said. 'I suppose I hadn't really thought about it like that before.'

'Every day's a school day. Now you've been made aware of it, you won't be able to stop noticing it. Although hopefully you'll take preventative action by being more aware of those in your surroundings.' I knew I was being a bit preachy, but he seemed prepared to have his eyes opened to the issue.

'I shall consider myself told.' He paused. 'But you, a humble female? I hadn't noticed. If only.'

I made as if to lightly punch him.

He grinned. 'Do you want to lead the way, then? I shall spend the rest of the walk contemplating my growing paranoia about my male privilege, and of course, the apparently unnatural length of my neck. Nobody's referred to me as a giraffe before. Don't they also have incredibly knobbly knees? I'm going to develop a serious complex by the end of the day.'

'Don't worry too much about it. Extra-long scarves are all the rage. And at least you've got the option of wearing trousers to hide any knee knobbliness, which puts you at a distinct advantage over the giraffes.'

We walked the rest of the way to the park side by side, Leo making a point of smiling politely and stepping into the road to let every woman in the vicinity walk past him. Judging by the delighted beams he was getting in response, he was making quite a few people's days. Whether he was doing it for the attention, or because he'd genuinely taken my words to heart, I couldn't quite tell, but at least he appeared to be thinking about it.

Although it was the Easter holidays, there were still plenty of students hanging around in the University Parks making the most of the warm mid-April sunshine. We passed a study group sprawled out on the grass, earnestly discussing their favourite Roman emperors, a collection of amateur acrobats practising their tumbling in full academic dress, and then a couple of postgrads who, taking up a bench apiece, debated whether to head into banking or follow their true ambitions of going into politics after university.

'They'd be better off getting some real-life experience first, if you ask me,' said Leo under his breath as we walked past them.

I smiled, amused that I wasn't the only one eavesdropping on the people around us. I suppose being a former policeman, he was used to paying careful attention to his surroundings so he could assess the situation he was walking into.

'I'm guessing the banking profession isn't the kind of real-life experience that you're meaning,' I said.

He snorted. 'Absolutely not. It's always struck me as fitting that there is only one letter difference between the words "banker" and "wa—"'

'My sister's a banker.' I got in there before he could finish the insulting statement.

'My condolences to your family,' he responded irreverently.

'There's no need to be rude.' I frowned at him. I knew he

was being deliberately provocative, but I had to defend Caro. 'She's a lovely person *and* a good banker.'

'I didn't know the two things were compatible.'

'She looks after her firm's charitable donations and leads on ethical investments. She gets to direct millions of pounds towards the people and causes that really need it. Caro loves that she can make a difference in her role; it's all she ever wanted.'

'Good for her,' said Leo sincerely, although he ruined it with his next statement. 'Being a dreamy optimist obviously runs in the Fisher family.'

He laughed at the glare I was directing at him, and I reminded myself to stop rising to his bait. Once again, I wondered if I'd made an error in enlisting his help. I could be back at the library enjoying the peace of the break room rather than being deliberately wound up by this exasperating partner in crime-fighting. But I knew I wouldn't be relaxing there. I'd be stressing about what harm Scammer Brian might be about to inflict.

'Oh look, there's a bench by the river,' Leo continued, apparently oblivious to my internal conflict. 'Will it offend your feminist principles if I stride on ahead to reserve it for us? I'm sure you'll have noticed that there is a particular ruthlessness on display in this park when it comes to bagging prime seating with the best views, and you'll admit I have the advantage with my apparently giraffe-like legs.'

He didn't wait for my answer, but instead made quick work of covering the ground to the bench. I spotted at least two other people turn away looking disappointed and Leo's gloating grin from fifty paces.

He looked even more triumphant when I caught up with him.

'Check this out.' He gestured at the small plaque screwed onto the bench.

'In memory of J. R. R. Tolkien,' I read out loud. 'I must take a snap for the library's social media feed. I knew there was a bench in his honour in the park, but I've never managed to find it before. Here's hoping we can channel Tolkien's creative writing powers when it comes to putting together your SO Ox profile.'

Leo pulled a face. 'Perhaps, before we get on to that delight, we should have a chat about the messages you allowed me to read.'

I braced myself for the ribbing I feared I was about to get.

'The main things I noticed were that he's got a good grasp of grammar, he's very open to sharing his feelings, and he never once uses your name,' he said, ticking the items off on his fingers, his tone matter of fact, to my relief.

'The first two were things I liked about him. Call me a prissy pedant, but using "your" for "you are" is a bit of a turn off, to be honest.'

Leo let out a noise which I could only describe as a snigger.

'Laugh all you like, but a girl's got to set her boundaries.'

'Duly noted. You do you.'

'And he never uses my name? I hadn't spotted that. I know it creeped me out when someone else contacted me and kept dropping my name into every other sentence. Take a look at this.'

I quickly opened the app on my phone and scrolled to find the message.

Hey Kat, you're profile pic makes me want to know the secrets that are shining in you're eyes. Do you like to snuggle like a cat, Kat? I bet I can make you purr, Kat.

Leo pretended to vomit. 'Wow, that's something else. What a creep. And extra negative points to him for his "your slash you're" errors.'

'Exactly, definite red flag right there.' I gave an exaggerated shudder. 'Is it any wonder that I was so open to Brian's more sensitive – and grammatically correct – approach?'

'Unfortunately, in Brian's case, I think the lack of use of your name is a red flag for a different reason. It made me wonder if he's been copying and pasting the same, apparently heartfelt, messages to all his marks.'

I shouldn't have been surprised by this revelation, but it still hurt. I'd invested a lot of myself in my replies to Fake Brian, pouring thought into my answers to his questions, and genuinely caring about the ups and downs he detailed of his life. It was mortifying to imagine the shadowy fraudster getting a kick out of my innocent responses, gleefully anticipating his pay day. To my embarrassment, I felt tears pricking my eyes. I stared angrily at the path, willing myself to get it together. I was not going to waste any more emotional energy crying over past mistakes.

'You've only got an hour for lunch, haven't you? Perhaps we should move on to discussing whether or not I should join the site. I'm still not convinced it makes any sense,' said Leo.

I was grateful for his tactful change of subject.

'Well, as you're being so funny about wanting to use my login details, it seems only sensible that you should have your own method of accessing the app.' I decided to hold back on the other part of my plan, namely that we should take our investigation to the in-person events. It would be enough of a battle getting him to sign up to SO Ox. 'Given Brian's voice, I'm 90% certain that our target is male,' I continued, 'but if he has managed to play the system to set up multiple profiles, what's to stop him pretending to be a woman and targeting the blokes too? I mean, he'd need to avoid the voice notes tactic, but you've seen his messages, I'm sure he could find other ways of being convincing.'

'Hmm.' Leo still sounded dubious.

'What are you so afraid of?'

'Did I say I was afraid? I'm not afraid at all. I just think it's a waste of our time, but you're the boss. Sign me up, if you insist.'

I smothered a smile at Leo's defensiveness. 'Okay, as you're so relaxed about this, I'll do the typing and you can concentrate on enjoying your sandwich. Hand your phone over.'

He looked like he was going to argue with me, but the appeal of food got the better of him and he reluctantly gave me his device before unwrapping the greaseproof cover of his pack-up.

'Smells nice,' I said, briefly distracted by the appealing aroma that emanated from his clearly home-made meal. The man obviously had skills. 'What's on the menu?'

'Paws off, Fisher. You can get your own falafel and Mediterranean veg wrap.'

'Mmm, fancy lunch. That sounds fal-afelly good.' I couldn't resist saying it.

'If I was still in the police, I'd arrest you for crimes against the English language with that terrible pun. And, by the way, I want to see everything you type on that profile, and I reserve the right to veto the lot of it.'

'You're determined to be as difficult as possible about this, aren't you? If I didn't know better, I'd say you don't trust me.'

'Trust has to be earned,' he said, in a holier-than-thou voice.

'I prefer to think the best of people until proven otherwise,' I said.

'And how's that working out for you?'

'Touché. Now, why don't you concentrate on eating your lunch while I get this sorted out?'

He opened his mouth to talk back, but his stomach let out a grumble instead. He smiled and shrugged, then started polishing off his delicious-looking meal.

Meanwhile, I tapped a few buttons and took a quick bite of my disappointingly ordinary shop-bought cheese sandwich while I waited for the app to load. It was tempting to have a quick browse through Leo's internet history while he was focused on food, but my conscience got the better of me. He'd been respectful of my boundaries when I gave him my login, after all. Besides, although he appeared to be absorbed in his lunch, I suspected he'd be quick to notice if I started nosing around things I shouldn't.

'Okay, first thing's first, we need a picture of you for your profile. They don't let anyone join without one. Smile nicely,' I instructed.

I held his phone up and managed to capture a snap of his scowling reaction to my request.

'Ooh, it's definitely giving off mugshot chic,' I said, moving the phone quickly away so he couldn't see it to dispute my claim. Given that I'd caught him off guard, he actually looked annoyingly good in the picture, his moodiness coming across more like he was deep in important thoughts. 'You're in luck: some women really dig that slovenly haven't-shaved-in-days kind of vibe.'

He rubbed his chin. 'I shaved this morning, thank you very much.'

'Then you have impressive hair follicles. You could light a match on that stubble.'

'Look, I don't have to sit here and spend my precious down time listening to you abusing me,' he reminded me.

I was getting far too much enjoyment out of pushing his buttons, indulging myself with a little light revenge for his earlier comments to me. I needed to concentrate on the matter in hand.

'Okay, well, do you have a photo you'd like me to use instead? Anything will do, but I'd recommend not using one where you're kissing a giant fish.'

'I'm vegetarian, so there's zero chance of that. Do guys

really think they're going to get anywhere by using a photo like that?'

'Sadly, yes. It's surprisingly common. Maybe the ability to catch supper does it for some women, but alas, not for me. I just look at the picture and feel sorry for the poor fish which was probably happily swimming along minding its own business before it got rudely ripped out of the water. And let's not forget what the smell must be like. I might enjoy eating fish fingers, but I certainly don't want to be embraced by a man who has them.'

'What type of photo works best in your opinion? I'm asking from an investigative perspective,' he added hastily. 'I'm trying to build a picture of what impression our man was trying to give, and how it helped him lure in his victim. Sorry, his target,' he corrected. 'Basically, what was it about him that appealed to you?'

He sounded serious but I thought I detected a note of empathy in there, which I found reassuring despite how exposing it was opening up about something so personal.

I decided it was safer to keep things light to start with. 'It was the classic posing with a puppy picture that first attracted me to him. Big brown eyes, helpless expression, silky ears, that kind of thing.'

'And the dog was cute too,' he said with a grin.

'You know full well that I was referring to the dog. In fact, I was hoping Brian would introduce me to his puppy once we'd met. I've always wanted to have a pooch of my own. We have a family dog, but he lives with my parents in Yorkshire, so I don't get to see him as often as I'd like. And dog-sitting Robin so her dad, Gavin, can get a bed for a couple of nights at the homeless hostel doesn't really count.'

Leo shook his head. 'You do go above and beyond for your library regulars. In fact, I'm starting to fear that you enlisting me in this endeavour is some covert project to fix me, like you try to solve the rest of your patrons' problems.'

I looked at him. 'That's a very generous opinion of me. Do you need fixing?'

There was a brief pause.

'Don't we all?' he said, his tone completely neutral.

'Um, well, yes, I guess,' I said, surprised by his admission into making one of my own. 'You're not wrong there.'

An awkward silence descended on us, during which I feigned deep interest in a couple of mallards swimming lazily by. Leo seemed equally absorbed in devouring his wrap. I think we were both taken aback by the direction of the conversation. This was meant to be a business partnership, two acquaintances helping each other out in exchange for something the other wanted. It was not meant to descend into a therapy session. I'd already revealed too many weaknesses to Leo. It wasn't his reaction that I was worried about, more what the act of showing them to him might mean for me. I'd been hurt enough already by a man who, it turned out, didn't even exist in the first place.

Leo's phone vibrated in my hand.

'That's the app asking me if you want to log off because I've not typed anything in a while.'

Leo frowned. 'It's a persistent little blighter, isn't it?'

'I guess it doesn't like being kept waiting. Look, if you really don't want to join, I won't mind,' I lied.

But it would change my plans.

Chapter Nine

After a long pause, Leo sighed. 'In for a penny and all that. I suppose you've got a point about keeping our investigative options open.'

I tried not to look too pleased, sensing that he was still teetering on the knife edge of calling the whole scheme off.

'Okay. Shall I take another picture of you?'

'Let's stick with the mugshot photo,' he said. 'As I'm not trying to attract a date, I don't really care if it's not my best.'

'Are you sure? I can take another one, if you like. Unless you're shamelessly fishing for compliments.'

Leo pulled a face. 'Would I do something as superficial as that?'

'I know, I know. You're above such trivial considerations as personal appearance.' Easy for someone as good-looking as Leo was, I added silently to myself.

I uploaded the picture. 'It'll probably take a little while to appear,' I explained. 'The app uses AI as one of its safety measures to make sure there's nothing inappropriate in any images.'

'And yet Brian's plagiarised photos got through the checks? Another black mark against SO Ox's allegedly watertight security. Anyway, what comes next?'

'Well, most profiles have more than one picture so that you can get a more rounded idea of the person behind the images. You know, showing shots of you in different situations, like surrounded by loads of friends so you can make it clear how popular you are, or on glamorous holidays to show that you've got a spirit of adventure. You get the idea.'

Leo nodded. 'That makes sense. Go on then, what caught your attention about Brian's other pictures? He lured you in with the puppy snap, and then the other pictures increased your interest because of what exactly?'

I considered my answer. 'He looked kind,' I said eventually, realising that I'd been drawn to this particular quality because it had been lacking in previous relationships. I wished my honesty with myself, and Leo, felt more liberating, but I couldn't shake my sense of shame at longing so desperately for something which should be so basic.

'Interesting.' The word was loaded. 'And what exactly makes a guy appear "kind" in his profile pictures?' he pushed.

'It was something about his eyes. He had this look like...' I struggled to find the right words to explain myself. Besides, it was difficult to make a sensible argument when Leo was watching me with such an intense expression on his face. 'You're just trying to get me to admit that he looked hot in the photos.' I threw my hands up in the air in mock surrender, taking the opportunity to steer the conversation into more superficial waters. 'Yes, fine, I admit it, there was one picture where he was in his combat gear surrounded by the people he'd been helping, sleeves rolled up, strong arms, devastating smile, the whole dreamboat thing. If that makes me incredibly shallow, then I have no defence.'

'I don't think it's shallow to admit when you're physically attracted to someone,' said Leo. 'That's a pretty key part of a successful relationship.' His voice was softer than usual, more intimate.

I felt my cheeks turn warm as my mental image of Scammer Brian's picture was replaced with one of Leo in a similarly heroic stance. I found myself glancing down at his arms, imagining the strength of the muscles concealed beneath his jacket, wondering what it would be like to be held in his embrace. I gave myself a mental shake. What was wrong with me? I looked back up, forcing my features into as unflustered an expression as I could manage.

Leo cleared his throat, and took on a more business-like tone, 'And scammers often use pictures harvested from people in the military. The armed forces have a certain cachet to them; plus, people are naturally more trusting of those in uniform.'

'It's even more disappointing to fall into a trap catering to a stereotype. I'd hoped I was better than that,' I quipped, still trying to get myself back onto an even keel.

Leo was warming to his subject. 'Another reason fraudsters often claim they're in the military is that it supplies them with a ready-made excuse as to why they can't meet up easily. Or they'll pretend to be working offshore on an oil rig, basically any kind of role where they have a high status and plausible reasons to be difficult to get hold of sometimes. Rule 101 from scammer school.'

'I wish I'd known that. Now you say it, it sounds so obvious.'

'You live and learn. Anyway, we're getting off point. I'd prefer to stick with just the one photo on this app. The less attention my profile attracts, the better.'

I toyed with teasing him about posting a picture in police uniform but, remembering his previous reactions to any mention of his time in the force, I decided it was better to leave that area well alone.

'Okay, if you're determined to stick to just the one photo, I guess we need to carry on to the next section which is writing a short personal statement, followed by a quick-fire quiz about your likes and dislikes. Then we fill out the security questions, upload your proof of Oxfordshire residency, and wait for you to be approved.'

'And is my approval also down to artificial intelligence, or does a human get involved at some point?'

'Good question,' I said. 'I can't remember it being mentioned in the terms and conditions. Let's add that to our list of things to find out.'

'Of course, she has a list.' He rolled his eyes.

'I thought it would be the best way of keeping organised and on track. How did you do it when you were carrying out investigations in the police?'

'The gaffer gave us our instructions and sent us on our

way. And I quickly learnt that it was best to keep my speculation and thoughts to myself, rather than writing them down in list form. The defence can demand that your notes are made public, you see.' He frowned, and I wondered once again what it was that had made him so wary. 'Right, so you wanted a personal statement? That sounds uncomfortably like applying for a job.'

'I suppose it's not too dissimilar,' I replied, double-checking the requirements and desired word count. 'Although this statement is aimed more at describing your personality traits than your skillset. I wouldn't worry too much about it. It's just something along the lines of "Hi, I'm an aspiring business owner based in Oxford, and I'd like to meet an outgoing woman for fun and blah blah blah."'

'Fun and blah blah blah, got it in one.' He raised an eyebrow, and my mind suddenly filled in what 'blah blah blah' could stand for. Why did I keep going down this unwanted path? Maybe it was a weird reaction to the Brian situation, a kind of delayed sense of frustration that the man of my dreams had turned out to be nightmare material, but I could really do without it. I could feel myself blushing but, thankfully, Leo didn't seem to notice as he continued with his theme. 'I think it would make perfect sense to advertise one's skills on a dating website and inform a woman what one can bring to the table. She should be aware that I'm practical and know my way around DIY. For example, I can fix a leaky tap in the ensuite and, when it comes to the bedroom, I'm incre—'

'Yes, alright, too much information, thank you very much, Leo,' I interrupted him, irritated that certain internal organs were already reacting to his unfinished sentence, despite the instructions from my much more sensible brain to ignore him.

'I was going to say that I'm incredible at hanging curtains and putting up pictures,' he said, the affected innocence contradicted by the wicked sparkle in his eyes. 'If your mind went to other places, then that's on you.'

I decided it was safer to take another bite of my sandwich rather than try to come up with a response to his deliberate provocation. Thankfully, he seemed oblivious to my self-induced discomfort.

'Okay, how about this? "Hi, my name's Leo. I live in Oxford and I enjoy good food and travelling."'

I responded with an exaggerated yawn. 'That's rather generic, don't you think? I mean most people like those things. It would be pretty unusual not to.'

'Generic was exactly what I was after. The blander the better, if you ask me. Why, what did you put in your statement?'

I thought about lying, but he was going to find out sooner or later. To be honest, I was amazed, and touched, that he hadn't used his access to my account to read it already.

'I wrote a short poem actually,' I admitted, embarrassed to reveal the amount of effort I'd gone to. Having held out against online dating for so long, fearing it would reduce my love life to the same level of passion as selecting a purchase on Amazon, I'd hoped that my thoughtful verse might attract the attention of someone who would share my love of the written word, a real gentleman who would reply with a similarly grand gesture, demonstrating his intelligence and romantic hero credentials. In retrospect, and judging by Leo's bemused expression, it had probably made me jump right to the top of the list of gullible victims ripe for the picking. I'd given of myself because that was what I'd been hoping for in return. But in reality, I had just made myself even more vulnerable to exploitation.

Leo stood up suddenly and cleared his throat.

'A poem? Let me guess. Did it go something like this?' He started declaiming a verse with the seriousness of an actor delivering a Shakespearean soliloquy in the West End.

'There once was a librarian called Kat,

whose dream suitor was a man with a rat.

She signed up to SO Ox,

found a man who could box,

now her mum's buying a brand-new hat.'

He finished with a flourish, and then bowed and pressed his hand to his chest as if moved by the applause of an invisible audience.

Although I should have been annoyed by his teasing, I couldn't help laughing at his impressive improvisation skills.

'Gosh, he's a poet, and I didn't know it,' I said, knowing that my retort was pathetic in comparison. 'I was hoping someone would respond to my efforts with poetry themselves, and now it's finally happened. I mean, a limerick wasn't quite what I was anticipating, but I'll take it.'

'You deserve better than Brian,' Leo said as he sat back down next to me, his voice suddenly serious.

I blinked at his unexpected kindness.

'We're getting distracted. Time is ticking,' he added. 'What was next? My likes and dislikes, wasn't it?'

I checked my watch.

'You're right, I should be heading back in five minutes. Let's be quick about the next section. How about this? Likes – vegetables, cute fluffy animals. Dislikes – criminals and eating meat?'

His laugh sounded rather forced. 'Not far off.'

'We probably need a little more detail, otherwise you're going to look suspicious,' I said. 'You mentioned you enjoy travel earlier. The app gives a prompt asking about particular places you'd like to visit and why. I put Japan in cherry blossom season and Canada in the autumn for my answer.'

He nodded. 'Both beautiful destinations at beautiful times of the year. Definitely giving away your romantic side there, in case he hadn't worked it out with the poem.'

'Brian said he'd visited Japan when he got some leave during a deployment in the Far East. Only, of course, now I know the pictures he shared with me from that trip actually belonged to the soldier whose photos he ripped off. He must have been rubbing his hands together when he saw my profile. Maybe that's another reason he targeted me.'

'I wouldn't get too hung up on the why. He's probably been trying his tricks with half the women on the app.'

'Nothing special about me.'

He shrugged. 'Be fair. There's no correct response to that statement, is there?'

'You're right. Okay, if you don't want to add any more

detail, we're nearly done. Just the final few quick-fire ones to polish off.'

He shuddered. 'Quick-fire questions? We're back to the screening process on a job application again.'

'I guess, in some ways, the app is asking people to fill in an application for the ultimate role – as someone's life partner. That's how I took it, anyway.' More fool me.

'As previously stated, that's a role I am not applying for. Okay, hit me with them, let's get this over and done with.'

'Dogs or cats?'

'Parrots,' he said defiantly.

'Sadly, there isn't an option for parrots.'

'That's a shame. Parrots are very intelligent creatures. I once encountered one who'd witnessed a crime and was able to tell us who'd done it. The defence lawyers tried to argue that the bird wasn't a credible witness, but the jury couldn't get enough of it.'

I stared at him. 'I can't tell if you're being serious or not.'

'Blame it on still having a policeman's terrible sense of humour.' His eyes twinkled. 'Okay, I'll go for dogs, then. They've got the reputation of man's best friend for a reason, right? Next question.'

I scrolled down. 'Country or town?'

'They're asking a lot, aren't they, forcing humans who are notoriously complex beings to place themselves within such a binary choice?'

'It's only meant to be a bit of fun,' I said. There was being a private person, and then there was Leo. His determination to remain an enigma was something else.

'Country.'

'Oh, snap, me too. Sweet or savoury?'

'These questions are dreadful. I really don't know how anyone would expect to find their life partner using them. Again, I'd prefer to tick the "other" box and say it depends on what mood I'm in, but, if we're having to generalise, I'll go for sweet on this occasion.'

'Running or rowing?'

Leo laughed. 'Tell me the app is based in Oxford without telling me the app is based in Oxford. In my experience, most rowers also do a fair bit of running as well to help build their cardio. Pick whichever one you like. Are we nearly done?'

'Only two more to go. Theatre or cinema? And yes, before you say it, I agree that they should let you tick both boxes.'

'I guess it depends on the show. I'll say cinema because I reckon a lot of people will answer the opposite to make themselves appear more cultured, and I'm trying to keep a low profile.' He sat up straighter. 'Right, I'm bracing myself. What is the definitive final question which will reveal whether I'm decent boyfriend material or not?'

'Would you rather cook, or wash the dishes?'

Leo tried to grab the phone from me. 'No, you cannot be serious. Is that really the final question?'

I turned the phone round so he could see it. 'I promise, that's what they've asked. I suppose it could be interpreted as a way of revealing whether you're a creative person or prefer more practical tasks.'

'That's assuming there's some degree of creativity in the cooking. What's to stop a guy from checking the cooking box and thinking proudly of the cold beans on burnt toast which is his signature dish? What did Brian go for?'

'Actually, the quick-fire questions are randomly generated for each user. He had much more interesting questions like, "going out or staying in?", "book or movie?", and "love or money?".'

Leo made a noise which sounded suspiciously like a snort. 'I'm pretty sure he wouldn't have answered that last one truthfully.'

'Obviously not. So, what is it: cooking or doing the dishes? Come on, Leo, it's time to reveal the real you. What are you passionate about? What makes your heart beat faster?'

Even though I was obviously teasing him, his face took on that shuttered expression it always did when he was being asked anything personal.

'I prefer to spend my down time in places other than the kitchen. Pick whichever you like. I've got an appointment to get to.'

Chapter Ten

A notification from SO Ox pinged on my phone screen as I arrived back at the library alone, wondering whether Leo really did have an appointment, or more likely, whether it had been a convenient excuse to make a speedy exit and swerve my questions. The man was clearly determined to remain a closed book. Which was fine, of course it was. Just because we were working together, it didn't mean he had to bare his soul to me, even though I felt I'd been doing a lot of that to him.

I clicked onto the app and saw that Brian had already got back in touch. The speed of his response made me feel like he was watching out for me, and not in a good way. I read his message and rolled my eyes, wondering how I'd ever been taken in by him in the first place.

Hon, I'm so glad that you're ok. I missed our heart to hearts. I've been reading back through your messages which have been sustaining me during a challenging period. The post-mission debrief is nearly over, and I'm looking forward to spending time with you once it's all done. It's taking longer than expected because the situation on the ground was worse than we realised. We're already planning our next aid drop, although the powers that be say there are issues with the funding, and without funding, there's no chance of helping those who so desperately need it. It's a huge worry. I wish there was more I could do. My army wages only go so far. I know you'll understand my frustration, being the gorgeous caring person that you are. We'll be together soon, but until then, sending all my love, Brian xoxo

He was trying to be slightly more subtle in his money-grabbing approach, but the emotional manipulation was still present, the pressure to offer financial support to back his work with these unnamed people who were suffering because of some unspecified disaster. Obviously, I had no intention of doing any such thing, but I could see how I might have felt compelled to if I hadn't finally cottoned on to his nefarious objective.

It would probably be best to play ignorant to try to force Brian into making an overt demand. If I expressed shock, and said something along the lines of I wished I knew how I could help, that might make him show his hand. Or would that sound strange?

'Are you heading in or out?' Library regular Gavin brought me back to reality. I hoped I hadn't been blocking the doorway for too long as I considered my situation.

'Sorry, guys, I was miles away,' I said, leaning down to

scratch his loyal pooch, Robin. I swear she grinned at me. 'I was going back into the library, but I guess my mind had other ideas.'

Gavin laughed. 'Don't worry, it happens to me all the time. But sometimes it's good to let the brain go into neutral and see what emerges from the subconscious rather than overthinking things.'

I nodded. 'You know what, that's just what I needed to hear right now. Thank you.'

'Always happy to help,' he said. 'Speaking of which, can I make a contribution?'

I looked at him blankly. 'What do you mean?'

He gestured at my phone. 'Sorry, I couldn't help seeing part of the message on the screen. It sounds like your friend needs some donations. Is it a charity he works for? I can't give much, but they do say that every little helps, right?'

He fished a pound coin out of his coat pocket and offered it to me. I thought my heart might break.

I reached out and squeezed his arm. 'That's so kind of you, but please don't worry. The situation is all in hand, I promise. You put that money back where it belongs, in your wallet.'

'Are you sure?' he said, the coin still held out towards me. 'Only I know what it's like to go through hard times, and I've got enough to cover myself for tonight. I'd hate for someone else to be struggling when there's something I could do to help, even if it's not much.'

'I'm certain. I'm going to sort everything out.'

If I'd been determined to put a stop to Scammer Brian's activities before, now I was even more motivated to track him down and bring him to justice. Gavin lived such a precarious existence, yet the briefest glimpse at a message from Brian had had him wanting to offer financial help, which he could ill afford. How many other vulnerable people like Gavin would be similarly taken in? I needed to up the ante.

Now that Leo was a fully signed up member of SO Ox, it was time to explore the next stage of my plan: that was, to book us onto one of the events run by the app and take the investigation into the real world. It couldn't happen soon enough. Scammer Brian was back in contact with me, and goodness knows how many other potential targets.

When I got home from work that night, I finished typing out a reply to Brian in which I hopefully sounded suitably sympathetic, like I was teetering on the brink of offering money, then I turned my attention to the app's upcoming events diary. I needed to find something happening in the next few days, then I could contact Leo and present him with a considered plan.

The first event I spotted was the promising-sounding Single Mingle which had a little red banner stating that it was nearly fully booked. I scanned through the details. It was basically a speed-dating event dressed up with a catchier name. Each participant had five minutes to talk to the person opposite them on the table, then a bell would ring and everyone would move around. I experienced a clutch of nerves. Never mind that it wouldn't leave much opportunity for screening potential Brian suspects, but it sounded like my version of hell. I was used to meeting lots of people on a daily basis in the library, but that was for work. It was easier to pretend to be confident and outgoing in a familiar, safe environment where I had an official job title and was surrounded by friends and colleagues. I knew it would be a very different matter turning up at a bar and facing a bunch of strangers, with a weight of expectation in every interaction. That kind of event was designed for extroverts, who would thrive in the challenge to make a connection in less than five minutes. I was more of a slow-burner, someone who preferred a quieter, steadier approach to getting to know new people.

The real-world events had been part of SO Ox's appeal in the first place, although I'd started talking with Brian so soon after joining that I hadn't attended any of them. Under normal circumstances, I would never have chosen to go to the Single Mingle. No, the book club or the cookery class were much more to my taste; events where there was something more going on than just checking each other out, where people had a chance to bond over shared interests and connect on a deeper level. I was far more likely to get to know a person by finding out their reading tastes or seeing how they reacted following a complicated recipe, than by enduring a quick-fire round of questions before a bell rang.

But Brian was definitely good at the patter and at making a quick impression. Wasn't that exactly the kind of event that he was likely to attend, if he was bold enough to get up from behind his computer screen and try his scamming in person? He'd be able to meet a dozen or more potential targets in one night.

The more I thought about it, the more I realised it could be the perfect way to advance our investigation. And if I could rope Leo into coming along with me, that would be even better. I could screen the male attendees for potential Brians, while he could subtly try to find out if any of the women had fallen for the same despicable advances that I had. But coming up with the plan was one thing. Getting Leo to agree to it was quite another…

'Absolutely not,' was his forceful response after I delivered my sales pitch. I briefly held the phone away from my ear and wondered if it would have been better to text him instead.

'Scared at having to talk to a bunch of women?' I challenged, trying a different tack.

'I'm not going to dignify that with a response.' He didn't even sound annoyed, so confident in his ability to attract and entertain. I envied that poise.

'I honestly think this is the most productive next step we can take,' I said, sitting forward on the sofa as I pressed my point. 'The only reason I can come up with for you digging your heels in like this is that you never had any intention of helping me in the first place, and that you've been stringing me along in exchange for access to Doris's business expertise.' It was a low blow, but I couldn't think of another way of getting him on board with my idea.

'I'm sorry that you have such a poor opinion of me,' he said, instantly making me feel guilty, although his next words replaced that with indignation. 'But it would be utterly foolish to take on that kind of operation with just the two of us and no kind of backup. And let's face it, only one of us has any actual experience of investigative work. Criminals are much more wily in real life than they are in the pages of books.'

I stood up and started pacing in exasperation.

'I wish you'd stop treating me like I've got my head in the clouds. I do know the difference between fiction and reality. We'd be each other's backup. And it's hardly like we'd be going undercover as drug dealers. It's a members' event on a Thursday evening in an upmarket bar in Oxford. The worst that could happen is that someone drops their drink.' Or that I chickened out. But I was keeping that particular fear to myself.

Leo sighed. 'And in the highly unlikely event that our scammer does make an appearance, what happens then? Do you plan to confront him? Have you thought about how he might respond to that? Everything you're saying is based on assumptions. We haven't had the time to build a proper profile of Brian James, and it's dangerous to go into any situation without detailed intel. All we know is that he has a good grasp of the English language – or that he bothers to use spelling and grammar checks at any rate – and has the ability to build connections with people online relatively quickly and gain their trust.'

'Exactly. I reckon that ability will translate into the real world as well, otherwise why not use a different app that doesn't offer in-person events?'

'Your optimistic logic astonishes me.'

'Surely, it's worth giving it a try? And I could listen out for his voice at the event as well.'

'There is that, I suppose, although there's every chance he's a master mimic and can put on a different voice to leave you voice notes.'

'We had a phone call once, not long after we first started chatting,' I said.

'One phone call? Why didn't you say so before? That changes everything.'

'That's great, then.' I settled back down on the sofa.

'I was being sarcastic. And yes, I know, it's the lowest form of wit. But I can already guess that the phone call was brief and the connection was bad, so that probably rules out any useful information which you think you might know from it.'

I decided it was time to play my ultimate hand. 'Look, if you don't want to come with me, that's not a problem, I'm perfectly happy going by myself.'

I could almost picture Leo's grip tightening on his phone in frustration at my stubbornness. 'Fine, if you're going to be like that and refuse to listen to my advice, you leave me with no choice.' He sighed. 'I'll book onto the event and pick you up an hour beforehand so we can agree on how to handle the evening,' he said, with as much enthusiasm as if he was arranging an appointment with the dentist.

'Looking forward to seeing you then,' I said, but it turned out I was addressing only the dial tone.

Chapter Eleven

Leo wasn't in a better mood when he arrived at my place on Thursday evening.

'Is that what you're wearing tonight?' was his opening gambit as I opened the front door.

I looked down at the yellow polka dot dress in confusion. 'I thought I might as well get some wear out of it. I bought it to meet Brian, after all. It seemed appropriate to use it in the continuation of that purpose. Why, what's the matter with it?'

'Nothing,' he said quickly. 'You look very ... nice.'

The way he said it, 'nice' was definitely not a good thing.

'Oh.'

Despite the negative associations of the dress, I had felt good putting it on again, like I was reclaiming it. The reason I'd chosen it in the first place was for the confidence boost, and wearing it tonight had felt like donning a suit of armour to protect me from whatever the night might bring.

I certainly didn't need validation from Leo, but on the other hand, it would have made me feel better about the whole evening if he'd sounded more positive about how I looked.

'Don't do that,' he said.

'What?'

'You look like a puppy who's had its dinner snatched away,' he responded.

'It's just that I've never heard a supposed compliment delivered with such disappointment. And given your previously stated preference for parrots over puppies, I'm even more insulted. Have I done something to offend you?'

Leo frowned. 'Look, you won't want to hear it if I say anything, so it's probably best we stop this conversation here, and get this evening over and done with.'

'You can't say that and then expect me to drop it! What is it that you can't bring yourself to say? Given that you've not shied away from making it very clear that spending the evening in my company is the last thing you want to be doing, I dread to think what it is that you're keeping to yourself. Why don't you just come out with it? This investigation partnership isn't going to get very far if we're not honest with each other.'

He tried to stare me into submission, but I glared back at him, determined not to back down.

Eventually he sighed in exasperation. 'Fine, if you insist. But you're probably going to hate me for it, I'm warning you now. Look, I know you've got great faith in the safety measures the app has. Or at least you did until the whole Brian thing. But the reality is that neither of us has a clue who's going to be turning up to this Single Mingle nonsense. You could end up sitting opposite a mad axe murderer for all we know. The crux of it is that I feel really uncomfortable with us continuing with this ridiculous idea and you putting yourself at risk in this way. Especially when you're looking like … that.' He gestured up and down at me.

'Again, I must be missing something here. Are you suggesting that the way I'm dressed will in some way provoke murderous behaviour? Because I have the right to dress exactly as I like.' I put my hands on my hips, facing him down with my best power stance.

'I know you do. I told you I was going to mess this up and make you get all annoyed with me. All I meant was that you look like sunshine, and I'm concerned that this might be an evening full of clouds.'

My stomach gave a surprised little flip. I wasn't sure how to react to that.

I went for a simple, 'Thanks.'

He cleared his throat and made a show of checking his watch. Was the great Leo Taylor actually embarrassed?

'The sad thing, Leo, is that every time a woman leaves the house, and all too often when she's still in it, the "what if" thought crosses her mind. The mad axe murderer phrase is the one we usually deploy to add some humour to what is, unfortunately, a genuine fear. But this isn't a surprise to you, is it?'

He avoided meeting my gaze. Were my words bringing back memories of cases he'd worked on? He remained quiet.

'Having worked for the police, you probably know all about the bad things that can happen to people.'

His nod was reluctant. We were definitely on sensitive territory here. I was more convinced than ever that there was something deeper to his departure from the police than merely an ambition to be his own boss.

'Which is why I really think we'd be better sticking to the trapping him online plan,' he tried one last time.

'But I'm not going into this alone,' I reminded him. 'You'll be there too. Won't you?'

Leo sighed. 'Seeing as you're determined to go through with this, you leave me with no choice. I still think this is a seriously bad idea.'

'You could at least try a little optimism.' Goodness knows I could do with it. His cynical attitude was making me even more nervous about the event.

'I can't, it gives me indigestion,' he said.

'Okay, well, let's agree on how we're going to handle the event before we walk down there. Will that make you feel any better? Why don't you come in for a few minutes?'

I didn't wait for him to respond as I went back inside. After a moment's hesitation, he followed me and perched awkwardly on the armchair, making my living space feel even smaller than usual.

'I think we should pretend we don't already know each other, and if we need to communicate during the evening, we can text,' I suggested. 'Nobody will pay any attention to people checking their phones regularly. You'll need to try to bring the conversations around to dodgy app experiences during your speed dates, and I'll keep my ears open for

Brian and attempt to work out if the guys are really who they say they are.'

'And what will you do if you happen to recognise Brian's voice?'

I hesitated, knowing that Leo was not going to find my answer satisfactory. 'I thought I'd confront him and try to get him to confess, then call over a member of staff.'

'You'll have to do better than that.' He leaned forward. 'Look, I know you don't like being told what to do, but will you take some advice from me?'

I nodded. 'That's why I hir— asked you to help me, after all.'

'The objective this evening should be purely fact-finding. I know you're keen to prevent him causing further harm, but we don't want to rush things and risk him going to ground. So, I was thinking it might be best if you assume another persona while we're there, as a safety net, if you will. Katherine is a common enough name, but your job is relatively unusual.'

'We live in Oxford, remember. Trust me, there are more librarians around than you could possibly imagine.'

'Fair enough,' said Leo. 'But I reckon it would give you an extra layer of security if you say you have another profession. You don't want Brian to recognise you before you find him.'

'There's an obvious flaw in this plan, and that is that he's seen my profile pictures. Brian knows exactly what I look like. I only left him a couple of voice notes – I find talking into the ether a bit awkward – but he might also recognise me from them.'

'If you found it awkward, your voice probably reflected that, so it's a slim chance. And everyone looks different in photos from real life.'

'Rude. I hope you're not suggesting *I* was catfishing *him*?'

'Absolutely not, only that cameras see things differently to the human eye. Speaking of which...' Leo nodded towards my glasses case on the mantelpiece. 'None of your photos on the app show you wearing those, do they?'

'No, but they're hardly going to radically transform my appearance,' I said.

'And, if I remember correctly, your hair is down?'

'I can put it up, but again, I'm still the same person.'

'I know that. But I have a feeling that our suspect won't have paid a huge amount of attention to your pictures. He cares more about the words you write because they give him the clues as to how to target you most effectively.'

'In any other context, a man who prioritises personality over superficial looks would be the perfect guy,' I sighed.

'It's not just men who are guilty of such behaviour. If you ask me, the reason Beauty fell for the Beast was that she liked the look of his library,' said Leo with mock seriousness.

'Sensible woman.'

'It's worth a try, though, don't you think?' he pressed.

'I suppose so,' I said reluctantly. 'Only, please, no buttoned-up librarian jokes.'

'I wouldn't dream of it. Besides, for the purposes of this evening, you'll be, what, a rocket scientist? A brain surgeon? What do you fancy?'

I considered my options as I wrestled my hair into an approximation of a French twist, and quickly zipped into the bathroom to take out my contacts.

'I think I'll be a writer,' I said on my return, putting on my specs and checking my hair one final time.

Leo nodded.

'That works. Come on, then, Ms Brontë-in-waiting. I guess we'd better get this evening over and done with.'

And with that less than resounding battle cry, we set off.

Chapter Twelve

Leo went into the bar first to carry out 'advance reconnaissance' as he put it. To be honest, I was probably safer going in there at the same time as him rather than loitering around outside, but if me staying back for a few minutes kept his mind at rest, then it was a price I was willing to pay. I lurked at the end of the street watching the other arrivals to try to get a sense of my potential speed dates while trying to remain as inconspicuous as possible, which wasn't the easiest of tasks given that I was wearing a bright yellow dress. I'd also inadvertently selected a popular smoking corner and kept being distracted from my surveillance attempts by people asking for a light, or blowing clouds of synthetic-scented smoke from their vapes in front of my face.

Everyone arriving at the event looked pretty normal, but I knew I shouldn't take them at face value. Scammer Brian could actually be the jumpy-looking bloke who'd walked around the block three times before finding enough courage to go in, or perhaps he could be the gym bunny who'd nearly marched into someone because he was too busy checking out his appearance in the windows. Or he could even be the harassed-looking guy in a suit hovering around the entrance with an iPad. Actually, scrap that idea. That had to be the organiser ticking everyone's names off as they arrived. I wondered if I could get a sight of the guest list. Perhaps, if Leo caused a distraction inside, the man would put down the iPad to see what was happening and I could check it.

I smiled to myself. I was getting carried away. Names on a screen were meaningless without being able to match behaviour to them. I could hear Leo's voice in my head urging me to be sensible and stick to the plan we'd already discussed. There was no point going off-piste at this early stage and making him back out altogether.

I checked my phone. Still no message from Leo with the all clear. I'd give it another thirty seconds, and then go in anyway. If I stayed out here much longer, I was going to develop some kind of chronic condition from secondary smoke inhalation. Either that, or I was going to lose my courage. The longer I waited, the more my stomach churned. However much I told myself that attending the Single Mingle could be a key part of the investigation, the reality of having to endure an evening of speed-dating where I had to try to strike up a rapport and find out information about a bunch of strangers in just five minutes apiece was starting to hit home.

'Hey, Kat, what are you doing hanging around here?'

I turned round and saw Gavin walking towards me with Robin trotting happily at his side.

'Hi, Gavin, I'm just waiting for someone,' I improvised. 'Hello, Robin girly, how are you?' I bent down and stroked her behind the ears, welcoming the distraction. She responded by rolling on her back and baring her tummy for the same treatment. I obediently followed orders and laughed when she started joyfully kicking the air as I found a particularly ticklish spot. Robin always knew how to enjoy the moment and go with the flow. I wished I could do that.

'She's utterly shameless,' said Gavin, a tender expression on his face.

'She's a very good girl. And so glossy. She's definitely living her best life.'

'I'm glad you think so. Some people give me really dirty looks when we're out and about. They think it's cruel that she's on the street with me when she could be in a proper home. But she's family.'

'Of course she is. You only have to look at her to see that she'd choose to be by your side any day.' I straightened up. 'Any luck with the latest housing application?' I asked.

Gavin shrugged. 'It's been submitted and it's a waiting game, as always. But a single bloke with a dog isn't exactly high up on any of the priority lists. Still, at least the weather isn't too bad at the moment. We've got the tent and I'm doing a few odd jobs for people, so things are looking up. Doris has commissioned me to put some new bookshelves in,' he said proudly, then his happy expression fell. 'Only she's a bit funny about when I can come round and do the work. I suspect she's worried what her neighbours might think. I don't mind, though. I appreciate I'm not everyone's cup of tea.'

'Oh Gav, it'll be nothing like that. She told me just the other day that her son says she's got too many books, and he's worried he'll need to get the floor strengthened. She'll be trying to hide the bookshelf construction from him, rather than anything else.'

Gavin looked relieved.

I jumped as my phone buzzed in my hand, the signal from Leo that it was time for me to join him in the bar.

'Are you two going to be okay tonight?' I asked Gavin first. 'You know the offer is open for Robin to come and stay with me any time you want to get a space at the hostel.'

On a particularly wintery day, I'd once offered for Gavin to sleep at my studio flat while I went to stay with Moira, but he'd turned me down, insisting that he could look after himself. I'd spent the whole night awake worrying about him and Robin freezing in the cruel conditions, and had been relieved to get into the library the next day to discover that the shelter's rules about no pets had been scrapped for the duration of the cold snap. It was probably a good thing that Leo didn't know about that incident, because it would have confirmed his prejudices about me being too trusting. But I knew that Gavin was a decent bloke who'd fallen on hard times. I wished there was more I could do for him.

Gavin nodded. 'Cheers, Kat. She likes her occasional visits to stay with you.'

'But she's always much happier when she's back with her dad,' I said.

'I can't lie, she is. Anyway, I hope your friend arrives soon. I'd better get off. I've got the old penny whistle out and I'm going to do some busking on Broad Street. I was planning to use the bookshelf money to get a bed at a dog friendly place tonight, but I had to buy Robin some new food as the last stuff gave her a gippy tummy. I'm not far off what I need though, so hopefully a bit of music will earn me the rest.'

'Good luck. Hope you don't have to stay out long,' I said.

I fought back the urge to make up the difference myself, knowing that it was a point of pride with Gavin to earn his way.

He whistled between his teeth, and Robin sprang to her feet and back to his side. As the pair sauntered down the street, an idea suddenly occurred to me and I hurried after them.

'Gavin, would you be able to do an odd job for me tonight? And, in this instance, the use of the word "odd" is particularly appropriate.'

He looked quizzically at me. 'That sounds intriguing. I'm happy to help with anything, as long as it's legal.'

'It's one hundred percent legit. It just might sound a little strange, that's all. When I said I was waiting for a friend, it wasn't strictly true.'

I quickly told him about the Single Mingle and why I was attending it, knowing that Gavin would be the soul of discretion.

He nodded. 'Ah, I heard about your disappointment

from Doris earlier. Very sorry to hear that, I was. You deserve better.'

'That's very kind of you to say.'

'But you should be careful taking on that kind of bloke. He could be dangerous to get on the wrong side of.'

Gavin and Leo would probably get on really well.

'I'll be fine. I was wondering if I could hire you to keep an eye on the bar's entrance for the next quarter of an hour or so. The event begins at eight o'clock, and it said on the invitation that latecomers wouldn't be admitted.'

'Have you got a photo of this Brian bloke so I know who I'm looking for?'

'If only it was that easy.' I quickly explained about the stolen photos. 'Anyway, I was hoping you could keep an eye on everyone who's going in, and if there's anyone acting shifty, make a note of what they're wearing and, when you're next in the library, we can compare experiences.'

If truth be told, I didn't really expect anything useful to come from this bit of the operation, but it would be a way of making sure Gavin got his bed for the night, and that was what mattered.

'I can help,' said Gavin, and indeed, he did look a lot brighter than he had at the start of our conversation. 'But it doesn't feel right to take your money when I'm happy to assist for free.'

'Well, I won't feel right unless I pay you. It's only like putting up bookshelves for Doris, after all.'

'I suppose so. It'll be like my old army days. And at least I have the perfect disguise for carrying out surveillance. It's amazing how being homeless is as effective as Harry Potter's invisibility cloak.'

He was delighted by this analogy, but the truth in his words made me feel sad.

'What are your rates?' I asked.

'As it's been a while since I've been on stag, a tenner would be more than acceptable.'

'Are you sure? Given your military experience, I'd be happy to pay double that.'

He shook his head. 'You're alright. Half of it will get me over the line for tonight's accommodation, and the other half will put some credit on my phone. A man couldn't ask for more.'

'You're a good guy. Now, promise me, if you're not sure about anyone or you feel in any way threatened, you'll get out of here immediately. Not that I'm expecting any kind of trouble,' I added hastily, recognising that Gavin would probably do the exact opposite. I couldn't bear the thought of him and Robin coming to any harm because of me. 'All I need is your insight into the people attending the Single Mingle. They might be putting on a front in the bar, but I doubt they'll be doing the same when they're walking down the street beforehand. You can offer us a really useful perspective.'

'I'll take photos,' he said eagerly. 'I'll bring them to the library first thing in the morning.'

'I've got a day off tomorrow, so maybe we can catch up on the phone? But there's no rush. You've got to make the most of that comfy bed. Don't leave until check-out time, deal?'

He shook my hand. 'Deal. Come on, Robin, let's set ourselves up over there by the bike rack. We'll watch Kat's back for her, won't we, clever girl?'

Funnily enough, I did feel better knowing that the two of them were looking out for me as I walked down the road towards the bar's entrance.

The man with the iPad barely bothered to glance up at me as he launched into his spiel. 'Welcome to the Single Mingle by SO Ox. I'm Dom, and I'm your host for this evening. Are you on the list?'

'Yes, I should be,' I answered, deliberately not giving my name to see what would happen.

'Head straight in. Guests are gathering in the bar until the official start of the Single Mingle, which will take place on the mezzanine level. I'll explain what the deal is once everyone has arrived.'

I waited until I was safely across the threshold before turning round. 'Don't you need my name?'

He shrugged, his gaze moving past me and lingering on a pair of girls giggling by the entrance to the ladies' toilets. 'Yeah, I guess so.'

'It's Katherine. Kat for short.'

'Have a good evening, Katherine,' he replied, with little feeling behind the words.

I didn't provide a surname and yet he still let me in. So much for the 'exclusive event with a carefully curated crowd'. I could have been any random punter wandering off the street to try my chances. Maybe Leo did have a point about being on my guard tonight.

There was a low hubbub of chatter as I walked up to

the bar, trying to take in my surroundings without appearing like I was paying an unnatural amount of attention. Unfortunately, my veneer of bravery was already threatening to give way. The room was giving me serious flashbacks to the junior disco at school when the boys would all huddle together in one corner of the gym, beadily watched by the gaggle of girls at the other end of the room. Hopefully, the similarities would end there. I had enough on my plate without everyone gathering round to laugh at my name and accuse me of being a boring geek.

I caught Leo's eye, grateful for one familiar face at least, and automatically gave him a slight nod. He frowned in response and subtly shook his head, warning me that I needed to up my undercover game. I turned my back on him and pretended to be checking out all the bottles behind the bar, realising that the mirrored backs of the shelves would enable me to continue watching the other guests arriving. Maybe I wasn't going to be so bad at this surveillance thing after all.

At the moment, the women outnumbered the men by a ratio of about two to one. As it had been billed as a night for straight people, unless there was a sudden influx of men in the next five minutes, there were going to be long periods where many of us women would find ourselves dateless. I forced myself to look on the bright side. That could give me the perfect opportunity to have a chat with the other female members of the app and see if anybody else had interacted with the Brian James profile or had a similar experience to me. Leo on the other hand was going to be occupied all evening with dates. I wondered how he was going to react to that.

Unlike many of the other blokes, who were either subconsciously or deliberately preening themselves, Leo was standing a little apart, apparently completely unaware of the admiring glances he was attracting from the girls in their chosen corner, as he casually sipped at his beer. He gave off an aura of confidence, a man who was clearly comfortable with himself and his effect on others. Was he enjoying the fact that half a dozen females were unashamedly mentally undressing him? I felt suddenly protective, like I should go and stand between him and the hungry gazes of the other women.

'Can I get you a drink?' The guy behind the bar interrupted my thoughts.

'Um, I guess so. What have you got?'

He gestured at the menu. 'Pretty much everything you'd expect, and then some. That mirror comes in handy, doesn't it?' he said, nodding at the reflections I'd been staring at. 'Seen anyone who takes your eye?'

'I'm not...' I started to say, flustered that I'd been so easily rumbled. 'Maybe,' I corrected. 'Though it's impossible to tell until you speak to someone, don't you think?'

The barman shrugged, unwilling to be drawn into a deeper conversation about the laws of attraction. 'What did you want to drink?'

'I'll have a gin and tonic, thanks,' I said.

'Ice?'

'Yes, please.'

'This might take a second. I need to replace the gin bottle. It seems to be pretty popular tonight with all the ladies in.'

'Are there normally so many women at the Single Mingle?' I asked, seizing on the opportunity. 'I noticed on the app that this place hosts quite a few of the events run by SO Ox.'

'Men, women, I don't really pay much attention. All I notice is how many people are queueing up for drinks and how much I make in tips over the course of the night.'

I tried what I hoped was a disarming smile. 'I'm sure there's not a lot that goes on in here without you noticing.'

'You wouldn't believe the half of it.'

But whatever it was that he'd observed, he seemed reluctant to share. He started slicing a lemon, humming to himself. Time to try a different approach.

I sighed heavily. 'I think I made a mistake coming to this. Maybe I should cancel my drink.'

'It's nearly ready. You might as well stay and enjoy it. Sure, there are more girls here than guys, but it'll be a good night, trust me. Dom's great at what he does.'

'Does he organise all the events?' I asked.

'Yeah, Dom does pretty much all the jobs, from what I've seen. But then again, he is the one who founded the app. He's one of those techie genius types. Got halfway through a degree then quit for a more lucrative field. Works for some.'

'Ah, one of those sorts.' I nodded knowingly. You didn't have to live in Oxford for long to come across people who had the ability to turn everything they touched into gold, although Dom's hands-on approach was perhaps a little unusual. 'What's his surname?' I asked. It would be good to be able to do some digging on the man behind the app.

The barman raised an eyebrow. 'Fancy your chances, do you?'

'No, I... yes, I mean...' I started to deny it, then backtracked to try to keep my cover. 'Is he single?' I asked, hoping the barman would interpret my flustered manner as being a result of my attraction to Dom rather than anything else.

'Dom Markham is wedded to his work,' he replied. 'But maybe that's because he's not met the right person yet,' he added. There was little conviction behind his words, and it was obvious that he didn't think I would be that person. 'Here's your drink. Just tap the machine at the top with your card when you're ready.'

The conversation was clearly over. I paid the eyewatering bill, vowing to stick to soft drinks for the rest of the night, and moved to a quiet corner where I could continue my hopefully subtle observation of the other patrons. I took a sip and attempted to act casual, but my heart was beating fast as I thought about how the rest of the evening would go. My conversation with the barman had been clunky to say the least, which didn't bode well for my dates later. I tried to be positive. At least I knew a bit more about who was behind the app now. Maybe I could find an opportunity to ask him about their screening process.

On cue, Dom strode into the centre of the room.

'Ladies and gentlemen, welcome to the Domino Bar, and welcome to the Single Mingle by SO Ox.'

There was a muted murmur in response.

Dom frowned, and cupped a hand behind his right ear. 'I'm afraid you'll need to do better than that, folks. This could be the night you meet your Significant Other. No, scrap that, let's be confident about this. This *will* be the night you meet your Significant Other. Oxford is the city of the dreaming spires, and your dreams will come true right here. The stats don't lie. Eighty percent of SO Ox members leave the app within three months because they're loved up and off the market.'

There were a few tentative whoops which grew louder as he gestured for more.

'Yes, that's right. Eighty percent. My accountant hates me, but I don't do it for the money. I'm all about making those dreams come true. Can I get a "hell, yeah" people?'

I found myself joining in with the spontaneous burst of applause. A few seconds later, my phone buzzed.

A message from Leo.

> LEO
>
> Quite the charismatic love preacher, isn't he? Remember to keep your wits about you, Holmes.

I double-tapped to send an eyeroll emoji response, mindful that I couldn't pull the face for real without running the risk of someone spotting our communication. Scammer Brian could be in this very room right now, and if he was, I was determined to find him.

Chapter Thirteen

We all gathered around Dom while he started to explain how the Single Mingle evening was going to work.

'So, lovely ladies and gorgeous gentlemen'—there were a few appreciative wolf-whistles of varying pitches from across the bar—'it's nearly time to introduce yourselves to each other. But, before we get started, let me explain the rules.'

He paused and looked around, his gaze travelling to every single person in the room, making sure he had everyone's full attention.

'The rules are: there are no rules,' he shouted, to the obvious delight of the crowd. 'Unless I make them up on the spot, of course, organiser's prerogative. Gents, settle yourselves at a table. Ladies you will make your way round the tables in any order you fancy. No fighting over the hotties, girls.'

I sighed inwardly. Wasn't it equally as likely that the guys would argue among themselves about the women?

'I'm afraid we had some last-minute cancellations so there are a few more of you ladies than there are men,' continued Dom. 'But fear not, look upon it as a chance to enjoy a free drink, which you will receive courtesy of SO Ox, and to compare notes on your dates so far. Speaking of which, each date will last five minutes, after which time I will ring my bell. Yup, I could have gone for a fancy timer on my even fancier electronic devices, but we're going old school tonight. It means the power is in my hands. If I spot some chemistry starting to sizzle, I might feel inclined to stretch out those five minutes. It's the personal touch that makes SO Ox the exclusive experience it is.' He paused and examined the crowd again. Was it my imagination, or did his gaze linger on me? I self-consciously tucked a loose lock of hair behind my ear and tried not to stand so awkwardly. There was no way he could know why I was really here. I was being paranoid.

'Seeing all the uniquely beautiful and fascinating people who've assembled, I have great hopes for the matches that will happen this evening.' Dom carried on with his pep talk. 'And if you do meet the love of your life sitting across from you at one of these small tables, you have my blessing to declare yourself then and there. We don't stand on ceremony here. What's the point of waiting until the end of the night and filling out some form requesting another date when you could instead join us straight away for the Single Mingle after-party – otherwise known as the "Now you've matched, let's get smashed" event – which will be happening later in the exclusive basement bar. There's an extra charge, but then it's an all-you-can-drink job, so it's definitely worth it. Grab me during the evening to sign up.'

There was a smattering of appreciative applause, although I did hear a few people grumbling about having to pay more to attend the after-party.

Dom glanced down at his iPad. 'Right, was there anything else I had to say? Probably something about where the nearest fire exit is, but you're all grown-ups; I'm sure you can spot the neon "Emergency Exit" signs. Although please don't use them if you decide you want to make a speedy departure with your new beau, as the doors will set off an alarm and we could do without that kind of drama. Everyone happy? Then take a seat at the tables of destiny, boys, and we can get the evening started.'

The dozen or so blokes did as they were directed. I watched carefully as they moved into place, but quickly concluded that I wasn't going to learn much from studying their body language. Over-confident swaggers and nervous shuffles alike could be explained away by the nature of the evening itself and the adrenalin-inducing speech which Dom had delivered. Meanwhile, I was fighting the urge to shrink back in my corner, or even better, leave the bar and forget the whole plan. Now I was faced with the reality of trying to get useful information out of these people, I realised how totally ill-equipped I was to do it. And all the while pretending to be the kind of person who enjoyed going to speed-dating events. I pressed each fingertip in turn against the pads of my thumbs, wishing that I hadn't already finished my drink. I could have done with it as a prop, because now I didn't know what to do with my hands, and, although I knew I was signalling my nerves to everyone around me with the anxious tapping, somehow I couldn't stop.

'Looking good, gents, looking good,' Dom said, as the men settled themselves behind their tables. Then he turned to the rest of us. 'Now then, ladies, get ready to meet your match. I will ring the bell to signal it's time to take a seat, then I'll ring it again to start what could be the most significant five minutes of your lives.'

I gave myself a stern lecture. This was my time to step up and potentially make a difference. I deliberately thought about that moment in the library when I'd had the shock realisation that Brian was a figment of someone's imagination, and that my modest dream of a happy relationship had been used as a weapon to manipulate me. The person behind the fraud shouldn't be allowed to get away with it, and if putting myself through the stress of speed-dating in some way helped that cause, then I would need to woman up and get on with it.

While I was still shrinking into the shadows, a few people had started subtly shuffling towards the tables, eyeing up their preferred first dates. The room had quietened now, and the anticipation in the air was almost palpable, everyone pumped up by Dom's exuberant style. My stomach turned over once again. Could I be about to meet Scammer Brian? Leo reckoned it was highly unlikely, but there was a chance the man was arrogant enough to hunt his victims in person as well as from behind the safety of his computer screen. I scanned the faces of the men in front of me, trying to commit them to memory in case I needed to identify one of them from a line-up. Actually, did the police still do line-ups? I'd have to ask Leo.

I risked a brief glance across at him. He looked totally at ease, leaning back on his chair, long legs stretched out as he surveyed the women queuing up to speak to him. I supposed I should be grateful he wasn't putting his feet up, as he did in the library. Suddenly he looked directly at me and winked. I jumped as if someone had tapped me on the shoulder.

The urgent ringing of the bell was less of a surprise than the wink. After a moment of hesitation, the girls surged forward to get a space at one of the tables, at least two of them good-naturedly jostling each other to get to Leo's place first, laughter in their expressions. I hung back, telling myself it would be sensible to play the role of observer a little longer so I could be more strategic about who I targeted. I angled myself so I couldn't see Leo and the red head in the bodycon dress who'd come out as the victor. But, despite the general hubbub, I was sure I could hear his rumbling laughter as the introductions were made. I hoped he didn't allow himself to get distracted from the real purpose of being here.

'Oh no, you don't. There's no hiding around here,' said Dom, sliding up to me and putting his arm around my shoulders. 'We don't allow any wallflowers at SO Ox.'

'But all the tables are occupied,' I said. 'It's fine, I'll join the other girls at the bar and wait until the next round.'

I took a step to the side, subtly extricating myself from his somewhat overly friendly embrace.

He completely ignored me and raised his voice to address the room again.

'Ladies and gentlemen, forgive me, but there's a twist. Here at SO Ox, it's not about those who get there first, but those who graciously step back and allow others to go in front of them. I find it's always good to shake things up a bit.'

He took my hand and marched me over to Leo's table. If ever there was a time for the earth to swallow me up, this was it.

'Excuse me, but we're going to swap the ladies over for this first round. Don't worry, there's an extra-large cocktail as compensation.'

The red head pouted prettily, then sent a devastating smile at Leo.

'No hard feelings. Good things come to those who wait, after all,' she said. 'I'll see you later, Leo.'

'Looking forward to it,' he replied.

She sashayed back to the bar while I stared at the floor. I didn't need the extra humiliation of seeing the disappointment which I assumed would be on Leo's face as he watched her departing form.

Dom held the chair back with exaggerated politeness and gestured for me to sit down, which I did with great reluctance. This was totally defeating the object of the evening. Then he bounced away to repeat the move with the other women who hadn't got seats at the tables in the initial dash. Before I knew it, the bell had rung again, and my first five-minute date had started.

'What a waste of time, I'm sorry, Le—'

'Hi, I'm Leo,' he interrupted me before I could finish my apology. He reached out and shook my hand, subtly squeezing it in warning. 'I like travel and eating good food, but my favourite thing is good company. How about you?'

I sat up straighter, suddenly more alert to our surroundings. I'd been hoping to compare notes on what, if anything, we'd managed to find out so far, but the tables were spaced barely two feet apart. This definitely wasn't the place for a private conversation about our mission, and we couldn't exactly sit in silence while I psyched myself up for the next date. The only option left to us was to spend the next five minutes pretending that we really were on a speed date, which was the last thing I wanted to do. Could this evening get any more awkward?

I placed my hands flat on the table, pressing against it to centre myself. All I had to do was act natural and not make a fool of myself, while at the same time being aware of my surroundings in case there was any suspicious behaviour going on elsewhere. Easier said than done. I took a deep breath and tried to channel Moira's air of easy confidence. She'd never find herself stuck for words in this situation. She'd just go for it and not have a second's concern about being awkward or embarrassing herself.

'Hello, Leo, nice to meet you. I'm Katherine. I imagine I'm not the first to tell you that travel and good food are fairly universal pleasures. So how about you tell me what your definition of good company is? Or shall we make it fun, and I'll guess?' I tried to inject a flirtatious air into my tone but, having never been very good at that kind of thing, I went too hard with the accompanying attempt at flicking a loose lock of hair back and ended up whipping myself in the eye.

I blinked hard then glared at Leo, my injured eye already watering, daring him to laugh at me. But instead, he gamely picked up my cue of fake flirtation and responded by slowly and deliberately lowering his gaze to my lips, then back up to my eyes, his smile growing wider.

'I'm always up for fun,' he said. 'But I'd rather talk about you. How about I guess what you find pleasurable first?'

He deliberately lowered his voice on the word 'pleasurable', parodying a practised seducer in a manner which I couldn't help reacting to. I cleared my throat, hoping he hadn't noticed my involuntary quiver. He was far too good at this game, and that riled me, not that I wanted him to realise that. I had to go on the offence myself.

I shrugged my shoulders, and giggled like he'd just said the funniest thing I'd ever heard. 'Sure. You can guess. I'm an open book.' I toyed with fluttering my eyelashes at him, a come-hither move which always seemed to feature in seduction scenes in Doris's romance novels, but given my already watering eye, I'd probably give the impression I was developing some kind of infection, so I decided against it and repeated the overly girlish giggle while twirling the lock of hair around my finger.

'Your laughter is like a wind chime trilling brightly in the breeze,' said Leo in a voice which I could only describe as a purr. His expression was of pure devilment. He was totally getting a kick out of watching my terrible attempt to play the flirt.

'Sorry, I think I just threw up a little,' I responded without thinking. A couple of heads turned in our direction, eyebrows raised at my sudden change of tone. I forced out another trill of laughter and fixed Leo with my best devoted expression. 'What I meant to say is that your voice sounds like a safe haven in a storm,' I improvised rapidly to save the situation, again drawing on my knowledge of the library's cheesiest erotica. I held my palm against my chest to emphasise the point, all wide eyes and breathy keenness. If Leo was determined to mess about and go down the clichéd seduction route, I was going to give as good as I got.

Leo managed to turn his responding snort of disgust into a deep rumble of amusement.

'You'll always be safe with me, babe,' he said, his voice dropping by half an octave and taking on a slightly Hollywood twang.

I raised an eyebrow at him. 'Babe?' I mouthed.

He shrugged apologetically, lips twitching with humour.

'You give me good vibes too, sugar,' I said, huskily. Actually, the huskiness was an unintentional bonus caused by the effort of fighting to stop myself laughing. This wasn't getting me any closer to tracking down our target, but I had to admit Leo was a very amusing partner for fake flirting. It actually felt kind of liberating to play at seduction with him and be as outrageous as I liked, safe in the knowledge that this was all for fun and there was no hidden agenda. It was certainly making me feel a little less tense about the speed dates yet to come.

'That's me, all about the vibes,' said Leo. 'But we're getting off topic. I was about to read your mind and deduce your greatest pleasures, Katherine.'

He sketched the shape of an imaginary crystal ball between us. I reached out and pretended to pick it up and throw it over my shoulder. He might be play-acting but, knowing my own tendency towards having subtitles in my facial expressions, combined with Leo's uncanny observation skills, I decided I'd rather not subject myself to his fortune teller routine.

'But sugar, they've changed since I met you. Just being here with you is now one of them.' I couldn't resist teasing him.

'I feel the same. How is it possible to experience such a sense of connection in such a short space of time?'

For a moment I thought he was going to reach out and take my hand.

'Having a good time, you two?' asked Dom, suddenly appearing by our table, looking between us with great interest.

'Just covering the basics, favourite colours and pizza toppings, that kind of thing,' I said breezily, willing him to go and make small talk with another table instead.

'Good stuff. You guys look like you're hitting it off. Do you fancy longer than the allotted five minutes?' Dom asked with a lowered voice. 'It's a one-time offer.'

'We'll stick with the prescribed five,' said Leo. I couldn't decide whether to be relieved or offended by the speed with which he answered the question.

'Fair enough. In which case, I'll disappear so you can make the most of your final minute,' said Dom.

'We need to be more careful. If you go too hard, our neighbours are going to expect us to run off together rather than staying for the rest of the evening,' I hissed quietly.

'Sorry, but it was fun while it lasted,' whispered Leo, then continued at a more normal volume. 'You said earlier that you're an open book. I reckon that's a dead giveaway that you like reading.'

I relaxed, glad that we were returning to safe ground.

'You've got me there. I wear my heart on my sleeve, quite literally,' I said, gesturing to the small stack of books tattooed on my inner wrist.

'That's a good quality to have. If perhaps one which can leave a person vulnerable,' said Leo, a more serious note in his voice. 'I bet you think the world of fiction is infinitely preferable to the real world. I can empathise with that, but it's something to be careful about. It can lead to all kinds of heartbreak. Real life doesn't always play out into a happily ever after.'

'Thanks for the warning, but I'm quite aware of that. I've recently been thoroughly inoculated against those who seem like they could have walked straight out of the pages of my favourite novel. If they sound like they're too good to be true, then they probably are.'

Leo nodded. 'A tough lesson to learn.'

'One I'd prefer not to dwell on any longer,' I said lightly. 'So, go on then, what else do you think I find pleasurable?'

Leo held my gaze steadily. 'You have an open and bright

expression, which tells me you're the sort of person who wants to truly experience every moment and take joy in it.'

'You sound like you're describing a dog. That's exactly how Robin behaves when she's following Gavin around the library ... where I often write. My friend Gavin who has a dog called Robin,' I added hastily, remembering that Leo wasn't supposed to know who I was talking about, and that I was meant to be pretending to be a writer this evening.

'Dogs have the right attitude to life. It's very simple for them – they want affection, good food and a comfy bed. And they'll sacrifice the latter two for the first one.'

'All very sensible things to long for. As you say, it's a shame that us humans are so much more complicated than that. It takes far more to please us.'

'I'm not sure if I completely agree,' he said. 'The affection and comfy bed sound good to me, particularly when they're combined.' His eyes sparkled in a manner which shouldn't be legal. 'Your pleasures'—again, the word was unnecessarily drawn out—'are positive ones, I reckon. I could guess the bog-standard long walks on the beach stereotype, or spending sunny afternoons with friends, or even better, lazy mornings with a lover, but I think I'm going to go deeper than that.'

There was something hypnotic about how his lips formed 'lover', the way the word came out so softly. And that was when I realised I was drifting into dangerous territory, that I was losing the ability to see the teasing edge in the funny flirtation game. I couldn't risk lines getting blurred and allow myself to believe that this exchange was turning into something potentially more serious, more meaningful. My priorities were elsewhere. I needed to focus, and to take back control of the situation, before I got caught up in the fantasy of something that could never be and distracted from the real reason we were here.

'Those all sound pretty good pleasures to me. I'm not sure there's much more to be said. I'm a simple person, with simple tastes. How about you?' Surely it would be safer to turn the tables on him?

'Oh, don't do yourself down. You strike me as being the kind of person who has many hidden depths. But perhaps you're too scared to show them.'

No, he was determined to keep trying to get me off balance.

'Maybe that's because I'm yet to find the right person to share them with.' It was a stock answer, one I'd trotted out dozens of times in the library when well-meaning but busybody patrons had quizzed me about my relationship status. But it was harder to say to the first real guy to make my pulse quicken in a long time. The online fraudster obviously didn't count.

He nodded. 'Or maybe you have, but you just haven't realised it yet.'

The aggressive ringing of Dom's bell was a welcome interruption to a conversation which had become unnervingly intense.

'Good luck with your next date,' said Leo. 'Parting is such sweet sorrow.' The teasing voice was back again.

'And there you go revealing yourself as a Shakespeare fan. Or maybe it's the doomed love affairs that you're really in thrall to.'

'I've always been of the opinion that Romeo and Juliet could have solved all their issues by having a good chat. Mind you, they were too busy doing other stuff to talk properly,' responded Leo with a twinkle. Then he lowered his voice. 'Good luck, Holmes. Don't speak to too many strange men.'

'Hopefully you'll be the strangest of the night,' I countered, and made a beeline for the next empty chair before he could respond. Time to get on with what I was really here for.

Chapter Fourteen

The bell to signal the start of the next date had rung before I'd even sat down properly.

'Hi, I'm Katherine and I'm a writer,' I introduced myself, pretending that I was back in the safety of the library and doing nothing scarier than merely greeting a new member.

The man I was now sitting opposite didn't meet my gaze but mumbled something in response.

'Sorry, I didn't quite catch that.'

I smiled, hoping to put him at ease. He looked as nervous as I felt.

'I'm Brian,' he repeated.

My heart started racing and I had to fight to stop myself from gasping out loud. Surely it wasn't going to be this easy? Surely the first stranger I spoke to at this event wasn't going to turn out to be my quarry? I told myself to calm down and not jump to any hasty conclusions. Scammer Brian was arrogant, but he wasn't stupid. There was no way he'd just introduce himself to me like this. My rudimentary disguise wasn't that effective, and wouldn't he at least recognise something familiar about my features, given that he was sitting directly across from me? The most likely scenario was that this was a completely innocent man who happened to have the same name as the guy who'd tried to fleece me had used. But I'd be on my guard, just in case. At this stage, it probably wasn't a good idea to completely rule anyone out.

'Brian, as in B-R-I-A-N?' I spelled it out.

He pulled a face. 'No, I'm Bryan with a Y,' he corrected, as if I should have realised that for myself.

That wasn't conclusive evidence either way. I needed to question him to establish whether he was a credible suspect.

'Lovely to meet you, Bryan.' I dialled up the charm.

He responded with a grunt, which left me with the strong impression that he did not feel the same way.

I paused, waiting to see if he was going to take the conversational lead. In the unlikely event that he was the fraudster I was looking for, I assumed he'd soon make it obvious. He'd have to acknowledge our online connection and explain his initial apparent indifference to me on meeting in person, wouldn't he? And clarify why he spelled his name differently on the internet.

The silence stretched out between us. If he carried on like this, it was going to be a very difficult five minutes.

'How long have you been a member of SO Ox, Bryan?' I asked. Time to attempt some subtle fact-finding.

He looked offended. 'Why do you want to know?'

I forced out a light laugh. 'No real reason. I was trying to make small talk. I've been an online member for a couple of months, but this is my first in-person event, all very exciting. How about you, have you been to many of the events?'

'Nah, it's my first IRL one too,' he admitted reluctantly.

Unless he was a very good actor pretending to be incredibly socially awkward, I was growing more certain this couldn't be Scammer Brian. For a start, although Single Mingle Bryan had barely said anything, his voice was totally different from the confident, playful tones of my online beau. And the bogus Brian had always been so assured in his communications with me, taking the lead and never being short of something witty to say. I couldn't see the man in front of me having the get up and go needed to execute a fraud. Wouldn't a scammer try to charm the pants off everyone he met?

But a niggling doubt occurred to me. What if his rudeness was because he did recognise me and had somehow guessed my real motive for being here tonight? Perhaps what I had interpreted as a cold attitude was actually an underlying threat? Or was I overthinking the situation, on edge because of all Leo's warnings? The reality was that the fraudster was in a very safe position because I had no idea what he actually looked like. Nevertheless, I subtly glanced around, feeling decidedly jittery and double-checking where my closest escape route was, just in case.

'And how are you finding the event?' I asked, trying to maintain a calm tone.

'It's okay,' he said.

I'd happily turn him into the police, scammer or not, purely for his inability to sustain a conversation. The man needed to give me something, otherwise we were going to start attracting attention because of the lingering silence between us. The five minutes with Leo had flown by. Dom must be messing around with the timings because this date was dragging.

'What do you do when you're not attending Single Mingles?' I tried a different tack.

'As I said, this is my first time here,' he responded, taking the question literally.

'Sure. So, what do you like doing in your spare time?' I asked instead.

'Hang out with mates. Get jobs done.'

He seemed determined to answer in words of one syllable. And still he was showing no indication of wanting to ask me anything in return.

'What do you do for work?' I might as well just interrogate him, if he was going to act like this for the rest of our five minutes.

'IT.'

Given his job, he'd probably have the technical know-how to commit online fraud, but I was becoming more confident that he wasn't our man. There seemed to be no spark of anything going on in his head. I seriously doubted a bloke who was this boring and uninterested in company would be capable of the intelligence and charisma needed to be the romance fraudster I'd encountered.

'Is there anything you'd like to ask me?' I tried one last time to get the conversation going.

He barely looked up from his close examination of his nails, which were particularly grimy, incidentally.

'What did you say your name was again?' The question ended with a yawn. He didn't bother covering his mouth and I was subjected to an unwanted glimpse of yellowing teeth and a waft of stale curry.

'Kimmy-Sue,' I said, the first random thing that came into my head. He didn't even blink at my sudden name change. Yup, the guy was totally indifferent to me. How utterly devastating, I'd be crying into my pillow all night. Not.

I checked my watch. We still had a whole two and a half minutes to go. I waited another thirty seconds to see if he'd make the slightest bit of effort, then got my phone out and started reading a book on my Kindle app.

I could have kissed Dom when he rang the bell twenty seconds earlier than expected bringing the dullest of encounters to an end.

'Goodbye, Bryan, enjoy the rest of your evening,' I said, not even trying to hide the delight in my voice that it was time to move on.

'What?' he said, blinking and looking around him like he'd been in some kind of trance. Then he sat up straight and started smoothing his hair down, his features contorting into what I assumed was meant to be a welcoming smile. The red head in the bodycon dress was heading towards his table. Good luck to the poor woman. I guess I just wasn't his type. What a shame. Still, on the plus side, I was now fairly convinced I could rule him out from my non-existent list of suspects. I couldn't imagine him having the dynamism necessary to be as entertaining online as Scammer Brian had been.

Time for speed date number three, or two, depending on whether I was counting the five minutes with Leo. Best not to think about that. I steeled myself for further disappointment and followed the direction of the crowd to my next encounter. Now that I was on a roll, I might as well keep going. I might even start to get some enjoyment out of the evening. Leo certainly seemed to be having a great time.

My next date was a stereotypically Oxford guy, almost to the point of parody, right down to his floppy hair. As soon as I approached his table, he stood up and walked around to help me into my seat; a gentlemanly move, if it hadn't been done in such a studied fashion. Or maybe I was being too quick to judge. I reminded myself to keep an open mind. My gut instinct wasn't necessarily to be trusted. If it was, I wouldn't even be at this event tonight trying to track down a fraudster.

'I'm Marcus, by the way,' he said. 'Marc to those who matter. I'd be very happy to count you in their number. And tell me, to whom do I have the pleasure of speaking?'

His vowels were extended with the lazy ease of the truly self-confident.

'I'm Katherine, although you can call me Kath, if you like,' I said, deciding to mirror his own introduction, although I took the precaution of altering my nickname.

'A delightful name, for a delightful person. I am honoured to be invited to address you thus.'

I was starting to think that the flamboyant posh-boy persona was being put on in an ill-judged attempt to impress. He'd picked the wrong audience for it. I wanted honest and straightforward all the way.

'How are you finding the event?' I asked. I already knew I was going to have to be more subtle about steering the conversation towards the areas I needed to investigate. Marc might be playing at the bumbling English gentleman, but I sensed a steely edge of intelligence behind the façade. It hadn't escaped my notice that he was wearing a tie belonging to a college with one of the most fearsome academic reputations in the city.

'It's a wonderful occasion, and I feel privileged to be meeting so many fascinating women, such as your marvellous self. Good old Dommo really has the knack for bringing together the best of the best at his events. Always handy to have a pal in an influential position, don't you agree?'

'Ah, so you know the founder. And does that give you special privileges on the app?' I asked, pretending to sound impressed.

He tapped the side of his nose. 'Now that would be telling. But tell me more about you. You must be a Single Mingle virgin. I would definitely have remembered meeting you at a previous event.'

'It is my first. How about you? Have you been to many of them?' I batted the question straight back at him.

'Does it make me look like a player if I answer yes to that?' Marc smiled self-consciously. 'I confess that I first joined when I moved to the city a year ago, right back at the launch of the app, so yes, I've been around the houses a bit on it.' He glanced about and lowered his voice. 'Before I came here, I was working in Cambridge. Don't like to say these things too loud. University rivalries and all that.'

I laughed, then quickly stopped when I realised that this was one thing he definitely wasn't joking about.

'Anyway, it seemed like a good way of getting to know people in my new home city without having to go through the painfully awkward process of approaching strangers in clubs and the like, you know how it is. Besides, it's small change to be a member, and it's important to have a hobby, hey? Enough about boring old me, how about you? What drew a delightful woman like yourself to SO Ox? Surely you must be fighting the chaps off every time you step foot out of the house?'

It would be easy to be flattered by his generous manner of address, but I suspected he was like this with everyone he spoke to, and behind the apparently laid-back air of charm, I could tell that I was being carefully assessed. I'd also noted his not-so-subtle reference to being well-off, as I think I was meant to. It was probably part of his usual patter, but judging by his expensive-looking watch and extremely well-tailored suit, I thought he probably wasn't exaggerating his well-to-do status. If he had no financial motive, then he was unlikely to be Scammer Brian. Unless he was, and he was getting a kick out of manipulating people online. I wouldn't be completely surprised by that. On the surface, he seemed to be entertainingly harmless, but something about him put me on my guard. I decided he wasn't in the clear yet.

'I suppose, like you, I was looking to make new connections in the city,' I replied. 'I've lived here for several years, but I'm a writer, which can sometimes be a solitary business. It's harder to meet people when you're not doing a standard nine-to-five role.'

Marc nodded. 'I concur. A writer? How simply marvellous.' That definitely sounded patronising to me, but I smiled politely back at him. 'I'm a lecturer at the university,' he continued. 'Now that the powers that be have decided that students are most definitely off limits, it does reduce one's dating pool somewhat.'

He laughed again, a throaty chuckle which made me want to shudder. I fought to keep control of my features. How could the man complain so casually about not being able to date his students? Never mind the fraudster I was seeking, here was another type of predator waltzing around in plain sight.

I wanted to walk away immediately, but the rules of the evening dictated I was stuck for the next three minutes, unless I wanted to create a scene. It didn't feel worth it. Yet.

'Have I shocked you?' he asked. 'Don't worry, you're much more my type. The students can get so needy. Tiresome, really. But I can tell that your needs would be quite different.'

The affable gentleman routine had all but disappeared now, replaced by sheer unashamed sleaziness.

I pushed my chair back an inch, preparing to leave.

'Let me see if I can discover what those needs might be,' said Marc. I'd like to say he was unaware of the effect he was having on me, but unfortunately it was the opposite, and that was clearly part of the appeal. 'Show me your palm. I may be a Physics professor, but trust me when I say my knowledge of the physical is just as good.'

Before I could react, he'd taken hold of my right hand and pulled it towards him with a surprisingly hard grip.

'Erm, can I?' I tried to remove my hand from his grasp, but he was determined not to let go.

He traced his index finger along my palm.

'They do say that, for women, the right hand shows the traits you're born with and the left hand is the experience you've accumulated throughout your life. It's always interesting to see how much experience a woman has. I shall compare the two palms in a minute.'

'I'd really rather you didn't,' I said. I glanced around, gauging my best route out of this situation.

'This is your heart line,' he continued, ignoring my protestations completely. He was now digging his nail into my skin as he traced the lines. It wasn't quite painful, although it was certainly uncomfortable, but if I snatched my hand away now, I would probably get scratched in the process. The five minutes must be nearly up, surely?

'Interesting. This crease in your palm is telling me that you fall in love easily. Lucky old me.' He looked up briefly and I nearly flinched at the calculating expression in his eyes. 'Hmm, but the way it touches your life line tells me that your heart is broken easily too. Not a great combination, right? Poor old Kath.'

Despite the fact that I knew Marc was making the whole thing up, what he was saying was too close to the truth for me. Yet another reason to bring this situation back under control.

'Perhaps we should move on to another topic,' I suggested. 'Have you…'

I was about to ask him another question aimed at advancing my investigation, but he took the words right out of my mouth by moving his steely grip further up my arm.

'Sexy tattoo. Goodness me, your pulse really is beating fast for me,' he said, pressing hard against my skin.

The strength of his hand wrapped around my wrist was bruising. I wanted to retort that the reason my heart was racing was because he was frightening me rather than because of any erotic reaction, but I had a horrible feeling that expressing my fear might be even more of a turn-on for him. I was just assessing how best to extract myself from his grip and the situation altogether, when he let out a surprisingly high-pitched wail.

'The lady asked you to let go.'

Leo had appeared behind Marc, grabbing his arm and twisting it up behind his back. Judging by the puce colour Marc's face was turning, it was not a comfortable hold. But despite this, Marc kept his grip on my wrist with his other hand.

'Steady on, old chap,' said Marc. 'You're interrupting my date.'

'You're damn right I am,' said Leo. 'In my opinion, dates should be mutually enjoyable, and it's very clear to me that this lady is not enjoying herself.'

'I'm not. But it's okay, I'm fine,' I insisted. 'Let's not make a scene. I can handle this. Marc, please will you let go of me?'

Marc completely ignored me, as unfortunately did Leo.

'I'll ask you nicely one more time, let go,' he said. His voice was calm and measured but there was an air of controlled threat beneath his words. I'm not sure what was making me more cross – the fact that Leo was interfering when I really didn't need his help, or mortifyingly, that I was actually rather turned on by his action.

I made a conscious effort to lean into the righteous feminist rage and frowned at him, telegraphing with all my might that he needed to take things down a notch. Heads were turning towards us, the room becoming quieter as people leaned forward to eavesdrop on what was happening. So much for my plan for incognito investigating. This whole embarrassing confrontation was clearly going to be the subject of everyone's conversation for the rest of the night.

I twisted my wrist, sensing that Marc might be about to loosen his grip, but just as I completed the move, Leo pushed Marc's chair forward, effectively trapping him between it and the table. He simultaneously leapt towards me and wrapped his arm around my waist, whispering something in my ear that I couldn't properly process, and hustled me out of the bar before I was fully aware of what was happening.

'Excuse me, but this lady is taken,' he called back towards an astonished Marc, his voice echoing around the bar. We couldn't have made a more dramatic exit if we'd tried.

Chapter Fifteen

As soon as we got into the street, I broke free of Leo's hold and spun round to confront him.

'I can fight my own battles, thank you very much,' I said, trying my hardest to keep my voice steady as I moved a safe distance away. If I stayed close to him for any longer, I was worried I might lash out at him in frustration, or worse, inexplicably find myself back in his embrace thanks to some primal instinct I knew I was better off ignoring. My heart was pounding so hard I thought I could hear my blood rushing through my head, and my waist was tingling, still experiencing the warmth from where his arm had wrapped around it.

'Of that I have little doubt,' he said.

'Then why did you feel the need for that ridiculous performance?' I waved my hand in the direction of the bar we'd exited at speed.

Leo's lips twitched. If he dared to smile at me right now, I wouldn't be responsible for my actions.

'Ridiculous? That's the first time any aspect of my performance has been called ridiculous. I obviously need to work on my technique.' His voice was low, so I had to lean in closer to hear what he was saying. Was it my imagination, or had his gaze dropped briefly to my lips again? Last time he'd done it in jest, but now I wasn't sure I wanted that to be the case, and I didn't know how to feel about it. I flushed, experiencing an unwanted flashback to moments earlier when he'd practically scooped me up, his breath warm against the nape of my neck as he whispered, 'Let's get out of here.' A centimetre closer and he could have dropped a kiss on the sensitive skin there. I shivered. Why was I allowing myself to get distracted by such a ridiculous and unwanted idea? Leo had acted in a completely overbearing manner, swooping in to save me when I hadn't asked for it, and most certainly did not need it. Just because such alpha he-man action would have been followed by a swoon-inducing snog in Doris's romance books, didn't mean such things would happen in real life. Thank goodness. The last thing I wanted was that kind of complication.

'Are you cold?' he asked. 'I would offer you my jacket, but I left it behind in the bar in our haste to depart.'

'*Your* haste to depart. Don't let me stop you going back in to claim it,' I snapped, still battling to get myself back in line.

'I think perhaps it's best for both of us to steer well clear of that bar. Your over-eager friend might feel the need for a show of strength to try to rebuild his bruised ego.'

'He's not my friend. And add it to your expenses claim, why don't you?'

'I didn't realise I was entitled to expenses. That's good to know.' Leo smiled, supremely relaxed, as if we were standing in the street passing the time of day. In some ways, it would have been much easier if he'd shouted back at me. But I already knew that he wasn't that kind of person.

'You're not entitled to them. Our original agreement stands, although I'm questioning the wisdom of that right now. And, as usual, you're completely missing the point. I had things under control. I'm quite capable of looking after myself. I certainly didn't need rescuing, especially not by a galumphing neanderthal declaring that I was "taken".'

I'd definitely gone a bit far there, but I wasn't going to back down now.

'Galumphing neanderthal? You do fling some interesting compliments at me. Well, it didn't look very under control from where I was sitting, but if I got the wrong idea about what was happening, don't let me stop you going back inside to pick up where you left off. Be my guest.' Leo gestured towards the entrance.

I folded my arms and frowned at him. Much as I'd like to prove my point about being able to stand on my own two feet, there was no way I was heading back in there.

'I thought not,' he said quietly. 'Look, it's nothing to get het up about. Everyone needs a helping hand now and again. It doesn't make you any less of a person.'

Before I could respond, there was a burst of noise behind us as the door of the bar opened again and a loudly swearing bloke who I recognised from one of the other Single Mingle tables staggered out into the street, accompanied by the thick stench of alcohol.

Despite the fact that I was in the middle of delivering my strong independent woman speech, I couldn't help flinching at the noise and taking an involuntary step backwards.

Leo neatly sidestepped and placed himself between me and the drunk lurching slowly towards us, ready to shield me once again from any potential threat.

'Alright, darling? Can I get you a drink? Those stuck-ups in there were doing my nut.' The drunk gazed blearily towards me, his eyes unable to focus.

I rapidly calculated whether it was better to ignore him or politely turn him down.

'No, thank you.'

'Think you're better than me, do you?' he retorted in a tone which made me want to take another step back.

'I've got a boyfriend,' I said, looping my arm through Leo's. Much as I hated using the 'not available' defence I'd just been riling about, sadly I knew it was the only one that a lot of men would pay any attention to.

'Course you have,' slurred the drunk, before slapping Leo heartily on the shoulder. 'Sorry, pal, no hard feelings.'

Somehow, I wasn't surprised he'd said sorry to Leo rather than the person who actually deserved the apology.

I watched the man stumble down the street until he'd disappeared out of view.

'Okay?' asked Leo.

'I'm fine. Again.' I paused. 'But thanks for that.'

'It's no big deal,' he said.

Given that I'd been in the middle of bawling him out for intervening and blowing up our investigation at the Single Mingle, I was grateful that he'd not let it stop him noticing my apprehension at the appearance of the drunk and acting on it. But it was important that I made clear the difference in the two situations.

'Seriously though, I could have handled Marc back in the bar. He was sleazy and definitely a creep, but what could he really do? It wasn't like he could jump me right then and there. We were surrounded by people.'

'People who were actively looking away from what was happening right in front of them.'

Leo had a point, although I didn't want to admit it out loud.

'Look, it's been a long evening. I'm tired and I think it's probably time for me to head home,' I said.

'Good plan,' he said. 'The city centre's only going to get more feral as the evening goes on.'

'See you later, then.' I gave a little half wave and turned to walk to the bike rack, glad to clock that there was no sign of Gavin and Robin carrying out surveillance from its shadows. Hopefully that meant they were now safely tucked up at the dog-friendly hostel.

Leo fell into step beside me.

'Don't worry, you don't need to see me home. I left my bike here after work so I could get back more easily tonight. See, I thought of everything.' I omitted the fact that I'd forgotten to bring my bike lights, so I'd be pushing it home, rather than riding it.

He frowned. 'You don't have to talk to me, if you don't want to. But I would prefer to make sure you get back safely. Let's say it's for my peace of mind, if that's an easier pill for you to swallow.'

There was an edge to his voice. I figured it was the influence of his previous career coming to the fore again.

'I do appreciate the thought, but I managed to get around the city perfectly fine by myself before you came into my life, and I'm sure I'll do the same after we've both moved on.'

I knew I was coming across as rude, but he was still setting me off balance and the only way I could think to deal with it was to get on the offensive.

'I don't doubt it for a second. Call me old-fashioned, but I can't rest easy if I see a friend marching off into the darkness alone, particularly after they've had a bit of a rough night, even if they're doing their best to pretend that everything is "just fine".'

His imitation of my speech was uncannily accurate, and despite myself, I smiled. Time to give in graciously.

'Then, thank you. I appreciate your concern. It's good to be able to walk home with a friend.'

I hoped he didn't notice my slight stumble before I said 'friend'. It felt weird using that term for him. We were investigation partners. Our relationship was meant to be entirely professional, each of us assisting the other towards their desired goal. It was important that the lines didn't get blurred in any way. Once again, I stamped down on the strange stirrings of a very different kind of feeling towards him. 'Friend' didn't quite fit in that scenario either, but it was definitely a much safer term than any other, and safe was sensible. I had learned that lesson the hard way.

'Where's your bike? Or rather, where on the rack was it? I know they have a habit of disappearing in this town.' Leo thankfully seemed oblivious of my internal dilemma, and I welcomed the change of topic.

'Tell me about it. Someone once told me that the bikes in Oxford get stolen to order and sold off in Cambridge, and vice versa. You'd probably know all about that, being in CID, although maybe you were dealing with much more serious stuff. Anyway, the combination of hardcore locks on both front and back wheels, and Betty being the most basic of bikes, has managed to put the thieves off so far, touch wood.'

I tapped the side of my head.

'Of course, you'd give your bike a name,' said Leo with a laugh.

'It's probably a bad idea. If she ever does get nicked, I'll be devastated.'

Thankfully, Betty was still securely locked where I'd left her, and, even better, my helmet was still attached too and didn't contain someone's leftover kebab, which had once happened.

'May I?' asked Leo. 'Please note that I'm not suggesting you're incapable of unlocking your own bike, but given the vulnerability of yellow dress fabric and the potential risk of oily marks...'

'In for a penny, in for a pound,' I said. 'On this occasion, I will play the helpless female and graciously accept your offer of assistance.'

'There's nothing helpless about you, Kat Fisher.'

'And nothing gracious, either?' I got in there first before he could.

Leo laughed. 'There's never a dull moment when you're around, I'll give you that.'

He quickly unlocked the bike, also freeing my shiny gold bike helmet which he passed across to me with great ceremony.

'How about you carry the helmet, and I'll push the bike?' he suggested. 'A classic model by the way, excellent front basket capacity.'

'All the better for transporting as many books as possible.'

'Naturally.'

'We librarians have got to take our perks where we can find them, and one of those is being able to borrow more than the usual limit of ten books at once.'

'And could a librarian's friend also get access to those kinds of perks?'

'They'd have to be a very special friend for that,' I said without thinking, then immediately felt my cheeks glow as I realised how unintentionally suggestive my response could have sounded.

'Something to look forward to,' said Leo, although perhaps I had misheard him. After all, there was a lot of ambient noise from the crowds who were also wandering along Cornmarket Street.

We turned the corner onto the High, steadily making our way back towards my flat on Iffley Road. Tonight we seemed to be walking comfortably in step with each other,

Leo obviously still heeding my lecture from the other day and resisting his giraffe striding tendencies.

'So, what did we learn from tonight's event? Apart from that you have knight-in-shining-armour syndrome, of course,' I said lightly.

'It's been a long time since anyone referred to me as a knight in shining armour. I appreciate it's not necessarily a compliment, coming from you, but I think I'm going to take it as one,' he responded.

'Sorry. I'm not ungrateful, really, I'm not. But I did believe I was getting somewhere with that Marc bloke.'

'He certainly thought he was getting somewhere. Didn't it make you feel uncomfortable the way he was staring at your chest throughout the whole conversation?'

I grimaced. 'Sure, I felt like pointing at my face and yelling "I'm up here, you know", but it wouldn't have done any good. Sadly, it isn't an unusual experience. I once tried to retaliate by directing all my answers to a creepy guy's crotch, but it definitely didn't have the effect I was after. Eurgh.' I shuddered at the memory.

'Yikes, sounds awful. Okay, so putting aside Marc's sleazy behaviour and lack of basic decency, you still thought he might have some useful information?'

'He was telling me that he's been a member of the app since it was founded. That's not as long as you might think, though, as it's only a year old. I was really surprised. All of their marketing material and the information on their website give the impression that it's really well established, like it's been around forever. It was one of the factors that made me feel more confident about joining.'

'Interesting. So, they're good at marketing themselves, but it's a case of style over substance.'

'Definitely. The barman told me that Dom runs all the events, and he certainly seemed to be doing all the jobs tonight, even though he was pretty laid back about some of them.' I explained how he hadn't even bothered to check I was on the guest list when I arrived. 'Anyway, did you learn anything from your dates? Anything of use, that is?'

'I assure you I remained entirely professional throughout, despite some of their best intentions to distract me.'

'I bet,' I muttered under my breath.

'Sorry, what was that?' said Leo.

'Nothing. Did any of them pour their hearts out to you about being scammed?'

'As you know yourself, five minutes pass in a flash.'

Thinking of my boring Bryan-with-a-Y date, I wasn't sure I completely agreed with him about that.

'I'd imagine a trained investigator like yourself is adept at getting the information you need in less than five seconds,' I said, deliberately over-egging the flattery.

'Hmm. I'm good, but I'm not that good. Let me think, what did I learn? Some of the women were gifted their membership for free in return for agreeing for their profiles to be used in promotional material.'

'Lucky them. Although I'm not sure I'd like the idea of becoming the face of SO Ox.'

'They did say that they'd had to deal with more than the usual number of creepy messages, and one of them let slip that the app refused to do anything about them and threatened her with losing her membership for making false complaints.'

'Which is exactly what happened to me.'

Leo nodded. 'There are definitely issues with the SO Ox system. As to whether any of the women I met had also encountered our fraudster, I'm afraid, despite my best efforts, I drew a blank.'

'I guess we're going to have to up the ante,' I said, as we crossed Magdalen Bridge.

'I'm not sure I like the sound of that.' Leo cleared his throat. 'Look, please don't take this the wrong way, but given what happened tonight, I'd feel a lot better about this whole thing if you let me teach you some self-defence moves.'

I snorted, then quickly tried to disguise it as a cough when I realised he wasn't joking.

'Self-defence? Really? You actually think I'm going to need that if we go to another SO Ox event?'

'I think it's better to be safe than sorry,' he said.

I reached out and lightly touched his forearm. 'You're being very big-brotherly and over-protective. It's really not necessary, Leo. As I've told you many times, I can look after myself.'

For a second, I imagined him responding with a Mr Knightley-worthy, 'Brother and sister! No indeed', but he just shrugged.

'I know that a core of steel lurks behind the kind librarian exterior, but it would put my mind at ease. Humour me.'

I pulled a face at him, unwilling to show I was strangely flattered by his description of me.

As we approached my front door, I said, 'I've got skills already, you know. And I've always got a book on me. I reckon I could inflict some damage with a hardback.'

'Knowing you, you'd prioritise saving the hardback over yourself.'

He had a point there.

I watched him lock my bike up while I considered his suggestion. He hadn't gone as far as saying he'd back out of the investigation if I didn't do the self-defence lesson, but I could tell he was genuinely concerned for my safety. If agreeing meant he'd spend less time worrying about me and more time concentrating on tracking down our target, then that was a price I was happy to pay.

'Fine, you can teach me some moves. But don't say I didn't warn you.'

He waited for me to unlock my front door and switch on the light inside.

'Great stuff. I'll meet you at my gym on Saturday. I'll text you the address.'

'See you on Saturday. Thanks for walking me home.'

I leaned forward and brushed my cheek against his, an ordinary kiss of farewell. Only nothing felt ordinary about being so close to him. I took a deep breath to steady myself, but the heady combination of his subtle aftershave and the warmth of his stubbly face made me feel even more off kilter. For one mad moment, I thought about turning my head and moving my lips into contact with his. What would it feel like to press still closer to him, and allow myself to let go? I lingered for a moment longer than was strictly necessary.

'Goodnight, Kat,' Leo said softly, his breath tickling my ear, before he stepped back. 'Sleep well.'

Judging by the confused way I was feeling right now, that seemed highly unlikely.

Chapter Sixteen

I spent most of Friday writing texts to Leo and deleting them before I did anything so foolish as to actually send them. My one saving grace was that at least it was my day off, so I didn't have to go into the library and face him. The more I thought about last night, the more confused I became. I tried to tell myself I'd imagined it, but it did feel like we'd nearly had A Moment. But A Moment was the very last thing I wanted, and besides, I was pretty sure it hadn't been mutual. It had merely been another classic case of Kat getting carried away again. Hadn't I learned anything from my experience with Scammer Brian? The reality was that I'd been so susceptible to him because I was in love with the idea of being in love. Brian had been charming and effusive in all his communications with me. It hadn't taken much for me to fall for him, as I built him up in my imagination, nurtured by the constant loving messages he sent.

Leo, meanwhile, had been at times rude, overbearing

and bossy, but underlying it all, I knew there was kindness there, and he seemed genuine and honest in his dealings with me. Was that all it took for my ever-hopeful heart to transfer its affections? I needed to get a grip and be sensible. The capacity for getting hurt in this instance was even higher, because I'd actually met the man and got to know him for real. Got to know him on one level, I reminded myself. There could be a whole lot more going on with Leo that I had no idea about. After all, as a former policeman, he'd undoubtedly be highly skilled at putting on a persona to suit his surroundings and mask his real thoughts. And he'd never actually told me why he'd left a profession which he claimed to have felt so strongly about.

No, I needed to protect myself. Now was not the time to get distracted by nebulous feelings which couldn't be trusted. I needed to concentrate on my goal of bringing down a dangerous romance fraudster. Then I could return to the sanctuary of my books, immerse myself in the safe, fictional versions of romance, and enjoy a peaceful existence in real life without the complications brought about by unpredictable men. And having made that promise to myself, I went for a walk around Christ Church Meadow, deliberately leaving my phone at home. It was better to be safe than sorry, after all.

The park was peaceful, a few joggers making easy work of the winding paths, while the occasional curious duck waddled past me as I lingered by the riverbank, relishing the quiet. This place had always been one of my favourite parts of the city, an oasis of calm away from the bustling streets where it was all too easy sometimes to feel like I was caught in a bubble, one which distorted my perspective on the rest of the world. It was good to stand apart from the intensity of the investigation and other life stresses for a few moments and just enjoy being surrounded by nature. But, for once, even here I found I couldn't settle completely. The sounds of the bells chiming from college clock towers every quarter of an hour were a constant reminder that time was passing, and with it, the likelihood of us tracking down Scammer Brian was surely diminishing, however optimistic I tried to remain about my mission.

I wandered on and found myself a bench overlooking the boat houses. Although most of them were shut up as the students were still on their Easter holidays, there was one door open from which emerged a team carrying a rowing eight. While they set about putting it in the water and rigging their blades, a couple of coaches launched the safety boat, laughing together as they watched the crew take their time getting ready.

'Come on guys, we haven't got all day, you know,' shouted the female coach.

'We need to make the most of this good weather before the wind gets up later,' called another voice which I instantly recognised. Leo. How many times had I come here to watch the rowers and never encountered him? And now, when I was trying to get a bit of distance to help bring myself back under control, here he was. Just my luck.

I nearly got up and started walking away, but realised that the movement might attract his attention, so I hunched on the bench and tried to summon a shield of invisibility.

The safety boat puttered alongside the eight, Leo giving

bits of helpful advice while the rowers settled themselves into their seats. Once they'd finally pushed off, Leo and his colleague followed along at a steady pace. The team looked like novices judging by the frequent splashes and direction changes of the boat. A couple of the rowers were obviously finding it stressful, voices raised as they clutched onto their oars, yelling at their teammates to go more steadily and balance the boat up. But as they made their way down the river, they slowly started finding their rhythm, working together, not against each other, as they pulled the blades through the water and followed the guidance and encouragement from Leo and his colleague.

Finally, they reached the Head of the River and started to make their turn to come back towards the boat house. The safety boat spun round more quickly and backed off to give them space. Judging by the laughter on board, Leo was in his element, relaxed and happy. Even at this distance, I could see his smile and appreciate the way it lit up his face. I felt an unwanted pang of envy that I wasn't the one sitting beside him, able to join in with his jokes with casual ease without worrying how he might or might not feel about me and whether I might or might not be worthy of his attention. Because wasn't that what was really at the root of my doubts and insecurity? That feeling of not being worthy, of not actually deserving to be loved? It seemed to come so easily to most people, yet for me it felt like the hardest thing in the world. Previous relationships had fizzled out, guys declaring that they wanted to keep things casual, then, within months of them breaking up with me, I'd see posts on social media announcing their engagement or similar.

They weren't keen on commitment when it came to me, but would go all in with someone else. Why wasn't I ever enough? And then Brian had come along, everything I'd ever dreamed of and more, seemingly with none of the game-play that I'd endured before. No wonder I'd been such an easy mark.

I gave myself a mental shake. There was no point in sitting here and wallowing. It wasn't going to change anything. I needed to focus on the positive. While other people might have crumbled after experiencing what I had been through with the fraudster, after an initial wobble, I had got back up again and come out fighting, refusing to let it define me. That proved I was a strong person, surely? It was hard to ignore, but I didn't have to listen to the horrid voice in my head telling me I was unlovable. How other people viewed me was up to them, but I should probably try to be kinder to myself in the future. As for the crush on Leo: well, yes, I had developed one, I could admit that to myself. But, for now, it was sensible to put that to one side so I could concentrate on bringing down Scammer Brian. I would need all the headspace I could find to make that happen.

I got up from my bench and walked back through the park and headed home, pretending to myself that I couldn't care less whether Leo had spotted me or not.

Inevitably the first thing I did when I got back was to check the messages on my phone. There were two missed calls from Gavin and the briefest of texts from Leo giving directions to his gym. He made no mention of his rowing coaching, and I resisted the temptation to ask him about it, ringing Gavin straight back instead.

'Hello, this is Gavin speaking,' he answered the phone in a very proper fashion.

'Hi, it's Kat, I'm just returning your calls. I'm really sorry I missed them.'

'Oh, thank goodness. I've been worried something bad had happened at that event last night.'

'Oh Gav, I'm so sorry. I'm absolutely fine, I promise. I just left my phone at home when I went for a walk.'

'That's a relief.'

'Thank you so much for standing guard yesterday evening. How did you and Robin get on?'

'Pretty well, if I do say so myself. We hung around for half an hour, as you suggested, and I took careful notes about every man who walked in that building. They mostly seemed fairly ordinary, but there were one or two who seemed a bit off.'

'Go on,' I said.

'It's hard to explain. It was more of an instinct rather than anything hugely concrete.' He was backtracking now, but I knew that Gavin's intuition was not to be unheeded. After all, he hadn't survived this long on the streets by ignoring it.

'I'm listening.' In fact, I'd sat down at my desk and pulled out a pad of paper ready to take notes.

'There was one guy who loitered outside for ages putting on a college tie before he walked in the bar.'

'Ah yes, I think I know who you're talking about. But there could be a simple explanation, like he might have been coming straight from somewhere else and not had time to change beforehand.' I decided to play devil's advocate to encourage Gavin to elaborate on his concerns.

'It was a new purchase. He took it out of a shopping bag and dropped the receipt on the ground. Robin went and fetched it for me.'

'She's a clever girl, Robin. What was it about the new tie that got you worried?'

'He could just have been trying to impress people, but I wondered if he was pretending to be somebody he wasn't. He seemed a bit shifty to me. There was something off about him.'

'Did he have floppy hair?'

'Yes, he did.'

'He definitely sounds like a guy I met who said his name was Marcus. He claimed to be a Physics professor, but he didn't act like any of the other university lecturers I've come across. Actually, it's fair to say he put the "letch" into lecturer.' I smiled at my own bad joke. At least it was a healthy reaction to what happened last night. 'Let me start my laptop and I'll look him up. I should have done that earlier. You can tell me about the other suspicious person you spotted while I'm googling.'

'Sure. The other guy had an iPad and he kept coming in and out of the building while the event was on. He was tapping away on that thing like nobody's business.'

'That sounds like the organiser, Dom. He founded the app. He struck me as being the kind of person who spends half his life on the internet. What was it about him that set the alarm bells ringing?'

'In truth, it's because Robin had a little growl at him that my suspicions were raised. Her judgment is usually spot on,' said Gavin. 'But then again, there was a tin can blowing around the street at the same time, and she always gets upset by the noise they make.'

I was only half listening to what Gavin was saying because I was so taken aback by what I could see on screen.

'You'll never guess what I've just found out about Marc.' I skim-read the article again, to make sure it was definitely about the guy I'd met last night. 'There's a piece in the *Oxford Mail* about him. According to this, he's been suspended from the university due to numerous "inappropriate behaviour" allegations from students. That certainly ties in with how he acted towards me. The article has a quote from him denying that he's done anything wrong and complaining that he's not receiving his full pay while he's on suspension.'

The cogs were turning quickly now. Marc's voice had sounded different to Brian's but it had been noisy in the bar.

Gavin tutted. 'He sounds like a wrong 'un. I hope my information helps.'

'You're a star, thank you so much. You've given my investigation a breakthrough.'

'I'm glad. People like that should face their comeuppance. Well, I'll leave you to it. It's time for Robin's dinner. She's very particular about such things. See you at the library next week.'

'Looking forward to it. And make sure you give that gorgeous girly a belly rub for me.'

As soon as I finished talking to Gavin, I hit dial on Leo's number, then just as quickly cancelled the call. At the moment, I only had a hunch, and while I was sure that Leo would be in full agreement with Gavin and me that Marc was indeed a 'wrong 'un', I knew that the next thing he'd challenge me on would be what evidence I had to back up my theory. And he'd be right to. I needed to find some actual proof.

I settled myself back down in front of my laptop and set to work researching everything I could about Marc. This was where my librarian skillset could finally come into its own. Before long, I discovered that he'd also left Cambridge University under a cloud, rather than to take on new challenges as he'd told me. The local press was vague, quoting an official statement saying that he'd resigned for health reasons, but the student paper went further, citing an unnamed source in the science department who said that an investigation had been started about claims of bullying.

I dug deeper, paying to access the records of county court judgements and discovered that Marc had two against him for unpaid parking fines. That hardly made him a criminal mastermind, I reminded myself, but it did suggest a pattern of behaviour. The court judgements would have affected his credit score, and he'd been grumbling about his reduced pay in the *Oxford Mail*. Judging by his clothing, he had expensive tastes. Perhaps he was struggling to fund the lifestyle he desired. That would give him a financial motive to run a scam. Plus, he'd made a big deal about being friends with Dom, so he possibly had access to insider knowledge about the app which could make it easier for him to create a fake identity to scam people. The more I thought about it, the more credible a suspect he appeared to be. He had to go to the top of our list. I ignored the fact that Marc's was actually the only name on that suspect list.

I went to bed happy that night, full of anticipation about seeing Leo the next day and telling him what I'd discovered.

Chapter Seventeen

Calling the place Leo attended a gym rather overstated the facilities within it. I'd been expecting somewhere full of state-of-the-art equipment and intimidating athletic types flexing for selfies in front of full-length mirrors. I opened the door with apprehension and felt self-conscious as a chime went off. But that seemed to be the only concession to modernity in the ramshackle, shed-like building. It was sparsely furnished, with a few racks of weights and other simple equipment, and not a mirror in sight. At the top of the room, a large blackboard listed the 'WOD' or 'Workout of the Day' as I mentally translated thanks to having come across it in a book once.

'Shall we get started?' asked Leo, barely glancing across at me as he carried on setting up a crash mat.

'Good morning, Leo. How are you? Did you have a good Friday?' I asked, making the point that a little bit of polite small talk wouldn't do him any harm. Admittedly, I was also being deliberately sarky as a defence mechanism because, although I'd sensed the strength which lurked beneath his normally run-of-the-mill attire, I hadn't quite prepared myself for the effect of seeing him in gym shorts and a t-shirt which was almost indecently form-fitting against his strong biceps and broad shoulders. If he smiled at me now, I was a goner.

He raised an eyebrow. 'It was the same as any other Friday of late.'

'I had a lovely day, thanks for asking,' I said, still needling away to maintain the protection of his grumpiness so I could focus my attention on what really mattered.

'Fine, how was your day off?' he asked begrudgingly.

'Extremely productive.' I started explaining what I'd found out about Marc, pulling a collection of print-outs from my bag to support my reasoning. Surely, given the extent of the background dossier I'd compiled, Leo would have to agree that Marc had both the motive and the means to be Scammer Brian.

'That is a lot of paper,' said Leo, which wasn't exactly the enthusiastic response I'd been hoping for.

'Have a read, see what you think. You have to agree that I'm on to something.'

He fixed me with a stern look. 'Is this a delaying tactic?'

'What do you mean?'

'You made it very clear that you're not keen to learn self-defence.'

'It's not that I'm not keen; it's just that I don't think it's the best use of our time,' I said. 'I wish you'd pay attention and believe what I've told you countless times – that I can look after myself.'

'You may have mentioned it once or twice,' he said, in a manner which told me he still didn't believe a word of it. 'If I have a quick look through this file now, and promise to read it more thoroughly later, can we please get on with the lesson?'

I'd really prefer we didn't. Initially my reluctance had been purely because I wasn't the complete novice that he thought I was. But there was also the fact that being taught self-defence by Leo would mean having to grapple at close quarters with him and, given the confusing way I was starting to feel, that was an added complication I could really do without. However, he was clearly going to keep nagging me until he got his own way, and the longer he spent doing that, the less focus he would be giving to the investigation.

'I'm surprised you're calling me stubborn when you're acting like the very definition of it.' I sighed. 'If you absolutely insist, I guess that sounds like a fair compromise.'

He sat down on an upturned packing case to read through my evidence while I wandered over to take a closer look at the list of exercises on the blackboard. No wonder Leo had the appearance he did. These exercises wouldn't look out of place in an Olympian's training schedule. Or in a torture chamber, if you ask me. Nobody worked out like that unless they were seriously dedicated. Or seriously in need of distraction.

Eventually, Leo came over to join me.

'Okay, I think you've got a point about Marc. He's definitely one to keep a close eye on.'

'That's great, I knew I was on to something.'

'Don't get too carried away. All of this is circumstantial evidence. And I use the word "evidence" in the loosest possible sense,' he said.

'I also knew you'd say that.'

'I hate to be predictable, but, on the other hand, I'm touched to be the voice of reason in your head.'

I knew he'd only said it to wind me up, but I fell for the trap anyway. 'Don't flatter yourself. Smugness doesn't suit you.'

Leo grinned in that provoking way of his. 'At least you acknowledge that we're nowhere near being able to prove that Marc has an alternative identity as one Brian James.'

'What do *you* think we should do next?'

'I can tell from the way you asked that question that you already have a plan in mind.'

'You're right, I do. I was thinking I should message Marc on the app and ask him on a date,' I said, even though the very thought of it turned my stomach. 'I've continued communicating with the Brian James profile, but I'm stuck in a holding pattern, to be honest. Take a look at this.' I found the relevant exchange on the app and passed my phone over to Leo.

Any luck on the funding front? I'm guessing things over there are still terrible, judging by the way you're stuck at HQ. Is there no way you could get even a weekend pass out to meet up? You deserve some down time, and I'd love to spend it with you. Missing your presence more every second. Love, Kat xx

As soon as the funding is sorted, I'll be all yours. But until then, I am waiting and hoping for things to work out so we can be together. You have no idea how frustrated I am that I can't be with you right this second. You are in my every thought. Love, Brian xoxo

'Very smooth,' said Leo.

'As you can see, both of us are dancing around things. He's pushing without overtly coming out and saying he wants money, and I'm doing the same, but it's information that I'm after.'

'There's certainly no indication that he might have already met you – if your theory that it's Marc proves correct. Why do you think asking him out would prove that hypothesis?'

'If Marc agreed to meet me – obviously in a public place for safety – then I could try subtly quoting stuff from Scammer Brian's messages, or referring to bits of his back story, and see how he reacts. It could be a way of catching him out.'

Even as I said it out loud, I knew how many flaws there were in my plan, and judging from Leo's sceptical expression, he was about to take great delight in pointing them all out to me.

'That's an – how shall I phrase this? – interesting approach. But I think we'll need to come up with something better than that. For a start, don't you think he might be a teensy bit suspicious of your sudden interest in him, given your swift exit from his company on Thursday night?'

'And whose fault was that?' I retorted. Then after a

pause, I added, 'But thank you. In retrospect, I agree it was probably for the best to get out of there, and I appreciate you helped me do that as quickly as possible.'

Leo clutched his hand to his chest and gasped. 'I must be hallucinating, because that sounded very much like Ms Kat Fisher admitting at last that I was right and she was wrong.'

'Alright, alright, there's no need to gloat about it.' I shoved my elbow against his side with slightly more force than was needed. Without even hesitating, Leo blocked the move and spun me round so I was facing him.

'As you instigated things, this seems as good a moment as any to start your self-defence lesson,' he said.

'I'd really prefer to push on with the Marc investigation,' I said, trying to ignore the fact that I was practically flush against him now. All I needed to do was act nonchalant or, even better, try to keep the grumpy banter going, but it was hard to concentrate on behaving normally when I was being held in such close proximity.

'Don't worry, I'll be gentle with you,' he said. 'What shall we use as a safe word?'

I shot him a glance. That low huskiness was back in his voice, but his expression was completely neutral. Was he deliberately teasing me, or was my overactive imagination conjuring up double meanings to his speech that weren't actually there?

I cleared my throat and gave myself a stern mental lecture to get it together.

'If that's how this works, then perhaps you'd like to come up with one yourself, oh mentor of mine,' I said. If my words came out slightly more wavering than I'd have liked,

I hoped he'd blame it on my supposed nerves at learning self-defence.

He finally unleashed the grin which I'd suspected he'd been hiding all along.

'Mentor, hey? I'm honoured.'

'Don't get used to it.'

'You spend all day surrounded by books. I'm sure you can come up with an appropriate safe word. It has to be something that neither of us will accidentally let slip in normal conversation while we work on our moves.'

I couldn't imagine having a normal conversation while grappling on the ground with Leo. And now I wished I hadn't let my mind wander to the grappling on the ground bit. I was already discombobulated by the hold which was lasting for much longer than felt normal. This was going to get so awkward.

'Can't we just choose something simple like "stop"?'

'That's a bit boring, isn't it? Besides, most attackers don't follow orders like "stop". How about Darcy?' he suggested. 'I'm sure he won't mind us leaving his title out. It makes it easier to shout in the heat of the moment.'

I shrugged as casually as I could manage. Was he deliberately trying to provoke me?

'I seem to recall you have a particular fondness for Mr Darcy, using him in your SO Ox password as you do,' he added.

Yes, yes, he was.

'Sure. If that's what you're happy shouting when I get the better of you, then we'll go for that,' I said, pretending to be all sweetness and light.

'Don't worry, I'm certainly not underestimating you,' he said, in a relaxed tone which gave away that he was doing exactly that.

'I'm really not sure this is necessary,' I reiterated, giving him one last chance to back out.

'I know you think I'm overreacting, but if you'd seen some of the cases I've dealt with, you'd understand why I think it's so important,' said Leo. His relaxed, easy demeanour changed, his gaze becoming troubled. I could tell that the surroundings of the gym had faded and he was seeing something completely different.

I fought the urge to soften myself against him and transform this martial arts hold into a hug, sensing that he'd prefer a slap in the face to accepting any gesture that acknowledged he was in need of comfort.

'I'm sorry you've experienced things that have made you feel like this,' I said.

'The point is that I didn't experience them.' He paused, and I waited to see if he'd trust me with more. 'I had to deal with the aftermath, which is a special sort of helplessness,' he added eventually. 'I never want to see anyone going through that kind of pain again, especially not someone I c—know.' He cleared his throat.

I wondered what he'd been going to say before he changed his mind.

'I can understand that.'

'Which is why I want to teach you the basics of self-defence,' he said, his voice growing stronger again.

I nodded. Perhaps it was time to respond to his honesty with some of my own. I suspected that some of what I was about to say wouldn't come as a surprise to him, but it still felt important to mention.

'I appreciate the kind thought, Leo, but I promise, you don't have to worry about me. I know you think that I'm a bit of a softy, but I can handle myself. It's a sad fact that this kind of stuff is ingrained into most women's sensibilities. Walking home with your keys between your knuckles, texting friends to let them know you're back safely, avoiding going out by yourself after dark, otherwise known as the unofficial female curfew. I hate that it's this way, but we don't even think twice about doing that kind of stuff. I realised a while ago that I've been following the basics of self-defence since I was capable of independent thought.'

He nodded. 'All sensible precautions, and I acknowledge how frustrating it must be. And I appreciate that "frustrating" doesn't even do justice to something so wrong. But sometimes you need to up your game. Also, let's be clear that I don't think you're a softy at all. Actually, I think you're an incredibly strong woman who people misjudge at their peril.'

The internal glow I experienced at his words was almost strong enough to light up the room. But then he carried on speaking and completely undermined the compliment he'd just bestowed on me.

'But what about situations like in the bar when that dreadful bloke wouldn't let you go? What would have happened if I hadn't stepped in?'

I would have shrugged, but was mindful that I was still in what was essentially an embrace with Leo and figured the minimum amount of movement I made, the better.

'As we've already discussed, I was handling it fine. And you did step in, so there was nothing to worry about.'

Leo's hold tightened. I wasn't even sure if he was aware that he'd done it. I could feel his chest rising and falling with his breath.

'I won't always be there to step in,' he said. 'You say you were handling it, but what you were really doing was the classic thing of being polite and not wanting to make a fuss, hoping that he'd grow bored before things got even worse. Please promise me this – in the future, make a fuss. Don't give a damn about who's staring at you. The more people the better, in truth. Make a scene, raise your voice, and if it's still not working, get physical and defend yourself.'

I braced my hands against his torso and tried to push myself back so I could get a better look at his expression.

'If this is another version of the lecture about how we need to change our behaviour, rather than the perpetrator altering theirs, I'm not listening.'

Leo looked horrified. 'Absolutely not. I would never, ever accuse anyone of provoking an attack, or suggest that they'd not done enough to fight back against one. The offender holds all responsibility for the crime.'

'Good. Then we're in agreement. Yes, Marc was becoming a tad handsy, and I didn't like it. But I decided it was a price I was willing to pay because I thought I was getting somewhere.'

'So did he,' said Leo. 'That was part of the problem.'

'You're deliberately misunderstanding me. Look, I'm touched by your concern, and I know all this is coming from a place of good intentions. But I am a grown woman, and I am more capable physically than you give me credit for.'

'Just because you've read about how to defend yourself in a book, doesn't mean you can do it in real life,' he hit back. 'Let me help you arm yourself with some basic skills. You enlisted me for this ridiculous scheme because you wanted my professional guidance. This is one of the times where you should be taking it.'

I frowned. This was clearly a situation where I had to show rather than just tell.

'Okay,' I said, acting as if I was giving up on the argument. 'I have no desire to hurt you, but if you won't believe me, then I guess there's only one way to settle this.'

He looked relieved. 'Don't worry about hurting me. That's the object of the game. And I—'

'If you're about to say you doubt I could do that, think again, Mister,' I said, hooking my leg around his ankle and using the element of surprise to knock him off balance and reverse our positions so I was the one now holding him in place.

'Nice moves,' he grunted, as I placed my right hand on his throat. I didn't apply any pressure, but the warning was there. He might be pretending to be impressed, but my unexpected show of strength had certainly caused his adrenalin to kick in, judging by how rapidly his pulse was beating under my palm.

For a couple of seconds, I revelled in my superiority, then, without any warning, my own leg hook move was used against me and I found myself tumbling towards the crash mat on the ground. But just as I was bracing myself for impact, Leo grabbed me around the waist and pulled me back against him, this time with my back to his chest.

'Never underestimate your opponent's strength,' I said, trying to keep my voice steady as if I was passing comment on the weather. It came out breathier than I'd intended, which I blamed on the fact that I was once again held tight against six foot something of solid man. I briefly closed my eyes to get myself together, then suddenly pitched myself forward and equally as quickly let myself go limp, making him stagger. He only just managed to stop himself tumbling, but succeeded in rallying speedily enough to grab me before I broke free, and heaved me back into a close embrace.

'Precisely,' said Leo. 'And judging by the way you demonstrated that pearl of wisdom when tackling me, I'm guessing that your understanding of it has not solely come from books.'

I jabbed back with my elbow, pulling the full impact so I didn't wind the guy. I could tell that he was still going easy on me and it was only fair that I afforded him the same courtesy. He wouldn't be any use to the investigation if he was incapacitated by my self-defence moves at full strength.

'You guess correctly.'

Leo responded by leaning backwards, effortlessly lifting me off my feet. I could feel the vibration of his laughter against my back. I could have got myself out of the situation by a couple of sharp kicks backwards, followed by a repeat of the passive resistance move, but if I was being completely honest with myself, there was an element of enjoyment in being lifted by him so easily. It was at odds with my feminist principles, but a girl's got to get her thrills where she can find them.

'You are full of surprises. Go on, then. Tell me more,' he urged against my ear. 'How did you acquire your secret ninja skills?'

'The university is running an evening course on the women's liberation movement,' I explained. 'Have you ever heard of suffrajitsu?'

'Actually no, but I think I know where you might be going with this.'

'It's a technique which the suffragettes used during the fight for— That's completely underhand.' My explanation finished in a yelp because I suddenly found myself flipped around and pinned down on the floor with Leo bracing himself mere centimetres above me.

'Never forget the importance of the element of surprise,' he said, looking thoroughly pleased with himself. 'Ready to use your safe word yet?'

I assessed my situation and realised I was trapped. There was probably something I could do to get myself out of the hold, but my mind wasn't working at full capacity, rendered somewhat fuzzy by this far too intimate position.

I opened my mouth, ready to say, 'Darcy', but instead found myself saying something else completely.

'Maybe I don't want to use it.'

Chapter Eighteen

'And then what happened?' asked Moira, her expression agog.

'Can't the poor woman enjoy her meal in peace without being interrogated?' challenged Rami. 'Can I help you to some more roast potatoes, Kat?'

He didn't wait for a reply before adding an extra couple onto my already laden plate. I was in danger of slipping into a food coma after this generous meal, which was probably a good thing as I'd spent most of last night lying awake, mentally re-living that moment in the gym, and wishing that things could have gone differently.

'How can you be thinking of something so mundane as roast potatoes when Kat's in the middle of telling us about how she engineered it so Mr Sex-On-Two-Legs was pinning her to the ground and showing off his manly prowess?'

I nearly choked on my mouthful of Yorkshire pudding.

'Well, when you put it like that, perhaps you're right. That is far more interesting than roast potatoes, especially as

I've already polished all mine off,' said Rami, looking at me expectantly. 'Go on, Kat, tell us more.'

'Not you as well, Mr Moira,' I said. 'I've always had you down as the sensible one.'

'How rude,' said Rami. 'I'd have thought you'd have realised by now that I'm far from sensible. I take great pride in that fact, just ask Moira. I shall retaliate by withholding dessert – a very fine apple crumble, if I do say so myself – until you fill us in on every little detail.'

'Well said, love,' said Moira. 'As you can see, we both feel very invested in this. Besides, you've got to let your old married friends get some vicarious enjoyment from your thrilling life of singledom. Or perhaps not singledom anymore, eh? Should I be looking for a hat?'

She mimed putting one on at a jaunty angle.

I rolled my eyes. 'You're as bad as my sister, preparing to rush me down the aisle the second a guy even smiles at me. The pair of you have a completely unrealistic perception of my powers of allure.'

'That's a load of tosh,' said Moira. 'You could have any man you wanted, if you'd only believe in yourself. But we've had that discussion on many occasions, and I refuse to let you distract me from the main point. So, you and the luscious Leo were both on the floor, you pulled him closer and then … you kissed him, right?'

My pulse quickened as I remembered the moment. I'd reached up and touched the curve of his jaw, then tentatively traced my finger along his skin and towards his lips. His breathing had seemed to be unusually fast, although I'd told myself that it was most likely because of the exertion of picking me up and throwing me to the crash mat. I'd closed my eyes, daring myself to close the small gap between us, to be bold for once in my life, and make that first move. For a few endless seconds, I'd experienced a sense of joyous anticipation that the moment my ever-hopeful heart had been longing for was about to happen. And then...

'No, I didn't kiss him. Absolutely nothing happened.'

'You what?' said Moira, the outrage obvious in her voice.

'Nothing happened. You see, the gym has this chime which sounds whenever the door opens, and of course somebody chose that exact moment to come in, and Leo made good his escape. You could say that he was quite literally saved by the bell from having to let me down gently.'

'But did he want to be saved by it?' asked Rami. 'And how about you? How did you feel when you were interrupted?'

I took another mouthful of food to buy myself some time. I didn't need to think about my answer, but I wasn't sure whether I was ready to admit it to myself, let alone out loud, even if it was to two of my closest friends.

'I bet I know exactly how she felt,' said Moira sympathetically. 'But there's always the next time. You wait until I tell Doris; she'll be gutted that I've won the sweepstake.'

'The what now?' I asked.

Moira at least had the grace to look shamefaced. 'The sweepstake on how long it would take for you and the lovely Leo to get it on. The signs were there from the moment you first clapped eyes on him. She plumped for a month, but I said it would happen quicker than that. And I was spot on.'

'No, you weren't,' I said, mortified by the idea of being the subject of such a bet. 'Didn't you hear me right? Absolutely nothing happened. I was about to make a complete fool of myself, then the door chimed, Leo leapt away like he'd burnt himself or something, and I disappeared as fast as I could.'

'Hmm, leaving Leo longing for you to return and pick up where you left off, I have no doubt. Curses be upon that ruddy door chime,' said Moira. 'Never mind, the first move has been made. You'll be dragging him into the library stacks for surreptitious snogs before we know it.'

'I highly doubt it. Didn't you hear the bit where I said he couldn't wait to get away from me? The door chime gave him the excuse he was looking for to break free before he had to do the whole "I'm sorry, I'm just not that into you" thing. It was incredibly awkward. And it gets worse.' It was clear I needed to tell the whole story to stop Moira getting any more carried away. 'I should also mention that the person who came in was Leo's fellow rowing coach, who's clearly some kind of model in her spare time. I could never hope to get a look in when someone like her with legs up to the ceiling is around. Anyway, he went straight over to hug her and made this big deal about how delighted he was to see her, almost as if she'd rescued him from my evil clutches. Further evidence, not that I needed it, that he couldn't escape from me fast enough.'

'That seems highly unlikely to me. She's probably just a good friend. It reminds me of when I was first dating Moira and I thought she only had eyes for that chap from the Chemistry department,' said Rami. 'He was a perfectly nice guy, but I thought he was the devil incarnate until I found out the truth.'

'Actually, he was only my mate, and I was using him to try to make Rami jealous so he'd hurry up and see what was staring him in the face,' Moira finished the story.

Rami laughed. 'And I guess it worked. Because here I am decades later enjoying the thrill of being your lifelong companion, not to mention your chief chef.'

He reached out and interlocked his fingers with hers.

'But I put the bins out, so it's all fair. We're an equal opportunities household.'

'That's only once a fortnight, dear heart,' said Rami, his grin growing wider.

'Which makes them all the heavier, my darling,' said Moira, blowing him a kiss. 'It's taken years of resistance training for me to get to the skill level I'm at now.'

I relaxed back in my chair, enjoying their banter, and happy that their attention was diverted away from me.

But my respite was brief.

'Why don't you ask him who his friend is?' said Rami. 'That's what I did with Moira and, before we knew it, we were getting thrown out of the lecture hall for kissing on the back row. When it's meant to be, it's meant to be.'

'Because I'm not sure that it is meant to be,' I said. 'Besides, our relationship is purely professional, and that is definitely an unprofessional thing to ask. I have no need to know who he associates with when he's not working on the investigation with me. He's helping me catch Scammer Brian, and I'm going to help him write his business plan, that is all there is to it.'

'Oh, writing a business plan: is that what the young people call it nowadays?'

I swear Moira was actually sniggering. I ignored her and carried on. 'Once we've achieved our goals, we'll go our separate ways and he'll probably never even think about me again.'

I tried to ignore the pang of loss which I experienced at the thought. Was that really what I wanted? But the alternative was to put myself at risk of hurt and that seemed like an even more terrifying prospect. What if I told him how I was starting to feel, and he didn't feel the same way about me? Or worse, he did return my feelings, but only for a short time, like previous partners. I couldn't bear the idea of the pain which would follow. There were only so many times I could put myself through the emotional wringer. No, it was much better to protect myself by remaining focused and sticking to the plan.

'We'll see,' said Moira in a voice which warned she was already plotting how to bring about her version of a happily ever after for me.

'Shall I clear the table?' I suggested, needing a break.

'Good idea. I think the poor girl's had enough of the two of us grilling her for now. How about that dessert?' said Rami.

I collected the plates and took my time loading the

dishwasher, making the most of having a few minutes to pull myself together.

When I returned to the dining room, Moira looked up at me with a guilty expression. I experienced a clutch of nerves.

'What have you done?' I asked.

'Moira has something she'd like to confess to you,' said Rami.

She pulled a face, looking uncannily like the little children during story time at the library when they've pinched someone else's book but are trying to deny it.

Moira shot her husband a glance, and my anxiety increased.

'Moira darling?' prompted Rami.

She let out a huffy sigh. 'Fine. Your phone pinged when you were in the kitchen, and I may have taken a sneaky peek at the screen.'

'Okay, well, I tell you most things anyway, so I really don't mind,' I said, even though I knew that there was going to be more to this confession.

'And then…' Rami encouraged her to continue.

'And then I used your passcode to unlock your phone and reply to the message,' said Moira in a rush.

'I'm getting a very bad feeling about this. And that passcode was for emergency use only.'

Moira tried, and failed, to look sorry.

I sat down at the table and braced myself for the rest of her story. There was no way this was going to end well for me.

'It was a message from Leo.'

I nodded, trying to appear calm, even though my thoughts were running at a million miles an hour.

'Of course it was,' I said, because that was my kind of luck.

'He says he has to leave Oxford for a few days, but he'll be in touch about the next stage of the investigation.'

'Okay.' I really hoped his sudden need to leave the city had nothing to do with the incident in the gym. I cringed with embarrassment just recalling it again. 'Please tell me that you replied with something innocuous like a thumbs-up emoji and "have a nice trip, speak soon"?'

'Mm-hmm,' said Moira. 'Yes, it was definitely something like that.'

'Moi-ra,' said Rami, employing his best stern tutor voice. 'Don't you think it's better you come clean rather than waiting for her to read the message and find out the truth for herself? You're torturing the poor girl by stringing it out like this.'

'If you insist,' she said warily. 'So, I may have replied with something along the lines of how much I – by which I meant of course you – will miss him. And then I urged him to hurry back, and ended with some kisses.'

'How many kisses?' I asked, my face feeling hot at the thought, although it was ridiculous to focus on that small detail when the rest of the message sounded mortifying enough.

'Three, or thereabouts,' she said.

'Oh, that is not good. I've never even used one kiss when we've been texting and he's certainly not, either. And I can't believe you told him to hurry back.'

'I thought it was sweet,' said Rami wistfully.

'Then I shall hold you equally responsible for aiding and abetting her,' I said. 'You're both as bad as each other. Maybe I should text and tell Leo you hijacked my phone?'

'You could do that,' said Moira, 'but won't he wonder why your friends thought it would be appropriate to send such a loving message?'

'I'm certainly wondering that,' I retorted, my mind whirling as I considered my options.

'In fact, do you not think he might start to question whether there's some basis of truth in the text?' she pressed. 'That you really will be missing him while he's out of town?'

'Which you will be, it's obvious in your face,' said Rami. 'Has anyone ever told you that your expression gives away everything that's going through your mind?'

Leo had, not that I was going to tell these two and add fuel to the fire.

Before I could respond, my phone buzzed, setting my heart racing. I leapt forward to grab it before either of my so-called friends could seize it first and cause more trouble for me.

'How's he replied?' asked Moira. I could tell she was fighting the urge to jump up and read the text over my shoulder.

I tried to hide my excitement as I read the message, lingering over every word. Then I nervously scrolled back to see if the text Moira had sent really was as bad as I feared. She had been exaggerating about the number of kisses, but putting even one was bad enough after the whole self-defence class encounter. On the other hand, Leo's message had ended with kisses of its own for the first time, so maybe Moira had done me a favour. Or maybe I was reading far too much into a reflex response. He'd probably spent all of five seconds tapping out his reply and not thought twice about its contents. Whereas I was inevitably going to spend the rest of the night over-analysing every word and dreaming about potential hidden meanings.

'I'm not sure you guys deserve to know after invading my privacy like this,' I said, half teasing, half rebuking them.

'We're very sorry and we won't do it again,' said Rami. 'Will we, Moira?'

She exhaled resignedly. 'Fine, as you insist, we'll leave you to your own devices ... for now. But if you don't hurry up and make a proper move on that man, I may be forced to retract. You're a fool if you let fear get in the way of something that's staring you in the face.'

I decided it was best not to rise to that particular provocation. And I still didn't really want to share Leo's message. I wanted to hug it to myself and come to my own conclusions about it, rather than have my friends chipping in with what would inevitably be far too optimistic interpretations. But it was clear that they weren't going to let up until I did, so I read it out loud to them.

LEO

Hey Kat, I have to deal with a few things this week, but I will be back soon. It's time to take things up a notch.

At this point, Moira squealed at an unnecessarily high pitch.

'Don't get too carried away,' I warned. 'He's only talking about the investigation.'

I continued reading.

> LEO
>
> How are you with heights? SO Ox is running a 'Love Can Overcome Any Obstacle (Course)' event next weekend. It's basically a five-kilometre mud run with a pretentious name. I reckon it's the kind of show-off mass event that could attract our quarry. What do you think? Could be a good opportunity to listen out for Brian. Have booked my place. See you there. Xx

'Two kisses,' said Rami gleefully. 'He's already missing you. And he's practically said he's going to hurry back to be with you. That's how I'd interpret it, anyway.'

I raised an eyebrow. 'That's lovely of you to say, but you're an English tutor. You spend half your life coming up with alternative interpretations of text, the more implausible the better. Most likely what he actually means is that he can't wait to have a laugh at my expense while I struggle to climb a rope ladder. An obstacle course? There's nothing romantic about that.'

'Oh, I don't know. The app people obviously run it for a reason,' said Moira. I shot her a look. 'Okay, okay, I'll stop sticking my oar in,' she added, putting her hand over her mouth for good measure.

I tapped on the app to read more about the event.

'According to this, it's the most popular event that SO Ox runs. It's strange what appeals to some people. I guess it's worth a try. And the social they're holding after it will also give us more chance to ask questions. I suppose people might be less on their guard after spending a few hours charging around a muddy field coming face to face with their own mortality.'

I booked a spot, then quickly tapped out a reply to Leo before I could change my mind.

> Sounds like a plan. See you there.

My thumb hovered over the screen, then I shrugged. What harm could I do after Moira's message?

I edited the message, then hit send.

KAT

> Sounds like a great plan. Looking forward to seeing you there. Xx.

What had I let myself in for? It was probably a good thing that Leo wasn't going to be around for the rest of the week. I'd need all the time I could get to transform myself into someone capable of completing a mud run, while retaining enough energy to keep my cool around Leo and still conduct an investigation. The challenge was on.

Chapter Nineteen

In retrospect, it was a mistake to cycle the nearly ten-mile distance from my house to Woodstock where the obstacle course was being held in the grounds of Blenheim Palace. After a week of running to and from work, and spending lunchtimes clambering up and down the bookshelf ladders in the library as a makeshift training regime, I was already exhausted. But I was feeling nervous about seeing Leo again, so I decided that it would be a good distraction to cycle along the canal towpath and have a peek at the new floating bookshop on my way, rather than sit stewing on a bus, which would inevitably take around the same time to make the journey because of traffic.

Leo and I hadn't communicated much over the last week. I'd sent him a few messages updating him on my progress chatting with Scammer Brian, which he'd acknowledged, and he'd promised me he was reading through my research on Marc again. But any tentative attempts by me to move the conversation away from the investigation into more general topics had been met with even briefer responses. I tried to take some hope from the fact that he continued with the kisses at the end of his messages, but the more rational part of my brain told me they were merely a reflex, and that he was not actually interested in getting to know me better. I was becoming more and more convinced that he hadn't really left Oxford at all and had instead engineered a pretend absence in order to avoid me after I'd nearly kissed him at the gym. If that was the way he wanted to play it, then that was completely fine, I lied to myself. I would do my best to act as if everything was normal, and as if I hadn't spent the week catching myself looking for him in the library's business section and being sad he wasn't there.

I cycled along Blenheim Palace's imposing drive feeling quite smug that I was able to sail past the queue of cars, locked my bike up at a handy rack, then followed the lurid heart-shaped signs through the parkland to find the obstacle course. Despite having lived in Oxford for the past six years, I'd never visited this grand estate, but it still seemed vaguely familiar, probably because it had featured in so many film adaptations of my favourite books. If only Leo and I were here to enjoy a leisurely day together, on a date featuring a picnic and a romantic stroll among the deer perhaps, rather than having to haul ourselves around an obstacle course with the added hazard of everyone trying to hit on each other, even if it was in pursuit of the investigation. I gave myself a mental shake. Getting carried away with wishful thinking was not going to help. If he wanted to be just friends, that was absolutely fine by me. I would pretend the almost-kiss never happened and avoid the risk of more embarrassing near-misses by keeping a safe distance from him like in covid times, and everything would be completely normal.

I turned a final corner and stopped dead at the sight in front of me. The obstacles looked horrendous, and I wasn't even standing near them. I had no doubt that on closer inspection the sheer wooden walls and barbed wire tunnels would be even more terrifying. The app hadn't been lying in describing the event as popular. The place was thronged with safety marshals, and the field was full of the kind of people I immediately clocked as being 'professional competitors', decked out in Lycra and neon trainers which probably cost more than my monthly rent. The blokes were ostentatiously stretching their muscles, casually leaning against the fence and pulling meaty thighs towards their chests. I swear some of them were actually grunting to emphasise their testosterone-filled credentials, although it was hard to hear over the noise of distorted music thumping from the speaker system. As for the women, well, most of them looked like they'd come straight from central casting, all toned limbs, bouncy hair and perfect make-up. I really hoped they'd gone for the waterproof stuff because it wasn't going to last long once they encountered actual mud.

I shuffled on the spot feeling extremely self-conscious in my oldest workout gear and tattiest trainers. I'd chosen to wear scuzzy stuff knowing that it was going to get completely trashed during proceedings, but now I wished I'd put a bit more effort in. I was going to stand out for all the wrong reasons among this glamorous lot.

'Hey, nice to meet you, I'm Leo,' said the man himself, striding across and holding his hand out towards me. All my good intentions about remaining cool around him immediately seemed unachievable. His trainers at least looked like they'd seen some action, but his white t-shirt was probably going to go full-on Mr Darcy emerging from the lake as soon as he went near any of the water obstacles.

I swallowed.

'I'm Leo,' he repeated, still waiting for me to shake his hand.

With an effort, I pulled myself together. 'I know perfectly well you're Leo. What's with the introduction again?' I hissed.

'You're Katherine, are you? Lovely to meet you,' he said loudly, reaching out and taking my hand as I was apparently stuck in position. Blame it on the Mr Darcy wet shirt mental image. Then he lowered his voice, and whispered in my ear, sending a delicious shiver down my spine. 'I thought it made sense for us to be incognito again. This is meant to be a dating mixer after all. I figured other people might get suspicious if we arrived and immediately acted like we know each other.'

I forced my mind back to the practical, with some difficulty, and took a step back.

'But what if some of the people from the Single Mingle are here? They couldn't have failed to notice you dragging me out of there halfway through the event. And now you've pretended like we're meeting for the first time again, it'll probably have the opposite effect and make them wonder what on earth we're playing at.'

Leo chuckled. 'They'll probably think that we're a real-life couple and it's a kink we've got going on.'

My stomach did a funny little flip at the way he was so casually referring to us being a real couple. 'Do you reckon? I'm not sure I like that idea.'

He laughed louder. 'You're so easy to wind up. What does it matter what the rest of the people here think about us? Unless they like the look of one of us, they're most likely worrying about their own appearance and whether they'll pull by the end of the event.'

'Good. Then there's little danger of me attracting attention, as I failed to get the memo about sexy athletic wear and turned up looking like I'm about to take part in a school sports day,' I said glumly.

'Fishing for compliments, Holmes? You look pretty good from where I'm standing,' said Leo.

I got to enjoy the thrill of his admiration for approximately five seconds before he hurriedly clarified what he'd actually meant.

'At least you look like you stand half a chance of getting around the course. I don't rate the chances of some of that Lycra still being in one piece by the end of it. There's aerodynamically tight and then there's looking like the clothes have been spray-painted on. I'm surprised they weren't arrested for indecent exposure on their way here.'

'Well, if we're going to screen them as potential Scammer Brian candidates, we'll have to get a lot closer to them so I can listen out for his voice.'

'Lucky us. The perfect weekend entertainment,' said Leo.

'It was your idea. I was just the fool who let you to talk me into this,' I said. 'I could be at home enjoying a quiet Saturday morning, catching up on sleep after doing not one but two evening events at work this week. Sounds like a much better option to me.'

Even as I spoke the words, I knew they weren't strictly true. I was happy to be here with Leo, even if it did mean having to bear-crawl through a marsh later.

'It's all part of the bigger picture,' he reminded me.

'Hmm.'

'Chin up. We'll get through it together,' he said. I reckoned he was drawing on his rowing coaching skills to try to jolly me along. I didn't appreciate it. 'Shall we go and get our race numbers?'

'Race? Nobody told me it was also a race. The element of competition makes this infinitely worse.'

Leo smiled. 'It's only a turn of phrase. We'll take our time. It's meant to be fun. Besides, I can't think of anyone else I'd rather be spending my Saturday morning with.'

I shot him a glance. Was he being genuine or was this part of his patter for the benefit of our fellow attendees? But I didn't have time to dwell on it, because the founder of SO Ox had pounced on us.

'Happy weekend, guys, it's great to see you here. It's Kat, right? I never forget a face,' said Dom. 'Great you two have hit it off, but let's see whether it will stand the test of the upcoming obstacles.' He chuckled. I didn't join in. 'Here's your course map. Beer and wine are on tap for survivors, sorry, course finishers, and don't forget to visit the photo booth for your before and after pictures. Anyone who uses them as profile pics on the app will get a week's free membership.'

And just as quickly as he'd arrived, he was on his way to speak to another group of nervous-looking participants.

'I'm not sure whether to be flattered or concerned that he can remember who I am,' I said, somewhat unnerved by Dom's little speech. 'Let's take a look at the map and see what we've let ourselves in for.'

According to the map, the obstacle course started off with the 'Lung Burner', a half kilometre run up and down a zigzag course on what looked like the steepest slope in Oxfordshire's countryside. Never mind my lungs, I suspected my legs would be screaming by the end of the first haul up the hill. Then came 'No Man's Land' which was illustrated by some disturbing cartoons of barbed wire and exploding mines.

I pointed them out to Leo. 'The pictures are just for dramatic effect, right?'

'I guess we're about to find out. Anyway, you've got this. Your suffragette predecessors would never have let a bit of barbed wire get in their way, would they? I'm still finding bruises from our encounter last week.'

'I'm sorry,' I said, worrying that I really had hurt him. That was the last thing I would ever want to do.

'Actually, I've been meaning to talk to you about that,' he said.

Chapter Twenty

Here it was. The moment where he ever so kindly let me down and explained that he could never be interested in me that way. I couldn't bear to hear him say the words and then spend the rest of the day pretending that everything was fine.

'All in good time,' I said in an overly bright tone. 'I think we need to concentrate on talking tactics right now. What do you think the best way is of us getting around the course? Do we stick together, or divide and conquer? We might find out more information by splitting up. We can pretend to be struggling over the obstacles as a means of starting conversations with people. I'll certainly have no problem in making that seem realistic, and you can have a listen to one of Brian's voice notes before we set off, so you know who to keep your ears open for. Does that sound like a decent plan?'

I glanced down at the obstacle course map again, staring at the route to try to regain my composure.

'Divide and conquer? I'm not sure I agree,' said Leo. 'I figure if we stick together then we'll spend less time worrying about making it around the course in one piece, plus we'll be able to focus on asking questions and observing the other runners. That's what makes most sense from an investigative point of view, anyway.'

'I suppose so. Whatever's best for the investigation,' I agreed, wishing that his reason for wanting to stick together had been a little more personal.

'I'm sure there'll be plenty of electricity between us on our way round,' said Leo.

I looked up in confusion.

'The "Shocker",' he said, pointing at an obstacle on the route map, illustrated by a skeleton with a lightning rod of electricity aimed right at its skull from a lethal-looking frayed cable.

'You're doing that one first,' I said. 'It's what the suffragettes would have advised.'

Leo merely nodded in agreement rather than taking the opportunity to tease me further. Logically, I knew that the organisers wouldn't be allowed to put anything genuinely dangerous on the course but, given the way they'd let at least one fraudster operate within their supposedly safe environment, I wasn't sure I trusted their ability to follow health and safety guidelines.

A crackly announcement interrupted the rave music.

'Ladies and gentlemen, this is your five-minute warning. The Love Can Overcome Any Obstacle (Course) event is starting shortly. Now's your last opportunity for nervous wees and Dutch courage, although hopefully not at the same time. We'll see you and your future Significant Others at the start line. Oggy oggy oggy…'

A few half-hearted 'Oi oi oi!' responses were shouted back, but most people were heeding the advice of the organiser and hurrying to the Portaloos.

'Dutch courage? I'm not sure that's going to do anyone any good,' I muttered. 'Although, right now, I can see the appeal of sinking into an alcoholic haze. I can't believe you talked me into doing this.'

Leo took a slurp from his water bottle then offered it to me before he answered.

'Nice re-writing of history there, Fisher. I don't seem to recall you making any objections when I suggested it.'

That was because I hadn't wanted to appear like a wuss.

'Hmm. Well, next time, I'm going to pick the event,' I said.

'Then I shall look forward to attending the SO Ox Book Club,' he said. 'I'm sure it'll be all very civilised. What books do you think we'll have to read? Romances all the way, I expect. I'll ask Doris for some recommendations.'

'She'll have many,' I said. 'But I don't want to think of a scammer using novels to seduce unsuspecting women. I like to believe book people are generally good people.'

Leo smiled. 'I don't know; I'd have thought fiction would be right up his street. We'll keep our eyes open. Now, do you want to have a quick practice of the best technique to get over the walls before we set off?'

I responded with a haughty look. 'I'm sure we'll be fine improvising once we get there.'

What I hadn't thought through properly before I signed up to this event was quite how physical it would turn out to be. It soon became apparent that the only way we were going to be able to get around the course was by doing a fair bit of climbing, and that wasn't just of the obstacles.

I stared up at the fifteen-foot wooden fence in front of me.

'I can't see any hand holds on it, can you?'

Leo put his hands on his hips. 'Nope, that looks pretty smooth to me. Perhaps we should try another approach. If I squat against the fence, you can clamber up my legs, then onto my shoulders, then I'll stand and you should be able to get to the top that way.'

I blinked. Using Leo as a human climbing frame could get me into all kinds of trouble.

'Maybe if I take a bit of a run at the fence,' I said, pretending I hadn't heard his suggestion. The speed technique had seemed to work for the guy to my left who had leapt over the barrier with the elegance and ease of Spiderman.

'Be my guest,' said Leo taking a step back and crossing his arms across his chest as he surveyed me. 'I'll enjoy this,' I thought I heard him add under his breath. I shot him an annoyed glance to which he responded with an expression of offended innocence.

I walked a few paces away and once again stared at the fence.

'They wouldn't have put it there if it wasn't possible to

get over it,' I told myself. I managed to overpower Leo during our self-defence class; I could do anything I put my mind to.

I charged forward, at a pace I hadn't used since my one and only time as a member of my school's relay race team, and then flung myself at the fence. In my head, I'd seen myself effortlessly darting up the side like a parkour specialist, gripping the top, then climbing over with ease, with Leo applauding admiringly from afar, regretting that he'd ever doubted me.

What actually happened was that I went splat against the fence like a fly against a windscreen, emitted a strangled cry that went something like 'Nrfghhhh' and then fell backwards into Leo's arms. In truth, saying I fell into Leo's arms makes it sound much more elegant and ladylike than it was. In reality, I thumped into him with all the grace of a bag of potatoes, completely knocking the wind out of him and causing him to stumble and fall backwards onto the ground with me sprawled out on top.

Leo let out a similar noise to the cry I'd made when I hit the obstacle. I twisted round so I was facing him.

'Oh my goodness, I'm so sorry. Are you okay?'

When he didn't answer, I decided to check for a pulse, then ran my hands gently over his face as I continued my efforts to find any sign of life. Why hadn't I paid more attention in the library first aid session?

'Leo, can you hear me?'

I moved my ear to his mouth, straining to hear the sound of him breathing.

'I must say that's an unusual approach to delivering the

kiss of life,' said Leo, his words sounding more laboured than usual.

'Are you okay?' I asked urgently.

He finally opened his eyes and looked at me.

'When they advertised the obstacle course as a way of getting to know other people, I hadn't envisaged we'd end up becoming quite so closely acquainted with each other.'

I suddenly became hyper-aware of our position. It was like being back in the gym, only this time our positions were reversed. My boobs were crushed against the hard planes of his chest, my hands braced either side of his head, while my legs were wrapped around his waist. I tried to steer my mind away from the close proximity of other parts of our anatomy, but it seemed irritatingly reluctant to obey my orders. My breathing grew unsteady. I really hoped Leo attributed that to my fall rather than anything else.

I cleared my throat and tried to roll to the side, but I hadn't thought through the move properly and ended up taking Leo with me as my legs were still wrapped around him.

'You have quite the grip,' he said gruffly.

'Sorry, really sorry,' I said, awkwardly trying to disentangle myself but making things a whole lot worse. I prayed he couldn't feel how rapidly my pulse was going.

Somewhere in the distance, I thought I heard someone wolf-whistle at us, followed by the sound of a camera shutter firing rapidly.

'I think we might be about to become the poster children for this event,' said Leo. I could feel the rumble of his laughter against my stomach.

'Can this get any more humiliating?' I groaned. With one last effort, I managed to extricate myself from our compromising position and rolled onto my back so we were lying side by side.

'I can finally breathe again,' said Leo, throwing his arms out. One of his hands ended up resting casually on my stomach in a manner which just felt right. 'Shall we stay here like this for the rest of the event? It's pretty comfortable.'

But before I could answer his question or wonder more about the meaning behind it, I heard it: an unmistakably familiar voice. Only instead of being used to leave a seductive voice note full of fake declarations of devotion, this time it sounded strident as it urged someone to use their upper body strength to haul themselves up the fence we'd just failed to get over.

'Brian James!'

Chapter Twenty-One

'How disappointing you're still getting my name wrong after we've shared such closeness,' said Leo with a laugh.

'I'm being serious,' I said, sitting up straight. 'I heard Brian's voice.'

Leo joined me in an upright position, all laughter gone from his expression.

'Are you sure?'

'One hundred percent. I'd recognise those cut-glass tones anywhere. He's here. He's actually here.'

'Wow, I can't believe he turned up,' said Leo, which begged the question why he'd suggested this outing in the first place. But I didn't have time to worry about that now.

I stumbled to my feet and moved closer to the fence, trying to tune into that one particular voice among the rest of the shouting and hubbub. Leo stuck close to me, glancing around us as if expecting to fend off an attack at any moment.

'At least try and act normal,' I hissed. 'You look like Robin when she's spotted a squirrel. You're going to draw the wrong kind of attention to us.'

'Grab the lip of the fence and then haul yourself up,' urged the voice again. 'I'll keep holding on to your arms so you won't fall.'

The instructions helped me narrow down the candidates. There were currently two guys straddling the top of the fence. One was surveying his surroundings with casual ease, while the other was leaning forward in a more precarious position, holding onto a woman with stunning two-tone dreadlocks who was sliding back down in horrifying slow motion.

'You've got this, one more heave, then you'll be up,' said the guy who was helping her.

I took hold of Leo's arm and then stood on my tiptoes so I could whisper in his ear.

'It's that bloke, the one on the top of the fence. Not creepy Marc after all.'

Leo pretended that I'd said something hilarious, then wrapped his arm around my waist and leaned down to respond in similarly quiet tones.

'Muscle man?' he asked.

'The one on the left. Medium height, blond hair, unnecessarily skimpy vest. Listen to his voice, it's unmistakeable.'

Of course, now Leo was trying to hear him speak, Scammer Brian had fallen silent, accepting the grateful babble of thanks from the woman with the dreadlocks who was practically crying with relief that she'd finally conquered the obstacle.

'Okay, we'll have to make him speak again,' I said, starting forward.

'Wait a minute,' said Leo, rushing in front and blocking my progress. 'We need to think carefully about this. Remember that our target is at an advantage over us. He's seen your profile pictures. What do you think he's going to do when he spots you coming towards him? Disappear into the ether, if he's got any sense.'

I glanced down at myself. If my face was anything like the current state of my clothes, then I already had pretty good camouflage.

'I think I'll be okay. Besides, you said yourself that people always look different in photos from real life. I'm wearing make-up in all my pictures on the app. He'll never associate my current swamp monster vibe with Miss Neat from online.'

'A little bit of mud can't hide your shine. I really don't think it's an effective enough disguise,' he said. 'Maybe we should fall back and reassess our options from a safe distance.'

'You flatterer, you. But don't think pretending to be nice to me will distract me from the mission in hand. Now is the time to take action. This is the moment we've been working for.'

I wasn't going to let his switch into over-protective mode stop me. I hurried forward and started another attempt at climbing the fence. I couldn't risk losing sight of

Scammer Brian now. Applying the lessons I'd learned from my previous disaster, I took my time, seeking out imperfections in the wood to hold on to and carefully maintaining three points of contact at all times. When I was nearly at the top, I pretended to lose confidence and let out a fake whimper.

'Can somebody help me, please?' I said, cranking up my normally subtle Yorkshire accent to a level that bordered on parody, and keeping my head lowered, in case Scammer Brian did see past my muddy exterior and recognise me.

'I'm here to catch you. And hey, mate, can you move along a bit so there's space for her to sit at the top?' said Leo, cottoning on quickly.

'No problem, I'll move onto the next obstacle, unless you want a hand being hauled up,' replied Scammer Brian.

Gotcha. It was one hundred percent the voice I knew and had loved.

'We've got this,' I said, silently apologising to my fellow Yorkshire folk as I once again butchered my accent. 'We'll be right behind you.'

'See you at the next obstacle. Perhaps we could chat then?' said Scammer Brian with a suggestive waggle of his perfectly groomed eyebrows.

'Mm-hmm,' I squeaked. He was obviously using this as a hunting ground for fresh targets, just as I feared.

As soon as he'd moved on, Leo and I dropped down to the ground again. My heart was racing with adrenalin.

'We've got him. We've really got him,' I said, hopping around on the spot, unable to keep still. 'I can't believe how unassuming and normal he looks, apart from the dodgy vest, of course. Should we do a citizen's arrest? Is that even a thing? And if so, how do they work?'

Leo frowned. 'It's not a thing we're going to be trying in these surroundings.'

'But we can't let him get away with it,' I said.

'I wasn't suggesting that we do.'

'Okay, so what now? What would you do if you were still in the police?'

'I'd invite him in for questioning, but as we certainly don't have enough evidence for an arrest, it would have to be a voluntary interview.'

I nodded. 'That makes sense. As we can't exactly bring him in for an interrogation without revealing our hand, I guess our next step is to find another way to get enough evidence for that arrest. Then we can take it to the real police. I mean, the ones who are still serving. Sorry, I didn't mean to rub it in.'

He absent-mindedly put his arm around my shoulders and squeezed. 'Don't worry, you need to try harder than that to offend me. How do you feel about doing some surveillance? Now that we know what Mr so-called Brian James really looks like, we need to press home our advantage.'

'I think I can see where you're going with this,' I said. 'We follow him around the course, observe every interaction, and then tail him home so we can find out his address. Then I can go on to the electoral register at the library and see who the registered occupant of that address is, and then there we have it, the real identity of Brian James.'

Leo blinked. 'Okay, I hadn't thought we'd go quite as far as tailing him home. Perhaps that's a tad extreme. But the observing every interaction at this event bit sounds good.'

I shook my head. 'Where's your sense of adventure? This is the biggest breakthrough we've had. This time tomorrow our whole investigation could be successfully completed. Or at least, well on its way to being,' I added hastily, realising that I didn't feel the delight I should at the idea of accomplishing our aim. Because that would mean I no longer had a legitimate excuse to spend so much time with Leo.

'Let's see how we get on,' he said.

'Okay,' I agreed. 'We need to start now, then. We've spent too long talking about this already. I hope the next obstacle is a tough one so he's still stuck on it, otherwise we're going to have a job tracking him down again.'

It turned out to be practically impossible. We had to negotiate our way across a wide stretch of icy water by hopping across a series of tiny platforms which wobbled wildly as soon as anyone landed on them. Most sensible people were giving up fairly early on and trying to swim instead, but our quarry seemed determined to do the thing properly. He was currently balancing on the middle platform, urging the woman with the dreadlocks to leap across and join him.

'I'm a bit worried that she's going to be his next target,' I said to Leo as we pretended to be working out our strategy for getting across. 'He certainly seems to be very interested in her.'

'Then we need to get her away from him,' he replied. 'But to do that, we have to get across this water. Ladies first.'

His expression was gleeful.

'Oh no, I think, in this instance, I will let you lead the way,' I said. 'If only one of us is moving at any one time, the other can be observing what Brian's up to.'

I was pretty pleased with that excuse. In reality, I was wimping out at the thought of ending up in that muddy, cold lake. I knew the worst thing that would happen was that I'd get wet, but I couldn't tell how deep it was and I'd never liked the idea of being in water where I couldn't touch the bottom. Who knew what kinds of creatures might be lurking in the depths ready to grab hold of me? Not that I wanted Leo to know I was thinking that way.

He shrugged. 'Time to learn from the master,' he said, exuding confidence from every pore.

'Show off,' I retorted.

Leo winked. 'Isn't that exactly what this whole event is about? It's the human equivalent of chimpanzee chest-beating. I'm merely getting into the spirit of the occasion. Here I go.'

And with that he leapt from the shore to the first platform. For a moment I thought he wasn't going to make it, but he landed with effortless ease and then pulled himself up into a gymnastics-style salute to his imaginary audience.

Although I was actually impressed by his athleticism, I

pointedly yawned in his direction which made his grin grow even wider. Looking beyond Leo, I clocked that Scammer Brian had moved onto the penultimate platform, but there was no sign of the woman with dreadlocks. I scanned the swimmers in the water and realised that she'd joined their number and was doing a slow breaststroke alongside a man who seemed enraptured by every word she was saying. At least that was one less thing to worry about.

'Hurry up, Leo,' I called. 'Jump onto the next platform so I can make a start. There's a queue forming, you know.' What I actually meant was for him to get a move on, so we didn't lose sight of Brian.

I blamed myself for what happened next. Recognising the urgency in my tone, Leo didn't take the same amount of time preparing for his next leap as he had with his first one. He probably wasn't helped by the fact that he was now setting off from an unsteady surface. Whatever it was, he jumped and caught the front of his foot underneath the next platform. I watched as he tumbled forward almost in slow motion, hitting his ribs on the edge then rolling off the platform with an almighty splash.

I didn't even stop to think about it. I half-dived, half-leapt into the water and started a messy front crawl to where I'd seen him disappear under the surface. About two strokes in, the cold hit me, instantly turning my breathing into ragged rasps and numbing my brain, making me uncertain which direction I should be going in. I paused for a couple of seconds, forcing myself to take a deep breath and exhale slowly so I could get myself back under control, and then I resumed my desperate swim towards Leo.

'Are you okay?' I called towards him as his head broke through the surface. His expression was glassy and I recognised the effects of the cold shock that I'd just experienced.

Leo, being Leo, choked back an 'All good', before starting a scrappy doggy paddle towards the wrong shore. I drew alongside him and took hold of his shoulders, forcing him to tread water with me.

'Look at me, Leo, you're alright. Take a moment. Breathe with me. In for four, hold, then out for four. Okay?'

I counted the breaths for a couple of rounds and saw his air of confusion gradually dissipate, to my great relief.

'Right, let's get to safety,' I said, once I was confident that he could start swimming again.

'What about Brian?' he asked.

'We'll worry about him once we reach dry land.' Nothing mattered more than getting Leo to safety.

We took our time getting to the shore, and I was very grateful that a marshal materialised as we arrived and helped haul us out. I was shaking with cold, and Leo wasn't much better, although he was still pretending that he was absolutely fine.

'You're nearly at the end, folks, not long now,' said the marshal. 'One more challenge to get past and, as we know, love can overcome any obstacle.'

'Be that as it may, I think it's time for us to withdraw from the race,' I said.

'But what about Br...' started Leo.

'Everything else can wait until we've dried off and you've got your ribs checked,' I said firmly.

The marshal escorted us back to the race village and took us to the medical tent where I insisted Leo submit himself to the attentions of a first-aider.

'You'll have a nasty bruise in the morning, but I don't think you've done yourself any proper damage,' she said cheerfully after she finished examining him.

'Do you think he should get an X-ray to be on the safe side?' I asked, not even the impressive sight of Leo's bare chest distracting me from my worry.

'I am here, you know,' said Leo grumpily. 'It's nothing that a hot drink and a night in snuggled up with you on the sofa won't solve.'

My breath caught. I knew he was probably only saying it for the benefit of our audience, but for a moment I imagined what it would be like if he'd meant it for real. He'd probably wind me up no end when it came to hogging the television remote, but I was beginning to realise I'd rather spend my free time fighting and making up with Leo than with anyone else.

The first-aider looked between us with delight on her face.

'Aw, you guys, that's so sweet. I must tell Dom he's got another success on his hands. It'll give him a much-needed boost.'

'Oh, yes?' said Leo with affected casualness.

The first-aider looked around and then lowered her voice. 'Between you and me, I think he's close to giving up on SO Ox.'

'That's such a shame. It's bringing happiness to so many people like us,' I said, linking my fingers with Leo's. It was purely cover, I told myself.

He squeezed my hand back.

The first-aider sighed. 'I know. But just because an app's good at making matches, it doesn't mean it's profitable. In fact, it means the opposite. And Dom's a numbers guy at heart. The figures he cares about most are the ones on his bank statement. Right, I think you guys both need some dry clothes, then I'll have to move on to my next patients. The romance-to-damage ratio of this month's obstacle course seems to be somewhat off, if you ask me.'

We slowly made our way out of the medical tent, wrapped in silver foil blankets and dressed in identical Love Can Overcome Any Obstacle t-shirts and shorts, our wet clothing in a plastic bag. My underwear was still soaking, but I'd drawn the line at removing it in the medical tent, even though I had been able to duck behind a privacy curtain to get changed.

'I look like I'm a Sunday roast about to be put in the oven,' grumbled Leo.

'No need to make a meal of it,' I quipped. 'That metallic look does wonders for you; it really brings out the lines in your frown.'

Leo's expression relaxed. 'Don't make me laugh. It'll make my ribs ache even more than they already do.'

'Sorry, I didn't mean to make it worse,' I said, instantly feeling guilty. I felt even guiltier when he seemed to stumble over his feet. I put my arm around his waist. 'Lean on me, I've got you.'

'Now that's better,' said Leo. 'We'll warm up much more quickly if we huddle together,' he added.

I shot him a glance. Was his mind still on the practical, or was he actually glad to be close to me? Perhaps I should be brave and just ask him?

But before I could open my mouth, he looked suddenly alert and pointed at the finish line, which consisted of a line of blazing hay bales. Running towards them was a familiar figure.

'Scammer Brian's about to cross.'

We watched as our target sped up and leapt across the flaming bales with athletic grace.

'If he ever decides to go on the app using his own identity, that would make an excellent profile picture,' I said.

Leo frowned. 'Let's hope the photographer missed the moment.'

'Time for action. We need to follow him and see what he gets up to,' I said, already starting to move.

'Hold on a minute. We stand out like sore thumbs with these blankets. He's going to spot us a mile off.'

'Then we'd better ditch them,' I said, although I was reluctant to lose the much-needed extra warmth. I was even more reluctant when I realised there were underwear-shaped wet patches on my outer clothing. Leo was gentleman enough not to comment, but he must have noticed them, just as I'd noticed he had no such patches. I forced my mind away from that realisation and back to the matter in hand.

'What's the best way of doing this? Observe him from

behind some cover?' I was drawing on the last spy novel I'd read.

'Unfortunately, we're somewhat lacking in natural cover around here. I think anyone lurking behind a tree will attract suspicion from this crowd. I reckon we should try to blend in with our surroundings, and act like a normal couple while we join the queue for the beer tent like Brian has. At least he doesn't seem to have locked on to anyone else.'

The queue for the beer tent was long and full of people loudly comparing escapades and war wounds. Leo and I made meaningless small talk while we kept a close eye on our suspect, occasionally whispering observations to each other.

'He keeps checking his watch,' I said.

'He definitely looks like he needs to be somewhere soon. Places to go, people to scam and all that,' said Leo.

'Do you think you can hold the fort, and I'll go and collect our rucksacks from the baggage zone? If he's going to move off soon, we need to be ready to follow him. We're never going to have a better opportunity to discover his true identity.'

Leo pursed his lips. 'I guess you've convinced me. But we'll need to be really careful about how we do it. Agreed?'

I nodded, then hurried off, glad I'd had the forethought to pack a complete outfit change. However, the queue for the baggage zone was even longer than the one at the beer tent, and by the time I'd collected my bag and persuaded the steward that it wasn't a security risk to hand over Leo's rucksack to me as well, I didn't want to waste another moment on getting changed, even if it would make me more comfortable.

For one horrible moment, when I arrived back at the beer tent, I thought Leo had left without me. Then he materialised at my side.

'What took you so long? We've got to go. Brian's heading for the car park.'

Chapter Twenty-Two

If the obstacle course had been hard, it was nothing compared to trying to keep up with Leo as we ran through the grounds in pursuit of Brian.

'Come on, we're nearly there,' he said, seizing my hand which was incentive enough for me to put on another burst of speed.

'But what about your ribs?' I panted.

'Never mind them. If we don't catch up now, we're going to lose him, and all of this morning will have been a complete waste of time. Let's take a short cut.'

We dived off the path and then started scrambling up a slope which felt uncomfortably like the one on the obstacle course. Leo got to the top first and stopped dead, holding his hand up, signalling to me to be quiet, which was easier said than done, given the erratic nature of my current breathing situation.

'Got him. He's getting into a blue BMW, licence registration ending in Oscar Hotel Whiskey.'

I took a couple of seconds to translate the police speak into normal English.

'I'm parked on the next row,' he continued. 'Let's go.'

'What about Betty?' I said. 'I can't abandon her here.'

Leo blinked at me. 'You cycled here? What on earth for?'

'It seemed like a good idea at the time,' I said defensively.

'Right, you go and fetch her, and let's pray the traffic doesn't ease while we try to work out how to lower my back seat so we can fit your bicycle in my nice clean boot.'

'I'm telling you now that Betty is far cleaner than either of us currently are,' I said.

Thankfully, it took less time than feared to get everything stowed, and when I clambered into the passenger seat, Brian's vehicle was still in sight queueing for the exit.

'Let's get going,' I said, making a note of his numberplate before hurriedly strapping myself in. I mentally apologised in advance to Leo for the grimy river water which was about to soak through from my underwear onto his pristine upholstery.

Leo set off at a crawl, slowly easing the car into the line of traffic, and steering it so we were slightly sticking out into the centre of the road where we could keep a watch on Brian about five vehicles ahead.

Fifteen minutes later, we were only halfway down the drive. A harried traffic marshal had informed us that there were three separate events happening at Blenheim today, and unfortunately everyone had decided to leave at the same time.

'This is the worst car chase in history,' I said, starting to laugh as we crept forward another couple of inches. 'Maybe I would have been better on Betty, after all.'

'Hmm, with that gold bicycle helmet of yours, he'd spot you a mile off. No, this is probably for the best. We'll take it slowly and steadily and keep a couple of cars' distance behind him once we do start moving properly. We don't want to raise his suspicions when we're following him.'

'At least you've got a fairly nondescript car, so we won't stand out,' I said.

There was a sharp intake of breath from Leo. 'I don't insult Betty, so have the courtesy to do the same with Paolo.'

I laughed. 'You gave me grief for naming my bicycle, then it turns out you're equally as bad with your car. I knew you were a softy at heart.'

A sceptical 'Hmm' was his only response, but I thought I saw his lips twitch into a brief smile.

We finally emerged from the grounds of the palace and started moving at a decent speed.

'How good are you at your Oxford geography?' asked Leo. 'Can you work out where he might be going while I concentrate on following him? If we can anticipate what his next move is, it'll put us at an advantage and make it less obvious that we're trailing him.'

'I'll try, but I don't know this area of Oxford very well,' I admitted. 'And I'm better at bike routes than roadways.'

Fortunately, it wasn't long before Brian turned towards more familiar territory.

'I know where we are now. He's not heading to the

library, is he? What if he's on to us and luring us back there to confront us?'

I worried I sounded ridiculous. But to give Leo credit, he took my suggestion seriously.

'If he does stop at the library – and he'll have a job finding parking around there, as I know to my cost – we'll drive past, turn around in Wellington Square and you can ring whoever's working today and tell them to keep a close eye on him if he goes into the building. I don't think we're anywhere near the confronting stage of our investigation, and if, or when, we do reach that, we'll make sure it's on our own terms.'

'Moira's in charge today. I'll draft a text ready to send.'

We continued along St Giles', but when we got to the traffic lights, they turned amber.

'Oh, sod it,' said Leo, accelerating suddenly so we managed to make it through before they went red.

We were just in time to see Brian manoeuvring around another corner further down the road.

'He isn't going to the library, phew. But I thought for a moment he was heading for the Randolph Hotel,' I said. 'He would have to be doing really well out of the scams to be staying there.'

After another few minutes of careful driving through the centre of Oxford, Brian indicated left and turned into a small car park, tapping something against the barrier to let him in.

'We can't follow him in there. It's a private car park for the Oxford Grand,' said Leo. 'I'll pull into the waiting bay opposite. I'm going to cause an incident if we stop here in the middle of the road any longer.'

'I wonder what his connection to the theatre is? He obviously had a security pass to get him in there.'

'We might be about to find out. Look, isn't that him walking towards the stage door?'

We watched as Brian let himself into the building.

I sighed. 'Now what are we going to do? We can't follow him backstage, and they're hardly going to let us in front of house in the state we're currently in.'

'Speak for yourself,' said Leo with a grin. 'Now is the time when you learn the police officer's most undervalued but most important skill.'

'Which is?'

'Patience. We watch, and we wait. This is the most common kind of surveillance – prolonged periods of time sitting in a stuffy car and pretending to be invisible.'

'I'm normally pretty good at the invisible bit. But it's easier said than done when you're wearing soggy pants,' I said without thinking, then instantly regretted oversharing.

'If you want to change out of them, I promise I won't look.'

'You're alright. There are too many passers-by around for me to get away with a quick change.'

We settled into a companionable silence, staring at the door through which Brian had disappeared. I wondered what he was up to in there. For all I knew, he could be logging onto a computer and working on his next mark. It was immensely frustrating to be so near and yet so far from our target. I felt like marching into the building and demanding to see him. But who would I ask for? I didn't even know his real name, let alone why he was there. It was probably a safe bet to say he was working in some capacity, judging by the security pass, but which department was anyone's guess.

'You're far from invisible, by the way,' said Leo some minutes later.

'Oh,' I said, somewhat thrown by his unexpected comment. 'That's kind of you to say.'

'I'm not being kind; I'm being factual,' he corrected gently.

'Right.' I paused. But there was something about being in this confined space with him, both of us staring ahead, which encouraged confidences. 'I certainly feel invisible a lot of the time. Often, I think I prefer it that way. It's ... safer.'

He nodded. 'I can understand that. But is safer always better?'

'It absolutely is. Deciding to take a risk and put myself out there was what got me in this mess in the first place. I never want to be humiliated like that again. All in all, the sensible thing is to be glad that I can exist in the shadows and be the one whom everyone's eyes slide past as they search for someone more interesting.' Even as I said the words, I realised how pathetic they sounded. And potentially untrue. There was definitely one person I wished would notice me.

'More fool them,' said Leo. 'Anyway, I've always found you very interesting.'

Before I could ask him more about this unexpected

comment, I was startled by someone tapping on the car roof.

'This is a no parking zone,' said an officious voice from outside. 'I must ask you to... Oh hello, Leo, mate.' The voice suddenly became a lot friendlier as its owner peered through the window and recognised who was behind the wheel.

Leo turned the key in the ignition so he could wind the window down. 'Sid, what are you doing here? This isn't your usual stomping ground.'

'I volunteered to help with city centre foot patrols over the weekend, like the mug I am. Lot of sickness around at the moment, you know what it's like.'

'Some things never change,' said Leo. 'This is my...'—there was a slight hesitation—'friend Kat.'

'Nice to meet you, Kat. He leading you astray, is he, with his disregard for parking regulations?' Sid laughed at his own joke. 'How are you getting on, Leo? It's ages since I bumped into you. It was just before you got signed off, right? Is it true you've resigned now?'

Leo shuffled in his seat. I tried to pretend my entire attention was back on the stage door, aware that Leo was growing increasingly uncomfortable with the direction of Sid's conversation.

'It is. Pastures new and all that.'

Sid looked across to me in the passenger seat. 'Ah, I see. Well, you're a wise man. You've got your priorities sorted. Whatever you're up to now, it's obviously doing you a power of good. You look masses better than before.'

'Cheers mate, it's great to see you,' said Leo, clearly trying to draw the conversation to a close.

'Likewise,' said Sid. 'Look, you're obviously waiting for someone, and I know how shocking the parking is around here, so I'll turn a blind eye to you two lovebirds loitering in the loading zone. Staffing being what it is, nobody else will be around later to check, and I spotted the parking warden heading down the other end of town earlier, so you'll be fine. You take care of yourself, old buddy.'

And with that Sid strode off down the street, whistling cheerily to himself.

'Friendly guy,' I commented casually. 'You two used to work together, then?'

'That's right. He's a good sort is Sid. He can sometimes be a bit full on, but he's well intentioned,' said Leo.

I nodded, sensing he wouldn't welcome any further questions. If Leo wanted to tell me more, he would do, in his own time.

After a long pause, he cleared his throat. 'If you check the glove compartment, there should be a box of cereal bars in there. If you're hungry, that is.'

My stomach gave a growl of approval in response, which made him laugh.

'Thanks. Breakfast feels like a long time ago.'

I found the box and offered one to Leo.

'You can have first dibs,' I said.

'Probably wise. I'll have one to make sure they're still edible. Those things have been in there a while, ever since…' His voice tailed off.

'Ever since?' I pushed gently.

'...ever since I put them there when I was emptying my locker from work before I went on sick leave. Fifteen months ago yesterday, if we're going to be precise. I think even then I knew I wasn't going back.'

'I'm sorry.' It was an inadequate response to the obvious emotion in his voice.

'Don't be. I couldn't see it at the time, but I needed time away from the job. Like a frog in a bucket.'

I frowned. 'I don't quite follow.'

'They say if you put a frog in a bucket of boiling water, it'll immediately leap out to save its life,' said Leo. 'But if the frog is put in cold water to start with, then you gradually heat it up, it'll get so used to the increasing temperature that, by the time it reaches a fatal point, it's too late. The frog can't save itself. It's a horrible analogy, but looking back, it seems quite fitting for where I found myself.'

'That sounds really tough.' I waited a beat. 'You don't have to tell me if you don't want to, but I'm a good listener and I never share other people's confidences.'

There was a long silence.

'I still find it hard to talk about, but I trust you,' Leo said eventually. His words tumbled out, hesitant at first, then growing in confidence as he told his story. 'Being in the police was all I'd ever wanted. It sounds like a cliché, and certainly idealistic, but I wanted to help people and make a real difference to their lives.'

'There's nothing wrong with that. I wish more people thought like that when choosing their careers.'

'I got into the force at my first attempt and threw myself

into it wholeheartedly. I got a lot of stick for being on the graduate trainee programme. This was before they made everyone do a degree in policing. I felt I had to work harder and act tougher in order to be seen as worthy of my position.' Leo tapped his fingers against the steering wheel, beating out a nervous rhythm. 'It was even more difficult once I made it into CID. This time it wasn't the pressure from my colleagues, which had settled into more of a good-natured banter by that point, but rather the type of crimes we were dealing with – more complex, more emotionally draining. It was harder to track down the culprits, and even more challenging to build watertight cases against them. I lost count of the number of times I watched a criminal walk free because the evidence wasn't deemed compelling enough. Jurors have grown up on a diet of crime dramas on TV and often find it difficult to understand the difference between fiction and reality.'

'I can't imagine how frustrating that must have been for you,' I said. I was used to being a sympathetic listening ear for many in the library, but in most instances at work I was able to retain some level of professional distance. But as Leo's voice faltered, I had to fight the compulsion to reach across and hug the pain away.

'I was coping. And then one day, I realised I really wasn't. Something bad happened to someone close to me – Jill. You saw her briefly when we were having our self-defence lesson.' He paused, and I could tell he was picking his words extra-carefully. 'It was the type of thing that's always very hard to prove. But I worked damn hard to find that proof. We arrested the culprit. We built a strong case.

Jill was incredibly brave, giving evidence and remaining cool under the most gruelling of cross-examinations in court. But the judge wouldn't let the defendant's previous convictions for similar offences be shared, and worse still, the jury held Jill's calm and collected demeanour against her. They didn't believe what she told them and decided the evidence we presented wasn't enough. So, a guilty man walked free, and Jill had to find a way to move on with her life knowing that he was still out there.'

He cleared his throat, his eyes damp. I automatically took his hand, holding it tight. He didn't pull away.

'Sorry, I can't believe I'm still in such a mess about this,' he said.

'Don't apologise. It would be surprising if you weren't in a state about it.'

'It was the justice system at its very worst. Anyway, the perpetrator is on remand now and awaiting trial for a different crime. Jill has her good days and her bad days – the last week was the latter unfortunately, hence me going off radar for a while – but she's overall doing pretty well, even though she's livid that someone else had to suffer because her case failed.'

'I hope she's doing better now. She sounds like an amazing woman, and I'm sure she's glad to have your support.'

'Whatever Jill needs, I'm there for her.'

'I'm guessing that what happened to Jill was part of the reason you decided to leave the police?' I asked delicately.

'Yes. They euphemistically called it "burnout" on my sick note, but full-on depression would have been a more accurate description. I struggled to see a way forward and I could barely drag myself out of bed. They say it's important to talk, but I couldn't even string two words together or formulate a coherent thought. But slowly – too slowly – with help, the fog started to clear, and I realised I needed to take care of myself as well as others. So, once I was well enough to be sure that it wasn't the illness making the decision for me, I handed in my resignation. I muddled around for a bit, then began thinking about how I could take charge of my life again, maybe find a way to become my own boss. And that's when I started hanging out in your library and causing problems for you by putting my muddy hooves – was that what you called them? – on your furniture.'

'I've just about forgiven you for that,' I said, pleased when he smiled in response.

'But I can't escape in the library world forever, much as I'd like to. I feel pretty useless, if I'm totally honest. I was daydreaming about finding a way to start my own business which would help people, but in reality, I had zero purpose whatsoever until you came along and talked me into assisting you. And I'm not sure I've really made much of a difference there.'

'You've made all the difference to me,' I said simply.

I wished I was courageous enough to say more. Leo had been incredibly brave being so open with me. My instincts were urging me to ignore my insecurities and follow my heart, telling me that Leo was nothing like Scammer Brian. But still my self-doubt held me back, the fear of rejection and further hurt turning my mouth dry and filling me with panic. And then there was the situation with Jill. Leo hadn't exactly explained who she was to him. Were they just friends, or was there more to their relationship?

Perhaps some of my internal dilemma showed on my face, because Leo suddenly made the decision for me, leaning in close, his lips just a breath away from mine.

'May I?' he started to say, but I didn't let him finish. If I didn't seize the moment now, I never would. I closed the distance between us and kissed him. I forgot the reason we were here, forgot even that we were sitting in a car on a busy street. All that mattered was the wonderful pressure of his mouth moving against mine, the tickling friction of his stubble against my skin and the sensation of tingling warmth that had started in the depths of my torso and was now spreading throughout my body.

I tried to shuffle forward, then winced as the forgotten gearstick jabbed me in the ribs. Leo reached out and untucked my t-shirt, gently caressing upwards, soothing the ache away and replacing it with one of a very different kind. As I mirrored his action, his lips left mine and started slowly tracing the line of my jaw. Then his mouth moved onto my ear lobe and he whispered something. I took a deep, juddery breath, the roar of growing arousal deafening me to his words. All I knew was that I wanted him to carry on kissing me. I ran my fingers through his hair, pulling him still closer.

'The coast is clear; Brian's gone now,' said Leo against my lips.

Chapter Twenty-Three

'Brian's out of sight,' repeated Leo. 'He didn't spot us while he walked past the car.'

Finally, his words filtered through into my consciousness and I sat back in my seat, my heart pounding. I cleared my throat.

'Oh, er, jolly good,' I said, trying, and failing, to sound normal. A wave of humiliation was engulfing me and I couldn't even bring myself to look at Leo, scared at the pity which I would undoubtedly see in his eyes. I couldn't believe how stupid I'd been, how carried away I'd allowed myself to get. There I was thinking we were enjoying a genuine moment of mutual passion, when in reality Leo had instigated what had been the kiss of a lifetime, as a cover so Scammer Brian wouldn't spot us as he emerged from the theatre. What had been so real for me had apparently been purely practical for Leo, a mere surveillance tactic so we could stay incognito while Brian passed by.

'Did you spot which way he went while we were kissing?' asked Leo. 'You'd have had the better view of him from your position. I could only see so much in the reflection of the wing mirror.'

'No,' I squeaked. To admit that my entire being had been overwhelmed and that I'd been unaware of anything but the kiss would be even more mortifying, given that Leo had apparently managed to continue tracking Brian through the passenger wing mirror.

'About the kiss…' Leo started to say, but I didn't want to hear his next words, where he'd no doubt tactfully make it clear it had been born out of expediency and I should most definitely not read anything more into it.

'I need to go,' I said, already opening the car door.

'Brian's long gone. I don't think you'll be able to catch up with him,' said Leo, ever practical.

'I need to leave,' I repeated.

'Kat, we should…'.

But I didn't hang around to hear what it was that Leo thought we should be doing. The door slammed shut behind me and I set off at a near run.

'What about Betty?' called Leo after me.

I pretended I hadn't heard. I'd text later and ask him to drop my bike off at the library next time he was going. But I needed to get far away from what was now the most embarrassing situation of my life.

To give her credit, if my sister Caro was annoyed to have me turn up uninvited on the doorstep of her home in London a few hours later, bedraggled and exhausted, she managed to keep it to herself.

'Kat, love, what a nice surprise,' she said, giving me a big hug and hustling me inside, thankfully without bombarding me with questions first.

I responded by bursting into tears which made me even more cross with myself.

'Looks like you've had a tough day,' she soothed.

'You don't know the half of it.'

'Hmm, like that, is it? Well, I think the first priority is for you to go and run yourself a hot bath. Don't worry, we've got the house to ourselves, and it'll do Harry good to entertain himself on a Saturday evening for a change.'

I was grateful that Una, Caro's housemate and long-time best friend, was out, and I was too exhausted even to find the strength to protest against my sister cancelling her date night because of me.

'Have you got a change of clothes?' I nodded and shook my rucksack which I'd thankfully not forgotten to grab in my haste to leave. 'Good, then off you go. Take your time,' she ordered. 'I'm sure whatever it is can wait until you're feeling more human. I'll go and fix some supper for us. You come down whenever you like and we'll chat properly then.'

It was bliss to sink into the water and scrub off the remaining traces of the obstacle course. And when the spectre of Leo briefly appeared as I examined the gearstickshaped bruise starting to form on my ribs, I firmly told it to go away.

When I finally descended the stairs into Caro's basement kitchen, my skin still glowing from the heat of the bath, I felt a bit stronger. Which was good, as I was going to need all the strength I could muster to deal with the interrogation I was about to face.

'Who is he?' was my sister's opening line as she put a sizzling plate of macaroni cheese in front of me and I jumped on it. It was a very long time since breakfast, and I've never been one of those people who loses their appetite during moments of emotional turmoil.

'Mmm, this is good,' I answered eventually, between mouthfuls. 'What makes you think this is about a man?'

Caro raised an eyebrow and gestured at me, as if the answer was obvious.

'Fair enough, yes, it is,' I admitted. 'You remember I told you about that former policeman, Leo, the one I'd enlisted to help me track down Scammer Brian?'

'Ah. Him,' she nodded.

'I may have accidentally fallen for him. I know, I know.' I held up my hand to stop the interruption which was about to come. 'Yes, I let my love of love carry me away yet again, but don't worry, I'm absolutely fine. I'm drawing a line under the whole thing, which I know you'll agree is the sensible move, and I'm moving on completely unscathed.'

'You've always been rubbish at lying,' said Caro. 'A person who's "absolutely fine" doesn't travel hours by bus and tube to cry on their big sister's doorstep.'

'It was only because I was tired. It's been a long day,' I protested.

'My question is this: what's so wrong about falling for Leo?'

I blinked at her as she calmly took a bottle of wine out of the fridge and poured us a glass apiece. How wasn't she getting this?

'But you're always telling me that I need to realise the difference between the world of fiction and real life.'

'You'll recall that I made that point when you were waxing lyrical about one Brian James who you'd never even met in person,' she reminded me. 'You've admitted yourself that you'd built up this whole fantasy world around him. Whereas, judging from the many "Leo this" and "Leo that" messages I've been receiving, you've spent a decent amount of time with the guy and have actually got to know him, and pretty well too, judging by the way your face is suddenly turning tomato red.'

'Now you're the one whose imagination is getting carried away,' I said.

'I've a feeling we're getting to the crux of the reason behind your dramatic appearance.'

'There's no need to be so smug about it,' I muttered, before reluctantly filling her in on the events of the day. My description of the kiss was slightly more PG than it had actually been, but I could see Caro reading between the lines and coming up with her own version.

'I'm still failing to see what the problem is. My suggestion is that perhaps you and Leo reconvene in slightly more comfortable surroundings where there's less risk of getting arrested for public indecency. Job done.'

'Do I need to spell it out for you?' I raised my voice in exasperation, carefully enunciating every word. 'He only kissed me as a cover so Scammer Brian didn't spot us carrying out surveillance. He doesn't feel the same way about me.'

'I don't buy it. I know you've been holding back on me, but I can tell from your expression that was one hell of a kiss. There are countless other ways the pair of you could have avoided being spotted by that Brian bloke. Frankly, I can't see there being any risk in the first place that he'd clock you and immediately assume you were carrying out surveillance. People hang out in their cars all the time. It's a perfectly normal activity. Nobody assumes someone is going to be spying on them.'

'They might if they're up to no good. And we had the obstacle course t-shirts on. He might have seen us there and wondered why we were hanging around where he was,' I countered.

Caro took a sip of her drink and gestured at me with the glass. 'It's a pathetic argument and you know it. I think deep down you know it was a real kiss and that really frightens you. Because, while you can be fierce and brave when it comes to fighting for other people's best interests, when it comes to fighting for your own, you always let your anxiety hold you back.'

She was right. But accepting that fact was one thing, changing such an ingrained habit was quite another.

I jumped as my phone started ringing. Leo.

'Did I mention that he's way out of my league?' I said.

Caro shook her head. 'Get over yourself. You'll get far more out of life if you do. That whole concept of not being in someone's league is a nonsense, an easy excuse because you're too scared to make a proper move and run the risk of having your heart broken. But sometimes you've got to feel the fear, then put on your big girl pants and go out and do it anyway. It's an old cliché but when people get to their deathbed, it's the things they didn't do that they regret the most.'

The phone stopped ringing.

'He's not left a message,' I said.

'You could always call him back.'

'It obviously wasn't that important.'

I sounded pathetic, but that was how I felt right now. Caro reached across and, placing her hand over mine, gave it a gentle squeeze.

'Try not to worry. I wouldn't read anything into him not leaving a voicemail. You can ring in the morning and have a proper conversation with him then. You'll feel better once you've had a decent night's sleep,' she said.

If only it were so simple.

Chapter Twenty-Four

Inevitably, I lay awake most of the night wrestling with my thoughts, but when dawn came, I had made a decision. I would continue working with Leo in a professional capacity only, until we exposed Scammer Brian. As promised, I would then help him with his business plan and set him up with Doris's mentorship. Once all our obligations had been fulfilled, and if – when – I was still feeling like this, I would summon up my courage and ask him out on a proper date. And if the voice at the back of my head, sounding suspiciously like my sister, told me that I was still taking the coward's way out by putting it off, I could sensibly counter with the argument that I couldn't afford to get distracted. Not at such a crucial moment in the investigation, not when we were so close to bringing the fraudster to justice.

'Oh, hey, Kat, didn't realise you were visiting,' said Una as I went into the kitchen to grab breakfast. 'Good to see you again. Do you want toast? I was just putting some on.'

'Thanks, Una. How are things? What's the latest in theatreland?'

She pulled a face, while adding another two slices to the toaster. 'I'm at the prep stage for my next directing gig, gathering the team together, casting the roles and so on. It's basically the foundation work – somewhat faffy, but it has the capacity to make or break the show.'

'Sounds like a busy time. Drink?'

'Busy is one way of putting it, but that's how I like it. And I'll have a black coffee, if you're offering.'

I filled the kettle and scooped coffee into the cafetière, wondering if Leo was carrying out a similar morning routine. I hoped he wasn't feeling too sore after his accident on the obstacle course. Should I text and ask, or would that invite conversation of a more personal nature? What if he brought up the kiss? I really couldn't handle talking to him about it just yet. In fact, what I needed to do was come up with a cast-iron conversation topic for our next meeting to distract us from any awkwardness. And the only guaranteed way to do that was to decide upon the next step in our investigation.

An idea was starting to form in my head. 'How do you find the people you want to work with in the theatre?' I asked Una.

'Job interviews, word-of-mouth recommendations, trawling the freelancer and acting databases, the usual stuff.'

'So, if I was looking for someone who might be in the business, you could perhaps help me with my search?'

'Is this something to do with your hunt for that

scammer?' asked Una, grabbing a jar of peanut butter from the cupboard. 'Caro's given me the lowdown.'

I quickly explained the latest developments. 'I've had a brief look at the Oxford Grand's website to try to identify the guy, but the only staff members listed on there are the theatre manager and the press officer, and they don't have photos. He could be working backstage, of course, or be in the cast of their latest show. The cast list is up, but again, no photos. I was planning to google all the names, but if you've got access to some industry databases, that might make my search more targeted.'

'A bit of light detective work on a Sunday morning: why not? You sort the toast; I'll grab my laptop and we'll get searching.'

Caro wandered in sleepily a quarter of an hour later and found Una and I hunched together over the computer, sipping our coffees.

'Glad to see you're in a better frame of mind this morning,' she said with a yawn. 'What are you two up to, cackling away like a pair of Macbeth's witchy pals?'

'We might have got briefly side-tracked into casting an imaginary film adaptation of my life,' I said.

'Hmm, well, until your personal drama comes to a satisfactory conclusion, don't you think you're better focusing on reality?' said Caro, ever the practical one.

'Fiction's way better,' I retorted. 'And yes, I know you're going to say that's what got me into this situation. Okay, back to work, try this next name – Blake Jenkins.'

Una typed it into the actors' database.

A picture appeared on the screen, and I froze. There he

was, the man who'd been responsible for so much heartache and shame. Even though he'd been a whole lot muddier when I'd seen him in real life, I'd recognise those determined eyes anywhere.

'Gotcha,' I said, swallowing down the hard lump of rage and sadness, aiming for triumph.

'He's fit. I can see why you went for him,' said Una.

I shook my head, some of my coursing anger beginning to clear as I realised how close we were to finally getting Scammer Brian. 'He didn't use actual pictures of himself. He nicked some from a guy in the army. But this is definitely the bloke we spotted at the obstacle course and followed back to the theatre.'

'It's a shame he felt he had to use someone else's pictures. He'd probably still have done well getting dates with his own snaps,' said Caro, leaning over my shoulder and examining the screen. 'I guess he was scared of getting caught. Or maybe he has an inferiority complex. Like someone else I know,' she added pointedly, giving me a slight nudge.

'I don't know why you two are bending over backwards to feel sorry for him,' I said, pushing back and standing up to pace. 'Have you forgotten why we've been hunting him down? He wasn't actually looking for love at all, just an easy mark to make money from. I reckon he used someone else's pictures out of self-preservation, keeping his professional and personal life separate. Or rather, his two different professions apart from each other.'

'I thought most jobbing actors got positions in coffee

shops when they were between roles,' said Caro. 'Still, I suppose it shows initiative.'

'Well, this Blake Jenkins guy obviously decided to go down a different route,' I snapped at my sister, rising to her deliberate bait against my own better judgement. I should probably be feeling more victorious about the breakthrough, but suddenly I wished Leo were here instead of Caro.

'It's too easy to wind you up, little sis, too easy,' said Caro.

'Well, we've found out his real name at last. Blake Jenkins,' I repeated. It certainly had a strong ring to it. Definitely more hero credentials than Brian James. But, I reminded myself, there was nothing heroic about the way he'd behaved.

'That's what he's called on the actors' database,' corrected Una. 'It could still be a pseudonym. The site insists that everyone has to have a unique name. It saves the embarrassment of the wrong John Smith being called for auditions or getting his credits muddled up.'

'I have a feeling it is his real name. It has the same initials as Brian James, after all. I reckon he was sticking with what he knew.'

'And you're one hundred percent certain that this is the guy?' asked Caro, scrolling through the rest of his résumé. 'Look, he's got some audio samples on his profile. Why don't you listen to them? He left you lots of voice notes, didn't he?'

'He did,' I said, humiliation sweeping over me once

again. I couldn't believe I used to listen to his messages on repeat.

I clicked on the play icon and immediately shuddered as the scammer's rich tones rang out across the room. What made it somehow much worse was that he was reciting Shakespeare's Sonnet 116, arguably the most romantic poem in the English language. At one time, I'd thought Brian and I might have had a 'marriage of true minds' in the future. I gave myself a little shake. I needed to hurry up and confront Blake Jenkins, before he used this seductive poetry recital on some other unsuspecting target.

'He's got a good voice, I'll give him that,' said Una. 'If he fancies some non-criminal work, perhaps you could send him my way.'

'I'm not going to reward him for trying to defraud me.'

My phone rang before she could respond.

'Come on, Una,' said Caro, with a grin. 'I think this is our cue to make ourselves scarce. Judging by the expression on Kat's face, it's lover boy calling again. Do say hi from us. I can't wait to meet him in person.'

I could hear my heart beating in my ears as I answered my mobile. 'Leo, hi,' I said, worrying about the sudden breathiness in my voice, then hissed, 'Go away' at my sister.

'Sorry, is now a bad time?' he said.

'That wasn't aimed at you. It was intended for my big sister, who's extremely annoying.' This last bit was directed at Caro who, despite saying she would leave, was showing no sign of actually doing so.

She stuck her tongue out at me like we were children again, then reluctantly followed Una out of the room.

'How—'

'What—'

Leo and I both started speaking at the same time.

I laughed awkwardly.

'Sorry, you go first,' said Leo.

'I was going to ask how you are,' I said.

'Oh. I'm fine. How about you?'

He wasn't going to mention the kiss, then. That was good. A big relief, in fact. So why did I feel disappointed?

'All the better for speaking to you,' I said, trying to sound as normal as possible. 'I've had a breakthrough,' I quickly added, before I accidentally let slip something I might regret.

'That's good news,' said Leo, although he didn't sound as excited as I'd hoped he would. 'But you can tell me later, if you prefer. I don't want to keep you when you've got your sister round.'

'I'm at hers in London, actually. Bit of an impulse trip, but it's proved to be very productive because her housemate works in the theatre industry and she's helped me track down Brian James's real name. He's called – drumroll please – Blake Jenkins. And he's an actor.'

I even did a celebratory jazz hand. It was probably good Leo couldn't see me striding up and down Caro's kitchen as I attempted to work off my nervous energy.

'Not a very imaginative one sticking to his real initials,' said Leo. He sounded strangely subdued.

'Exactly. So, do you reckon we could go to the app, or even the police, with this new evidence?' I pushed, still trying to drum up some enthusiasm from him. 'Surely, they'd have to take me seriously now we can show that he's been using a false identity?'

Leo sighed. 'I wish it was that simple, but we don't have any proof of wrongdoing. It's not a criminal offence to use another name and someone else's pictures on a dating app, and although he was clearly out for money, he's still not made another outright demand in black and white. And there's no evidence that he's been targeting other people.'

I thought rapidly. 'Fair points. But how about this for an idea? We know Bri— Blake's job, so we know exactly where to find him and at what times he'll be there. What if I go and wait for him near the stage door after a show, and pretend I want to pick up where we left off in our last online conversation?'

I pictured Leo frowning at the other end of the line as he prepared to pick my improvised plan apart. 'Putting myself in Brian slash Blake's shoes, wouldn't I be highly suspicious if you suddenly came up to me, not even questioning why I look nothing like my profile pictures or why I was at a theatre in Oxford when I'd told you I was being debriefed at an army camp?'

I was grasping at straws here, but I couldn't seem to stop. 'I could give him an abbreviated version of the truth, that I recognised his voice at the obstacle course and managed to find him in Oxford when I couldn't keep up with him at the event. I'll ask him if he's dyed his hair, and pretend I've not noticed he's half a foot shorter in real life than he appears in his profile pictures. He'll probably be flattered that someone has gone to such an effort to meet him.'

I sank back onto a chair, exhausted by my mental gymnastics.

'Or he'll start worrying that he's got a stalker. I'm not telling you what to do but, as your friend, I'd advise you to reconsider.'

'I have to do something,' I said, a little more brusquely than I'd intended as I tried not to get caught up in overanalysing his use of the word 'friend'. 'We can't carry on forever like a budget Holmes and Watson, never achieving anything.'

'Morse and Lewis would be more accurate, given our usual surroundings,' said Leo, a genuine warmth in his voice for the first time in this strange conversation. 'And I'm offended that you'd describe us as "budget" anything. Haven't you just tracked down your man? I would say that makes you quite the crimefighter.'

'Yes, but it's seemingly not going to make a scrap of difference unless we can bring him to justice. I need to move on with my life. We can't keep going like this.'

'Sure, I understand,' said Leo, suddenly all business again. 'You're right. We sort out the Scammer Brian situation and then we can both move on.'

I wished he hadn't agreed so readily.

Chapter Twenty-Five

It was difficult to concentrate on work on Monday when I knew Leo was elsewhere carrying out surveillance on the man we now knew to be Blake Jenkins. I was worried about him being out there by himself, but Leo had refused to listen to my concerns when he'd dropped by this morning.

'Trust me, I'm experienced at this kind of thing. He won't look twice at me. As far as he's concerned, I'm just an average bloke hanging around in the street.'

I fought the urge to tell Leo there was nothing average about him, but now was not the time.

I tried a different tack. 'It's not fair making you do all the legwork. I don't want to take advantage of your good nature.'

'You aren't, I promise,' he said.

'And you really think you'll find out useful information by following him around for a while?'

'It'll help us establish his routine and usual haunts,

which means that, if – and it's a very big if – we go ahead with your plan of waiting near the stage door, I'll have a good idea of where he might suggest you go afterwards. With this kind of operation, the more preparation we can do, the better.'

'It sounds like you're coming round to my way of thinking,' I said.

'What part of "if" don't you understand?' he said, although his tone was benevolent.

'I know, I know. You only want me to be safe.'

'I care about you. Of course, I want you to be safe,' he replied before doing a swift about turn and stomping out of the library.

'My, oh my, we'll need to get air conditioning in here if you're going to carry on heating up the place with all that sexual tension between you two,' said Moira, appearing from behind the fantasy section where she'd been unsubtly eavesdropping. She fanned herself.

'Ha ha, very funny,' I said, looking anxiously towards the street where Leo had disappeared.

'He'll be fine,' she added. 'He's a big boy. He can look after himself. And he's got a point about the need to be careful. A wild beast is always most dangerous when it's cornered.'

That didn't make me feel any better.

Fortunately, I had a meeting with Doris about the seniors' social media group to distract me. Once we'd sorted out the logistics of her running a few sessions, I took the opportunity to ask her about assisting Leo with his business plan. I knew I should have done it ages ago, but I hadn't at the beginning because I'd been dubious about whether he'd actually help me. Then, as things progressed, I'd been selfishly putting it off because I didn't want our arrangement to end. But the delighted expression on Doris's face made me feel guilty I'd not asked sooner.

'You really want me to get involved? Are you sure? I've been out of the loop for a while. I could probably put you in touch with someone better.'

'There's no one better than you,' I reassured her. 'It's important to me that Leo's business gets the best possible start, and I know that you're the person to help him do that.'

She almost visibly grew in stature.

'You're very kind, pet. In which case, I'm more than happy to help. If you'll excuse me, I'll go and make a few phone calls to some old contacts who might know about funding opportunities for start-ups in Oxford. It doesn't do any harm to think ahead.'

She was so keen to get started that she forgot to ask whether her latest book reservations had arrived.

Helping Etta register new stock took up the next few hours, but I still couldn't resist checking my phone every five minutes to see if there was any news from Leo. I finally caved mid-afternoon and texted to ask if he was alright, but he left me on read. Logically I knew he was probably too busy to get back to me, but that didn't stop my mind skipping merrily down the catastrophising rabbit hole, and I started to picture all kinds of terrifying scenarios, ranging from Blake merely confronting him to Leo being pushed in front of a moving car. Eventually I sent an ultimatum.

> KAT
>
> Let me know you're still alive in the next half an hour, otherwise I'll call the police and get your friend Sid on the case.

A response came back within five minutes.

> LEO
>
> Am ok. Talk later.

Fair enough, Mr Chatty, if that's the way you want to play it, I said to myself, and buried myself in reshelving for the rest of the day.

'Gotcha,' I hissed later that evening, pouncing on Leo where he was lurking behind a large recycling bin at the far end of the Oxford Grand's car park. Somewhat to my disappointment, he didn't even bat an eyelid.

'I heard you coming a mile off,' he said calmly. 'Did you realise that those Converse shoes of yours squeak when you're on tiptoe?'

'Drat. And here I was thinking I was so much better at engaging stealth mode than you are.' I gestured at his high visibility waistcoat which was practically glowing in the dark.

'Au contraire. Hi-vis is a very effective disguise. Everyone assumes you're a workman with a legitimate reason to be hanging around. And if you're hanging around by the bins, it's even better. Nobody in their right minds wants to get too close to the smell.'

I wrinkled my nose. 'Now you come to mention it, you are rather ripe.'

'Maybe you can lend me some of whatever shower gel it is that you use. You always smell flowery and fresh,' he said unexpectedly.

I experienced a definite frisson at his compliment and what it might mean about how he felt towards me, especially as I religiously used unscented products so my sensitive skin didn't get irritated. Had I been a bolder person, I might have taken the leap and flirtatiously invited him to share a shower with me some time. But it was late, I was tired, and I wasn't suddenly going to undergo a personality transplant and proposition a man behind the bins, even if he did look exceptionally good in spite of his bright yellow safety gear.

'I'll tell you where to find the brand I use,' was my lame response instead. 'What have you learnt, Mr Bond, James Bond?'

'Hmm, that the reality of surveillance work involves a lot fewer martinis of either the shaken or stirred variety. Our quarry seems to be a man of fairly mundane habits. About the most exciting thing he's done today is buy coffee not once, but twice, and both times he went to chains rather than independents.'

'Definitely another mark against him.'

'He also did what he'd probably claim was a workout in the University Parks, but really he was preening and hoping to catch the attention of any passing woman.'

'Did he have success?' I asked.

'None whatsoever,' said Leo with a grin. 'I, on the other hand…'

I gave him a shove. 'I thought you were meant to be concentrating on the task in hand.'

'I'm only kidding. I was laser-focused on the target the whole way round. A group of dancing girls could have come up to me and I wouldn't have noticed. Besides, I'm a one-woman kind of man.'

I wanted to ask more when the stage door suddenly opened.

'Duck down,' hissed Leo. 'You need to hide in the shadows; I've only got one hi-vis vest on me.'

Blake Jenkins whistled to himself as he walked through the car park and down the street, passing only metres away from us. I held my breath, trying to keep as still as possible in case my unsuitable footwear revealed our position.

'Interesting, he still hasn't got back in his car,' muttered Leo. 'Maybe that means his digs are nearby. Are you up for some more field practice in surveillance?'

'What about my squeaky shoes?' I whispered back.

'Try walking normally,' he advised. 'I think it was probably your tiptoe technique causing the problem.'

He quickly removed his hi-vis and stuffed it into his rucksack.

'Right, I reckon we could pass as a couple heading home from a meal out. The key thing is to create a different silhouette in the dark. Shall we?'

He took my hand in his and we set off down the road, strolling casually as if we were merely enjoying the mild spring evening rather than on the trail of a master criminal.

The streets were bustling, even at this time on a Monday night, full of students eagerly catching up with their friends, having just returned to Oxford for the start of Trinity term. I tried to concentrate on our task, but it was difficult to give it my full attention when half of my brain was engaged in a joyous internal commentary about how right it felt to be walking through town like this with Leo. His clasp was gentle yet confident, and every so often his thumb delicately swept across my palm. I knew he was only doing it to subtly indicate when we should slow down or speed up to match Blake's pace, but I allowed myself to pretend there might be something more to it, relishing every moment of his soft touch.

But as we continued on our journey, my sense of unease grew.

'We're nearly at my flat,' I said quietly. 'He can't... He doesn't know where I live, does he?'

'Hold on, I think he's stopping,' said Leo, leaning towards me, the words more mouthed than audible. He pulled me behind a large stone gatepost, standing so I was further concealed in his shadow, and we watched as Blake Jenkins unlocked a basement flat only five buildings along from my own studio flat. The click of the door closing behind him seemed to echo down the road like a gunshot, and I jumped, despite my best efforts to remain calm.

'That is too close for comfort,' said Leo. 'Are you okay?'

I realised I was shaking.

'Yup,' I said, not trusting myself to say anything more in case I gave away that my teeth were chattering.

'Come here,' said Leo, and he pulled me close. There

was comfort in the warmth of his embrace, but I knew I couldn't allow myself to get too used to it. The reality of the danger which Blake could pose had suddenly come home to me, almost in a literal sense, and I knew I couldn't afford to get distracted at such a critical point. How long had the man I'd known as Brian James been living around the corner from me? Had he been watching me, using what he saw to help build a profile which he knew would appeal to me?

'Is there someone you could stay with for a few days?' Leo asked. 'I'm sure I'm being over-cautious, but it might be better for my peace of mind if you could be elsewhere, just until we've sorted out this situation. I don't feel easy knowing that he's staying so close to your home. Would Moira take you in?'

'Absolutely,' I said. 'The only issue is that she lives in the rest of the house above my flat. It wouldn't exactly be providing the distance we're after.'

'Then you'll have to come and stay at mine,' said Leo without hesitation. In any other circumstances, my heart would have been singing at the invitation, but it had been delivered in a decidedly impersonal tone, and I was aware the motivation behind it was purely practical.

I made a lukewarm protest, but I knew I'd feel physically safer staying at Leo's, even if I was running the risk of becoming even more emotionally vulnerable. I was grateful for his kindness.

'Will Moira worry about where you've got to?' asked Leo.

'I'll text her to say I'm staying with a friend,' I said,

already knowing that it would send Moira and Rami into a paroxysm of inquisitive excitement.

Leo lived in a pretty village several miles out of Oxford. He'd left his car at home, not wanting to run the risk of Blake Jenkins recognising it, so we got the bus back instead, sitting together on the top deck. I felt inordinately tired, the stress of the last few days catching up with me, and I had to fight the temptation to let my head rest on Leo's broad shoulder and doze off as the bus trundled its way through the countryside.

'I'm renting this place from a friend who's travelling abroad for a year,' he explained as he unlocked the front door, the outdoor light illuminating the chocolate box style cottage, complete with softly scented wisteria winding its way up the honey-coloured stonework. 'He says I can have first refusal if he decides to stay abroad and sell up. I'll miss him if he does do that, but I'll admit I've fallen for the house and wouldn't mind making it mine permanently.' He smiled. 'Of course, I'll have to have established my business properly by then in order to afford it.'

When I'd first met Leo, he'd struck me as being the type of bloke to live in an impersonal warehouse flat, full of shiny chrome surfaces and black leather sofas. But knowing him better, I could see why he felt so at home in this little house with its cosy, shaker-style kitchen and squishy armchairs. It was a comfortable and undemanding environment, the kind of place where you could relax and be yourself. Or it would have been, if I hadn't then started worrying about the sleeping arrangements. An only-one-bed scenario could lead to all kinds of complications which were probably best avoided, given the other dramas I was dealing with.

Fortunately – or unfortunately, as the braver side of my mind put it – Leo had a spare bedroom, and he'd thought of all the practicalities.

'Here's a t-shirt for you to sleep in. There's a spare blanket in the chest at the end of the bed if you get cold, and I'll put some towels out in the bathroom for you,' he said from the doorway. 'There's a new toothbrush in the cupboard which you can use. Feel free to bob downstairs and put your clothes in to wash and dry overnight so they're fresh in the morning for you. Have you got everything you need?'

Everything except you, I said silently. But this was hardly the time or the place. Leo was such a gentleman that, even supposing he had any interest in me in that way, he'd probably worry about taking advantage of my emotional state following the discovery that the scammer lived near me. And, while it would be wonderful to briefly forget my fears in Leo's arms, my troubles would still be waiting for me in the morning.

'Mm-hmm,' I said.

'Try not to let it worry you, Kat. We'll sort it all out tomorrow. All will be well.'

For a moment, I wondered if he was referring to my internal dilemma, then I realised that his focus, as always, was on the investigation.

'I hope so,' I said, thinking of both situations.

'Good night. Sleep well.'

'Night, Leo. You too.'

He seemed to hesitate on the threshold – or was that just my wishful thinking? – then he turned and went into his own room, the wooden floor of the hallway creaking beneath his feet.

I had a quick shower, put my outfit in to wash as offered, and settled myself in the spare room. Wearing Leo's clothing was a poor substitute for actually snuggling up in bed with the man himself, but I found comfort in it nevertheless, and drifted quickly off to sleep embraced by the subtle, clean scent of his t-shirt.

I woke in the middle of the night with a pounding headache and a desperate thirst, my adrenalin pumping after a vivid nightmare in which Blake Jenkins was chasing me through the streets of Oxford. I felt my way to the bathroom in the dark and took a long drink of some toothpaste-tasting water to calm myself down. I'm at Leo's house, I'm safe, I repeated in my head until my heart rate returned to normal. As I rinsed the cup out and put it back on the edge of the sink, the fabric of the t-shirt tickled the back of my legs. It felt so intimate to be wearing Leo's clothing, especially as I had nothing of my own on underneath. I thought back to that moment in the car when he'd gently stroked his palm across my ribs. How I wanted to experience that sensation again, only this time for real.

Back in the hallway, my eyes now adjusted to the gloom, I hesitated. There were two doors in front of me – my bedroom and Leo's. There was nothing stopping me from softly knocking on his door and asking to go in. Nothing but myself. But somehow in the timeless world of the dark, it felt like it would be easier to make that move, to tell Leo, and perhaps even show him how I really felt. As Caro would say, what was the worst that could happen? Do it, my heart urged. Just that one step forward could change everything. Why shouldn't I take a chance on happiness? I had dithered for long enough, telling myself that I wasn't worthy of a man like Leo. Perhaps it was time for me to stop listening to that voice of negativity and be brave enough to trust my heart instead. I raised my right hand, curling my fingers into a loose fist ready to rap my knuckles against the wooden door.

Then I heard Leo's voice inside the room.

'Yeah, of course. Try not to worry. It'll all be sorted soon, and then we can get back to normal. Night, Jill.'

My hand fell back down by my side. He was on the phone with Jill. His fellow rowing coach. The 'someone close to me' who he'd supported through the very worst of times. That was probably what he was doing right now, continuing to be a listening ear for a woman who was still struggling. But the niggling voice of doubt at the back of my mind suggested another explanation for the late-night phone call with its hushed, intimate tone. Perhaps Leo's relationship with Jill was even closer than he'd admitted to me. After all, he had made a big point of saying he wasn't in the market for a date when we'd started our investigation.

I'd interpreted that as him meaning he was content in his single status, but it was very possible that I'd got the wrong end of the stick. Had I once again allowed my imagination to see things that weren't there, to create another fictional happily ever after with a man who was equally unavailable as the so-called Brian James, although for very different reasons? Would I never learn my lesson? I turned on my heel and quickly fled back into my bedroom, praying that Leo hadn't heard the creak of the floor beneath my feet.

Chapter Twenty-Six

'Hope you slept okay,' said Leo the next morning when I went downstairs. I quickly examined his expression, worrying there was more to his words, but he seemed thankfully unaware of my midnight dilemma. He cheerfully poured me a coffee and set about preparing some scrambled eggs while I sorted the toast. I tried to ignore how right it felt, sitting around the kitchen table together and sharing breakfast, almost like a real couple. But that was out of my reach. There was the Jill factor to consider, after all. Although a nagging voice of reason suggested I'd latched onto that unknown because it was an easier excuse than the other obstacle standing in my way – my own self-doubt.

'So, what do you want to do now?' asked Leo, as if he'd read my thoughts.

It was a good question.

'Well, I can't stay with you forever,' I said, forcing a levity I didn't feel into my voice.

'I'm sure I could find some extra space for shelves to house your book collection,' he responded, matching my jokey tone. Once again, I searched his features, hoping to read something more there.

I gave myself a mental shake. What was the point in hoping, while I was still leaving so much unsaid? I would never know if a life with Leo was possible unless I found the courage to take a leap. Ultimately, the pain of potential rejection would be less damaging than the regret of not even trying, I told myself. Maybe it was time to follow through on the promise I'd made to myself when I stayed at Caro's, however much the prospect of doing so frightened me. As I had vowed, I would finish the investigation and then confess to Leo how I felt. And whatever happened next would happen.

'We need to bring this situation with Brian James to the endgame,' I said, leaning forward and fixing Leo with a serious look, determined to take that next step.

The relaxed humour disappeared from his face. After a moment's hesitation, he nodded.

'Okay, here's what I was thinking,' I said.

I elaborated on my stage door idea, then spent the next few minutes listening to Leo trying to come up with alternatives. When he eventually fell quiet, I shook my head.

'No, I don't see any of those suggestions working. And I don't think you do either. If I "accidentally on purpose" bump into him in the street, I'm worried it'll be easier for him to get away. And carrying on monitoring him without taking action isn't going to change anything. In your heart of hearts, you know that my plan is the best option we have.'

Leo frowned. 'I'm still certain we can think of something else which doesn't involve such a level of risk to you.'

'But I've already explained how we can mitigate that risk. I'm sure Moira will swap shifts with me so I'm free for Blake's matinee this afternoon.'

In fact, she'd probably be falling over herself to make the offer, imagining all kinds of starry-eyed dreams involving me wanting to spend a romantic day out and about with Leo, or perhaps even one where we didn't stray beyond his bedroom. I forced my mind away from that too-tempting image.

'I'll wait for Blake Jenkins after the matinee show, play the besotted innocent who's thrilled to discover he was really a "famous actor" trying to keep a low profile all along, and go from there. I've been messaging him about how very desperate I am to meet him, so hopefully he'll assume that I've taken the initiative. It'll still be sunny and there'll be lots of people around. And if he does get funny with me, I'll kick up a massive noisy fuss, exactly like you advised in our self-defence class.'

Why had I mentioned that? I needed to concentrate, not get nostalgic about rolling around on the floor with Leo in the gym.

'I still say it's a weak plan. There are too many variables in it. And because it's daylight it'll be harder for me to follow you both without being detected,' he pointed out.

I decided to ignore his interruption. 'Then I'll persuade Blake to come with me to a pre-arranged meeting point like the coffee shop around the corner, so you'll know exactly where we're going. We'll sit in the window where it's nice and public. And then I'll confront him.' I tried to sound as convincing as possible. Privately I agreed with Leo that my plan was full of holes, but I needed to do something to resolve this situation.

'Just like that, you'll confront him. It sounds so simple,' said Leo in a disbelieving voice. 'And then what happens? While I'd love for him to roll over and confess everything to you, unfortunately, I think it's highly unlikely it'll work out that way. At best he'll laugh in your face and deny the whole thing, then where do you go? You'll have played your hand and he'll have realised how flimsy our evidence is. And at worst, he could get very angry and lash out, public place or not. Angry people are unpredictable, and there are far too many unpredictable elements to this scheme already.'

'I don't think Brian slash Blake is the lashing-out kind.'

'He seemed pretty physical to me from what I saw on the obstacle course and when he was prancing around the park yesterday,' said Leo, subconsciously flexing his fingers as if already preparing for a confrontation.

'It's one thing showing off your strength in feats of endurance, quite another using it against a woman in full view of a busy coffee shop,' I said, hoping I sounded more confident than I felt.

'You're forgetting the fact that he's been living down the road from you,' pointed out Leo.

'I've been thinking about that.' In fact, I'd been doing little else since the middle of the night. It had been an easier worry to pick away at to distract me from my other, Leo-related concerns. 'I've come to the conclusion that it's a coincidence.'

'What is it that Sherlock Holmes says about coincidences? Something along the lines of there being no such thing,' said Leo.

'But I thought you had little faith in Sherlock Holmes as a detective? Besides, Conan Doyle isn't exactly consistent in pushing that line. Let's examine the facts. Oxford is an expensive city with limited places where a jobbing actor could afford to rent. The more affordable housing – and I use the word "affordable" in the loosest possible sense – tends to be in the Cowley and Iffley Road area, which is where I live. There are loads of shared houses around there in addition to the usual student accommodation. Besides, I did a search online last night. It turns out there is a theatrical digs in my street, and it's been established for some time. I've gone back through all my messages with the scammer, looking for any clues I might have given him about where I live. I was taken in by his spiel on the app to start with, but I was never so naïve as to say anything which would have allowed him to work out my address, I'm absolutely certain of it. Have a little faith in me.'

Leo pushed the coffee pot towards me, offering a top-up which I gratefully accepted.

'I do have faith in you. A lot of faith,' he said. 'But there are other means whereby he could have found your address. It doesn't take a genius once you've got somebody's full name, which you did share with him pretty soon. Plus, he knew where you worked and could have followed you home. Maybe he thought you own the whole house rather than living in a flat, and that's why he targeted you?'

'But there are clearly two separate entrances to my building, and two post boxes,' I reminded him. 'If he had gone to the extreme of following me, he would have presumably also carried out a much more thorough background check and realised that the effort-to-reward ratio in targeting me was simply not worth it. I'm a librarian earning barely more than the living wage. I'm not a secret heiress, more's the pity, and disappointingly I'm not sitting on a vast savings account. The only way I can afford to live alone is because Moira and Rami took pity on me and gave me a generous discount on rent. My one financial extravagance was joining SO Ox, and that turned out to have a cost far higher than I'm willing to pay.'

Leo took his time finishing his drink before he replied.

'I suppose you've got a point,' he conceded, but I could still see the worry in his eyes. 'Okay, so maybe him living nearby isn't such a huge consideration, but there are plenty of other risks.'

I reached out and took his hand. 'I know that, but they're mine to take. I'm not going to waste any more time allowing fear to get in the way. I need to take back control and set my own narrative, rather than passively letting things play out.'

As I said the words out loud in my effort to convince him, I finally accepted their truth myself. I was tired of believing that negative voice in my head that told me I wasn't good enough or brave enough or strong enough.

Actually, I was more than enough, and I wasn't going to let anxiety hold me back any longer. Yes, it was one thing to declare this from the safety of Leo's kitchen several miles away from the situation, but I knew I would find the strength to handle whatever Blake threw at me, and then whatever happened with Leo after that. Being afraid had left me standing lonely in the hallway. If I'd been bolder and more confident earlier, maybe I could have been on the other side of that door, lying next to him in bed as we came up with a plan together.

Leo's eyes raked my face, as if trying to see beyond my expression to glean my true thoughts. Eventually he nodded.

'Okay, let's do this.'

'Good. I'm grateful for your support.'

He shrugged. 'It's what anybody would do.'

I wasn't sure I agreed with that. Leo was one very special individual.

'There was one other thing I was going to do, but I'm not sure it's strictly legal, so if you don't want me to tell you about it, that's fine,' I added.

Leo frowned. 'You can't say something like that and expect me not to want to hear what it is. I'm not in the police force anymore, so I'm not under any obligation to report what you do. Providing it's within reason, of course.'

I grinned, wondering what he thought I might be up to. 'I'm going to covertly record my conversation with Blake Jenkins. And, even if he doesn't confess, I reckon the contents of the recording would still be pretty damaging to his acting career, if they were to ever get released on the internet.'

'Ah, so you're going to indulge in a little light blackmailing? A cunning idea, Ms Fisher.'

'Exploit your opponent's weaknesses: that's another bit of vital self-defence, isn't it, Mr Taylor? Blake Jenkins obviously still wants to make it in showbusiness, otherwise why would he be living in theatre digs and performing at a little-known regional venue? We're not law enforcement. We don't need to convince a jury that our suspect is guilty. We just have to convince our suspect that we'll make life miserable for him unless he starts to behave himself.'

'I definitely wouldn't want to get on your wrong side,' said Leo. 'It's a good idea, and I'll agree to it on one condition.'

'I'll remind you that I don't need your permission.'

He nodded. 'Of course you don't. But we're partners. In this investigation, I mean,' he added hastily. 'And partners never let each other go anywhere without providing backup. So, if it's okay with you, I'll sit at a nearby table in the coffee shop. I promise I won't get involved unless you want me to. But at least if Blake starts getting funny with you, as you put it, you know I'll be ready to help in any way that I can.'

'That sounds reasonable. And thank you for looking out for me. You can consider yourself employed as my bodyguard.'

Chapter Twenty-Seven

Even though I knew that Leo was lurking in the spot by the bins only metres away, I still felt incredibly exposed waiting for the man formerly known to me as Brian James by the stage door several hours later. The area was clearly not set up for admiring fans wanting to get a selfie or an autograph with a star. This was a purely functional exit and, judging by the detritus on the ground, it was probably also the place where theatre staff came to take their smoking breaks. I was conscious of the CCTV camera focused on me, but I pretended to be absorbed in checking my phone, hoping I looked innocuous enough, while I wondered how long it would take Blake Jenkins to emerge.

Leo and I had been two of a mere handful of audience members sitting through the matinee performance of *The Glass Menagerie*. Blake had played the role of the narrator and protagonist, Tom, who started the play by warning the audience that everything that followed might not be strictly true because it was based on his interpretation of events.

'Speaking his own truth, rather than the actual truth, sounds about right,' Leo had muttered under his breath disapprovingly, although he'd soon quietened down. I figured that, like me, he'd been so caught up by the story that he'd put his feelings about the duplicity of the leading actor to one side. When I'd last seen the play, I had particularly empathised with the character of Laura, a shy young woman who was trapped by her insecurities. I was afraid that, if I wasn't careful, I was still in danger of being too similar to her. But there was a big difference between us: although I definitely felt the fear about confronting Blake, and then about what might follow when I opened up to Leo, I was determined to act anyway. I wanted to take control of my own destiny.

'He's a powerful actor,' I'd said as the applause faded and the house lights came up.

'We always knew he was good. Maybe if he directed all his energy into acting rather than getting distracted by scamming, he'd get his big break.'

I thought about Leo's words as I checked my phone again. It had been twenty minutes since the show had ended, and the other members of the cast had left long ago. What could be taking Blake so long? I navigated to the SO Ox app, in case another message from Brian James had appeared. His latest one had made my skin crawl at the way he'd fluctuated between talking poetically about how he wanted to run his hands through my 'soft flowing locks' and bemoaning the cruelty of a world in which he couldn't afford to be there for the disaster victims. I was toying with sending Brian slash Blake a message asking for his bank details as a last-ditch backup plan, when a text from Leo buzzed onto the screen.

> LEO
>
> He's a no-show. Let's try another time.

Short and to the point, as always. I started tapping out a quick response.

> KAT
>
> I'll give it another five minutes.

However, before I could hit send, the heavy metal stage door opened with a clatter. I jumped and dropped my phone.

'Here, let me help you,' said Blake, reaching down and scooping up my phone before I could stop him. I thought I detected movement out of the corner of my eye from near the bins. I shuffled around to block Blake's view of that direction, and flapped my hand behind me in a back-off gesture which I hoped Leo would interpret correctly.

'Thank you,' I said as Blake handed my phone back. I quickly started recording while pretending to be checking it over for damage. 'No harm done, thankfully.'

'That's good,' said Blake.

Given how many hours – no, weeks – I'd wasted pining after and then worrying about this bloke, I was somewhat insulted that he appeared not to recognise me at all. Moira would probably say it was because he had balls of steel. I looked at him more closely, trying to spot a tell-tale sheen of nervous sweat on his upper lip or an anxious twitch of his fingers, but there was nothing.

'Can I help you with something?' asked Blake, his face the picture of detached politeness. In fact, he was already looking past me, no doubt thinking ahead to whatever he had planned for his break between shows.

'Actually, there is,' I said, adding what I hoped sounded like a flirtatious giggle for good measure. In none of the scenarios I'd played out in my head had Brian James slash Blake Jenkins looked at me this blankly without even the slightest glimmer of recognition, so I was having to improvise rapidly.

'I saw the show, and I thought you were amazing,' I gushed. 'You had me in tears.'

His expression brightened. 'Thank you. I really appreciate you taking the time to tell me. Would you like me to sign your programme?'

'I don't have one. But perhaps you could sign a napkin for me.' I forced myself to smile, even though I wanted to shout at him. The longer he continued this pretence, the more frustrated I was getting.

'Sure, do you have a pen?' he asked. I'd assumed he'd produce one of his own. A guy with the confidence to scam someone online would undoubtedly be the type to carry a Sharpie around with him on the presumption that he was big enough of a deal to be handing out autographs. He needed a wake-up call.

'I have to confess I don't have either a pen or more importantly a napkin.' I blinked, leaning into the character of a slightly ditzy seductress. 'But if you let me buy you a cup of coffee in the café around the corner, then I'm sure they'll be able to provide us with both.'

I was acting a part, but there was something pretty empowering about being so bold and just asking the guy out like this. If only I'd tapped into this side of my personality earlier to do the same with Leo.

Blake grinned broadly, his chest practically puffing up as I played to his ego. 'I can't refuse an offer like that. Let's go and get that coffee. What did you say your name was again?'

'I didn't. I'm Kat. Kat Fisher,' I said.

'Nice to meet you, Kat,' said Blake, still keeping up a front of polite ignorance. How long was he going to maintain this pretence?

'How are you enjoying Oxford?' I asked, trying to appear like I was making small talk as we walked towards the café.

'It's good to be back. I actually grew up here, then went away to drama school and travelled and toured for a while. I feel like I'm getting to know a new side of the city now I'm an adult here, with my own digs and everything.'

He held the door of the coffee shop open for me and I did a double-take, immediately clocking Leo already in there and sipping from a mug. How had he managed to get past without my spotting him?

He caught my gaze and sent the ghost of a wink in my direction, impossibly pleased with his subterfuge skills. I fought the urge to smile back.

'Why don't you grab us that table in the window while I fetch the coffees?' I suggested to Blake.

'Good idea,' he said. 'I'll have a venti iced macchiato with caramel syrup and an extra shot of espresso. Oh, and can you ask them for almond milk as well? I bloat when I have dairy.'

He ran his hand over his stomach, a self-conscious move rather than one intended to draw my attention to how flat it was, I thought.

'No problem,' I said. 'I'll do my best to remember the order.'

Blake laughed with genuine warmth, and I experienced a disconcerting flashback to those early voice notes he'd sent me. 'I know. It's massively pretentious, isn't it? But I've worked more than my fair share of barista shifts, and trust me, it's worth the faff to order it.'

'I'll give it a try too, then,' I said.

It took a while for the drinks to be made, during which time I maintained a subtle but careful eye on Blake. He seemed completely relaxed, checking his smart watch and staring out of the window, watching the world go by.

'Don't let your guard down. He's good at acting, remember?' whispered Leo as he brushed past me, apparently on his way to collect some more sugar for his drink.

'I'm not sure he's that good of an actor. And I thought you were sweet enough already,' I teased him out of the corner of my mouth.

'Very funny. Please be careful.'

Finally, the barista handed over the drinks, and I took them across to Blake.

'Two very fancy macchiatos, and a napkin and pen,' I said as I sat down opposite him. He reached out to do his signature straight away. I couldn't decide whether his slight hesitancy was due to having to sign on the rough surface of the napkin, or because he genuinely wasn't used to doing it.

'How long have we got? What time do you have to be back at the theatre?' I asked.

'Before the half. That's five to seven in normal speak. Everything in the theatre world runs five minutes ahead, don't ask me why.'

'Then there's no rush. We can take our time enjoying our drinks.'

'Cheers,' said Blake, clinking his cup against mine. 'You've made my day, by the way. It's not often I get asked for an autograph.' He gave a little half smile, almost as if he was shy making the admission.

The man was good, I'll give him that. In any other circumstances, I would have warmed to this self-deprecating air he was putting on. Despite myself, I was already starting to feel a little sorry for him.

Then I reminded myself of all the angst he'd put me through, how he'd manipulated me and preyed on my emotions. How he'd been so plausible and clever that the merest glimpse at one of his messages had had Gavin wanting to give him money; Gavin who had so little of his own to give. I needed to stand up to this man and stop him in his tracks before he caused any more damage.

'There's something important I need to talk to you about, Blake,' I said. 'Or should I call you Brian James?'

Chapter Twenty-Eight

I made the accusation at a slightly louder pitch than I'd normally use, aware that this question needed to come out clearly on the recording, and also out of concern that Leo might miss the key moment. As a consequence, it sounded more like I was a performer in a theatre delivering the cliff-hanger line just before the curtain came down for the interval.

Blake frowned in obvious confusion. 'Sorry, I think I misheard,' he said, although there was no way he couldn't have heard what I'd said.

'There's no point in pretending anymore, Brian. Why don't you come clean and admit what you've been up to?'

Blake Jenkins, also known as Brian James, shook his head, looking concerned. He'd obviously decided to play this scene like he was an innocent party who'd inadvertently come across a deranged woman.

'I think you've got me confused with somebody else. I'm Blake, not Brian,' he repeated, speaking slowly for good measure. 'Look, thanks for the drink and I'm glad you enjoyed the show and everything, but I should probably be going.'

'I'd prefer it if you stayed exactly where you are,' I said, letting the teensiest edge of a threat creep into my voice.

Somewhat to my surprise, Blake slash Brian sat back down on his seat and did exactly as he was told. I obviously had a greater air of authority than I realised.

'It's strange meeting you in person at last. You don't look anything like your profile pictures,' I said, tilting my head to one side and examining his face as if I was committing every single one of his features to memory.

He shifted uncomfortably in his seat.

'They may be a little old,' he admitted. 'I didn't realise we'd matched anywhere.'

'Ah, so you admit you're carrying out this scam on more than one app, are you?' I said, seizing on his mistake.

'Yeah, so I'm on a few dating apps. There's nothing wrong with that, right? Who isn't, these days? You've got to keep your options open. And I didn't know using old headshots counted as a scam. I apologise if you were disappointed. The life of a jobbing actor has obviously taken a bigger toll on my features than I realised.'

'There's using old pictures, and then there's using someone else's pictures altogether,' I said. 'You ripped off the photos of a genuine military hero to try and entrap me.'

'I did no such thing,' he said, so indignantly that I almost believed him.

'How do you explain this, then?' I brought the SO Ox

app up on my phone screen and found Brian James's profile. 'Look, here you are.'

I waved the phone in his face, hoping he didn't spot the little symbol in the corner of the screen which indicated that it was still recording this conversation.

'That guy looks nothing like me. And that isn't even my name,' he said, starting to laugh. 'I think we must be at cross-purposes here. You're mistaken.'

I took a deep intake of breath. I actually felt like slapping the man to get some sense out of him. How dare he sit there so blatantly denying all this and trying to make out that I was the one in the wrong? This was gaslighting at its very worst.

'That's the whole point. Of course, Brian James isn't your name. It's a pseudonym you use online when you're trying to lure unsuspecting women into giving you money by toying with their emotions and manipulating them into falling in love with you.'

Blake put on a very realistic expression of horror.

'That's a terrible thing to do.'

'Yes, it bloody well is. At least that's one thing we can agree on. So why did you do it to me?'

He shook his head. 'I'm really sorry that you seem to have fallen foul of this Brian James character but, hand on heart, I promise you he's not me. The pictures are of someone else completely.'

'I know that. And you're not going to convince me that easily. You stole someone else's pictures to help create distance between your online persona and your real life.'

'There are safety measures on SO Ox. You'd never be

able to get away with doing something like that,' he pushed back.

'And yet you did.'

'No, I really didn't. I admit I have a profile on SO Ox. Look, let me find it for you.'

I kept tight hold of my phone. There was no way I was going to let him stop the recording at this crucial moment.

He shrugged and got his own device out.

'Here, see. That's my handle, Actor Blake, and I've got my full name in the "about me" section.'

I wouldn't have recognised him from the headshot he'd used as his profile image. He was right: it *was* an old picture.

'Just because you're there in your own capacity, it doesn't mean that you're not also on there as Brian James,' I pointed out. 'You're not in the clear yet.'

'What happened to innocent until proven guilty?' he asked indignantly.

'That's a principle used in the court system. And I'm very happy to march down to the police station with you now and see what they have to say about it.'

It was a bluff, but he fell for it.

'Let's not do anything too hasty. What else makes you think that I've been pretending to be this geezer called Brian James?'

'Here's my proof,' I said, clicking on one of the voice notes that Brian had sent me. Thank goodness Leo had showed me a hack to make my phone play and record simultaneously.

'Hello, my gorgeous one. It's so good getting to know

you properly. I love hearing about all your interests and funny quirks. I'm trying not to get too carried away, but I think we're a match made in heaven.'

I cringed as the message played out, horrified all over again that I'd been gullible enough to fall for such a sickly-sweet playbook. But I felt even worse when Blake slash Brian started laughing.

'You actually have the cheek to laugh? After everything you've put me through?' I said. 'You are the lowest of the low, a disgusting, creepy manipulator who should be thoroughly ashamed of himself.'

My words seemed to have a sobering effect on him. He dipped his head as if in submission.

'I'm really sorry. I didn't mean to be rude. It's because I'm relieved. I was starting to believe what you were saying was the truth, and that I'd somehow been carrying out a scam without even knowing about it.'

'But it is the truth,' I retorted.

'Sorry, I'm not explaining myself very clearly here. As you know, I'm an actor.' Again, he did that self-conscious puffing up of his chest thing. 'I don't only appear on stage. In fact, I have a pretty broad portfolio.'

'I'm not trying to hire you for a job here,' I snapped.

'That's exactly the point. I was hired for a job. The founder of SO Ox, Dom Markham, is an old pal. We used to be at school together, before he got booted out, and we stayed in touch. Anyway, he approached me a few months ago asking if I'd record some voiceover adverts for the app. The idea was that they'd sound like messages left by a lover so people would get the idea of the calibre of date they'd meet on SO Ox. I do get a lot of voiceover work. My agent says I've got a very sexy voice.'

I took a deep breath while I tried to gather my thoughts.

'So, what you're saying is that the voice notes I received purporting to be from someone called Brian, were actually recorded by you for promotional reasons?'

'That's the nub of it,' said Blake cheerfully. 'I was wondering what had happened to them and why I hadn't heard them in use. Mind you, I wasn't that surprised. Dom's always been an old cheapskate. He barely paid me enough for doing them to cover a dinner out. He made a big deal of offering me six months of free membership for SO Ox as an extra bonus, but I'm not sure that's worth the angst.'

He leaned forward. 'I'm genuinely sorry. If I'd had any idea the recordings were going to be used like that, I would never have agreed to make them. I'm devastated you've been hurt in this way.'

And he did seem to be completely sincere. But there was still one thing that wasn't adding up.

'But what about the call? I once had a phone call with Brian James. The line wasn't good and so it only lasted less than a minute, but we definitely spoke in real time. How can you explain that?'

Blake frowned. 'I'd have remembered a phone call, especially with someone who's got as pretty a voice as yours.'

'Nice try, but you're not going to distract me with fake flattery. The advert excuse is plausible, I'll give you that, but you can't explain the phone call, can you?'

'AI,' said Blake suddenly.

'Pardon?'

'Artificial Intelligence. That's what Dom was doing his DPhil in before he dropped out of university. He must have taken my voice samples and used AI to create other sentences and conversations. Bloody hell, that's really scary. He could have impersonated me for all kinds of bad stuff.'

The outrage in his voice seemed genuine and, the more I considered his explanation, the more plausible it seemed. Who better to perpetrate a scam of this kind than the founder of the app himself? He certainly had the means and opportunity, and several people had independently told me that he wasn't doing well financially from the app, which would give him a motive.

'Apparently, he did. The character of Brian James was determined to get money out of me. Who knows how many other women he's been targeting on the app, using your voice? He's well placed to generate a proper money-spinner for himself.'

'It's terrible, absolutely terrible,' said Blake. 'Just think about the damage it could do to my career if this got out.'

I laughed. His self-centred response was actually the light relief that I needed from the intensity of the conversation.

Blake had the good grace to look ashamed of himself. 'Sorry, that was an awful thing to say. Of course, my first concern is about the poor victims of this dreadful scandal.'

In another life, I reckoned Blake would probably have made a very good politician with his ability to do a slick about-turn.

'Would you be willing to give a statement to the police about how he's used your recordings? It could be exactly the evidence we need to get them to open an official investigation. I imagine they'll be able to get a court order to investigate the rest of the app and look into Dom's financial status.'

To give Blake credit, his hesitation was only brief.

'I guess so. Dom can't be allowed to get away with this kind of behaviour any longer. The truth about SO Ox needs to get out into the public domain before he causes more hurt.' But then the doubt started to creep back into his voice. 'If that is indeed what has happened. Are you sure there can't be another explanation? Dom might have had a wild streak when we were kids, but he's always been a decent sort, very bright, that kind of thing. It seems a bit much to think that he'd need to turn to fraud like this.'

'It's surprising what people will do for money,' said Leo, coming over to join us. 'Especially when they're desperate. It's pretty clear that he's abused your friendship to get those recordings and use them to take advantage of people. Hi, I'm Leo Taylor, by the way.'

He held his hand out to Blake.

'Nice to meet you,' said Blake, a confused look on his face as he tried to work out who Leo was and what he was doing here. 'Are you Kat's friend? Boyfriend, perhaps?'

'Friend,' said Leo, a little too quickly for my liking. 'I'm a detective and I've been helping her get to the bottom of this scam.'

Blake sat up straighter. 'Right, it's obviously very serious, then.'

I glowered at him, although he seemed completely impervious to my irritation. I'd played his voice recordings and explained everything to him, yet he still couldn't quite believe me. Then, the minute a man came along and told him it was true, he was falling over himself to accept it? Unbelievable.

Leo caught my gaze and I could tell he knew exactly what I was thinking because he did the subtlest of eye rolls to show that he echoed my thoughts.

'Let's head down to the police station now, then,' I said.

Blake took a noisy slurp of his drink. 'Would you mind if we went on another occasion? I really prefer to get as much rest as possible on a two-show day.'

'But you told me you didn't need to be back at the theatre until thirty-five minutes before curtain-up,' I pointed out. 'And you didn't say you had to rest when I invited you here for coffee. Maybe the real reason you don't want to go to the police is that you knew all along what Dom was up to?'

He frowned. 'I promise you I didn't. I guess I'm running out of excuses. Sorry, I know I'm not being very helpful, but there was this phrase that Dom always used when we were at boarding school together – snitches get stitches. It leaves one with a rather nasty taste in one's mouth.'

Leo squeezed his shoulder, half in comfort, half as a gesture to urge Blake to pull himself together. 'That's what the macchiato is for. Good thing Kat got it in a cup-to-go for you. Look, don't worry that you're "snitching". It's only a phrase, mate. From what we've seen of Dom's MO, he prefers not to get his hands dirty. And if he's not done anything wrong, then he won't have anything to worry about, will he?'

I could see that Blake was still trying to come up with a reason not to get involved, but between Leo's hearty encouragement and my pleading expression, he was left with little choice.

We walked across town together to the police station on St Aldate's, Blake spending the whole journey looking around nervously as if he half expected Dom to leap out and try to stop him. To be honest, I felt pretty jumpy myself and wouldn't have been surprised if the SO Ox founder had pulled a stunt like that. I thought back to the two occasions I'd met him face to face, first at the Single Mingle and then at the obstacle course event. He'd seemed so ordinary and unassuming, acting like I was just another app member, even though we'd been exchanging messages for weeks. Or maybe even the written stuff had been generated by AI too. That could explain why he'd never used my name. He'd probably created a programme which mined all the great romantic works for their best lines. Brian James was even more of a fictional creation than I'd imagined.

As we got to the entrance to the police station, Leo pulled me to one side.

'How do you want to handle this?'

'I assumed we'd go to the front desk and tell them what's happened. That's what I did when I found a lost credit card in the street and handed it in there.'

'You're a thoroughly good person, you know that, right?' Leo smiled. 'But reporting someone for fraud is a little different from handing in a lost credit card. What I was trying to ask is, do you want me to call in some favours? I know you're perfectly capable of handling this for yourself and don't need me putting my size tens where they're not wanted.'

'You and your clompy shoes,' I said. 'As long as they're not on the furniture in the library, I'm pretty happy for you to put them wherever you like. You're right, I can deal with this, but I would appreciate your support. If you're happy to pull some strings to get things moving faster, I'd be a fool to say no.'

'Let me call Sid and see if he's on duty. He may not be in CID, but he keeps his ears open. A lot of my detective colleagues have moved on, otherwise I'd approach them directly, but Sid will know who's got the lightest workload at the moment, and who will deal with this the most sensitively and efficiently.'

Thankfully, although Sid wasn't on duty, he was happy to take Leo's call, and before we knew it, we were being hustled into an interview room where a friendly detective constable – 'Call me Laurie' – listened to my story and took copious notes.

'Thank you for giving a statement, Ms Fisher,' he said at the end of the interview. 'Leave it with me and I'll be in touch. Off the record, it looks like you've given us enough probable cause to bring him in for questioning, but we'll get a warrant and do some more digging around his electronic footprint first, so we're armed with as much information as possible. Don't want him to start wiping computer records, do we?'

'Absolutely not,' I said.

'Try not to worry,' said Laurie. 'I'm determined to get to the bottom of this, believe me. There are too many con artists like Dom out there. I shall have great pleasure in making sure he's taken off the streets. I'll also be your liaison officer, keeping you up to date with the status of the investigation. Any questions, here's a card with my contact details on, just drop me a message.'

As he escorted us out of the police station, he turned to Leo.

'You were here the other day with Jill Gladstone, weren't you? I thought I recognised you.'

Leo frowned, his body tensing. I instantly recognised him going into protective mode.

'Will you send her my best wishes?' continued Laurie, apparently unaware of Leo's discomfort. 'I'm really glad that she's doing so well, from what I hear. She must be so grateful having you on her side.'

Leo cleared his throat. 'I'll let Jill know you were asking after her,' he said gruffly.

'Goodness, that was quite the experience,' said Blake as we emerged onto the street. He was bouncing with energy, his earlier good mood completely restored. I suspected, under the right circumstances, he probably had what Doris would describe as golden retriever energy. 'I really must make some notes for myself, so I don't forget it. What incredible background research should I ever be lucky enough to get a role in a crime drama. I must suggest it to my agent. I think I'd make an excellent detective.'

'Undoubtedly,' I agreed, more because I felt the need to thank him in some way for helping unlock the mystery of Brian James, rather than because I had a strong opinion of his acting talents.

However, he looked thrilled by my apparent endorsement.

'Thanks, Kat. I really appreciate it. Look, I know we met because of a weird situation, but do you fancy going on a date with me? I owe you a coffee, after all, and I'd love to get to know you better.'

I was very conscious of Leo standing next to me. He was affecting disinterest, but I could tell he was listening to the conversation, although what his thoughts were on Blake's unexpected question was anybody's guess. What I really wanted to do was to say no to Blake, and turn to Leo and ask him out instead. But I'd just heard him promise to convey the detective's best wishes to Jill and I'd seen the way his expression had softened when he'd said her name. I needed to find out where I stood, but first I needed to turn Blake down.

'Blake, I...' I started to say.

Leo cleared his throat. I spun to look at him and was shocked by the mask-like expression he now wore.

'I'll leave you two to make plans and compare coffee orders. See you around.'

And then he turned on his heel and strode off down the street, quickly disappearing into the crowds.

'He's a busy man, obviously much in demand,' said Blake.

'Yes, he is.' I was far too aware of that fact.

'So, how about it? A proper date, this time?'

'Thanks for the invitation, that's really kind of you. But I'm afraid my feelings are engaged elsewhere.'

Blake smiled and shrugged. 'I wondered if that was the case. Ah well, I had to ask. Perhaps you'll let me know how you get on,' he added.

'Sure, let me have your number and I'll drop you a text when the detective gets back to me. I would DM you on SO Ox, but I'm not sure that's going to be around for much longer.'

Blake laughed. 'I think you might be right. Actually, I was hoping you'd let me know how it goes with your friend Leo. I'm an old romantic at heart. I can see a love story in the making.'

'That obvious, is it?' I said, aware I was probably blushing.

'He has it bad for you,' said Blake, nodding after Leo's retreating form.

I sighed. 'Actually, sadly it's the other way round. I have it bad for him, and he … well, I really can't tell.'

Blake laughed again. 'Oh dear, I'll leave you to work that one out for yourself, then. But if you don't ask, you don't get. Or in my case, you do ask, and you still don't get. The difference is at least you know you've asked.'

'Thanks. I've been coming to that conclusion myself. And I really appreciate you sticking your neck out to make the statement about Dom.'

He brushed away my gratitude. 'No problemo. I'll have quite the tale to tell my fellow cast members when I get back to the theatre. I bet they've spent their break doing boring stuff like the crossword and catching up on sleep. See you around.'

'See you.'

I watched Blake walk down the street in the same direction that Leo had gone. Then I turned the other way and wandered across town towards the canal. I needed to plot out my next move.

Chapter Twenty-Nine

I took a deep breath and savoured the vanilla-sweet smell of ageing paper. I always thought better surrounded by books, and the newly opened Oxford Bookship, which was moored by Isis Lock, seemed the perfect place to consider my next course of action. The canal boat's main cabin was crammed to the brim with an eclectic mix of new and second-hand volumes, and I instantly felt calmer standing in the embrace of so many words of wisdom and comfort.

'Are you looking for something in particular?' The friendly proprietor called through the doors from the deck where she was sitting in the early evening sunshine with an extremely large and very hairy dog.

'Just browsing,' I said.

'Sorry to disturb. It's my first week of doing this, and I still haven't worked out whether it's best to leave the browsers well alone or try to point them in the direction of something interesting. And now I'm disturbing you still further. You should complain to the manager.' She looked about her then pointed at her chest. 'Which would be me, Molly.'

I laughed. 'It's nice to meet you, Molly. Your bookshop is beautiful.'

She smiled proudly. 'Thank you. I love her, but then again, I'm biased. I was hoping the novelty factor of a bookshop on a boat might attract a few more sales, but it's early days.' Then she put her hand over her mouth. 'Sorry, that sounded like I was trying to guilt-trip you into buying something, which was really not my intention. Ignore me, I promise to shut up now.'

I took pity on her. 'Perhaps you could recommend something, after all.'

She jumped up eagerly, and hurried down to join me in the cabin, the dog following her closely.

'Don't worry, Hilda's very friendly. Now, what are you in the mood for?'

I scratched Hilda's wiry coat, grinning at the grunt of appreciation I got in return.

'I'm not sure. That's not very helpful, I know.' I paused, then decided there wasn't any harm in asking. 'Actually, what I'm looking for is something to help me feel confident ahead of an important conversation.'

Leo had once said to me, 'Romeo and Juliet could have solved all their issues by just having a good chat.' I knew that was what I needed to do. The prospect of laying my feelings bare and exposing myself in that way still felt utterly terrifying. But I was resolved to find the courage to do it.

Molly frowned thoughtfully. 'A challenge. I like it.'

She bustled along the shelves, happily humming to herself for a few minutes while I continued to enjoy some dog therapy courtesy of Hilda.

I was fully expecting Molly to recommend a self-help book, so I was surprised when she turned round and presented me with a paperback of *Gaudy Night*.

'It may seem a random selection,' she said, 'but I think the leading lady, Harriet Vane, is a great example of a strong woman who knows her own mind.'

Molly had unwittingly made the perfect choice for me. After all, Harriet Vane's example had inspired me to embark on my investigation and been the catalyst for the start of my partnership with Leo. I held the book close to me and felt my determination grow.

'Thank you, this is just what I needed. I'll take it.'

The next morning, I was tired but full of nervous anticipation, having spent most of the night lying awake rehearsing what I would say to Leo when I saw him in the library. What I hadn't expected was for him not to show up.

'You could call him,' suggested Moira, when she caught me lingering in the business section for the third time in as many hours.

'I could,' I said, straightening the chairs as if the reason Leo was a no-show was because the library furniture was askew.

'But?' prompted Moira.

'But I've only just recovered from a relationship which was conducted entirely remotely, and yes, I know it wasn't even a real relationship, but the principle still stands. I want to be face-to-face with Leo when I talk to him. Some things need to be said in person, rather than over the phone or by text.'

Moira squeezed my arm. 'That's fair enough. But there's nothing stopping you from arranging to meet up with him, rather than waiting and hoping for him to pop back in. Message and ask him to come to the library. You'll feel much better once you've taken some positive action. Besides, your fan club here feels invested in the outcome; you've got to give us something. We're all on tenterhooks.' She winked at me.

I knew Moira was teasing me, and that she'd do her best to keep Doris and the gang from gawping too openly, but her words came rushing back to me when Leo finally arrived at the library on Friday morning. By this stage, I'd about convinced myself that his conspicuous absence over the last few days had been because he was making the most of being able to be with Jill, now that he no longer had to spend all of his free time running around with me trying to solve the Brian mystery. I'd managed to instigate a brief text message exchange under the pretext of arranging when I could help him with his business plan and formally introduce him to Doris for the mentorship I'd promised him, but his answers had been frustratingly brief, and now I was worried that I'd given the wrong impression that this was the only reason I was still in touch with him.

That fear crystallised when he approached the front desk.

'How are you?' I said, my heart thumping in my chest. 'You've been missed around here. *I've* missed you.'

'I thought you might be enjoying some peace and quiet without me cluttering up the business section.'

'I'd kind of got used to having you around. Especially since you stopped putting your feet up on the furniture.'

I smiled at him but, although he smiled back, his face didn't light up as much as it usually did.

'I won't keep you long,' he said.

'Oh.' What I wanted to say was that he could keep me as long as he wanted, but there was already a queue starting to form behind him, and Moira and my other colleagues were nowhere to be seen, so I couldn't linger with him without starting a library revolt. If it had been Doris or Gavin in the queue, it would have been a different story, but I recognised some of the more truculent retired academics from the seniors' social media club and knew I would delay serving them at my peril.

Sure enough, one of them cleared his throat and looked pointedly at the large clock on the wall, tapping his foot impatiently on the ground, in case I hadn't got the message.

'If you can wait half an hour, it'll be my lunch break and we can take a look at that business plan we were discussing earlier,' I said to Leo, trying to sound professional in front of my increasingly tetchy audience, while attempting to convey through glances that there was much more that I wanted to talk to him about. But he seemed oblivious to my signals.

'Maybe some other time,' he said, in a tone which I feared implied never. My heart twisted painfully.

'Sure, no problem.' I forced a note of jollity into my voice. 'How can I help you now?'

'I need to return some books.'

'Okay, let me check them back in for you.'

I scanned the bar codes, taking my time over the transaction, and praying for Moira to return so she could take over and I could drag Leo off for a private word. But, as I got to the final volume, there was still no sign of the cavalry.

The computer bleeped a warning.

'Aren't you going to make him pay his fine?' asked the grumpy academic as I quickly silenced the alert.

'Sorry, I've been meaning to bring it back for a while now, but I got caught up with other stuff,' said Leo. 'Here, this should cover it.'

He slid a folded five-pound note across the counter.

'Keep the change,' he added, before turning on his heel and marching out of the library so fast, it was as if the fire alarm had sounded.

'But it's far too much,' I tried to call after him, but the heavy double doors had already swung shut behind him.

I opened the till and, as I unfolded the fiver to put it into the drawer, a note of a different kind fell out and onto the floor. I scooped it up and stuffed it into my pocket.

I dealt with the queries from the queue on automatic pilot, my mind on what the note might say. As soon as Moira reappeared, I darted into the depths of the library, taking refuge in the romance section to read Leo's message in peace, hoping that the love in the books surrounding me would find its way into the real world. However, the note seemed to be focused on the investigation, written in a typical Leo style: short and to the point.

Dear Kat,

Forgive the somewhat old-fashioned method of communication, but I thought SO Ox might have put you off the virtual kind. It certainly has me. Sid's tipped me off that the police are planning to pick Dom up at the next event – the Date My Mate do at the Botanic Garden tomorrow. How about one final outing together undercover? I'm guessing you'll say yes, so see you there. Time to end this charade once and for all.

Take care,
Leo xx

It wasn't quite the Captain Wentworth-style declaration I'd been dreaming about, and the mention of 'one final outing together' concerned me. I tried to take some hope from his affectionate sign off but, all in all, the note made me doubtful how Leo would react when I told him how I felt. But there was only one way to find out.

Chapter Thirty

Of course, the first person I encountered as I arrived at the Botanic Garden the next day was Blake, who hugged me like we were old friends.

'Kat, darling, it's so good to see you. You're looking gorgeous,' he said, kissing my cheek for good measure. I laughed at his theatrical greeting.

'I thought you'd decided you'd had enough of the apps for the time being,' I said.

He shrugged. 'I'd already booked this before events overtook us, and what can I say? The ever-optimistic romantic in me hoped that perhaps I might meet someone special here before the app gets shut down for good.'

'Shh, not so loud,' I said, squeezing his arm in warning and looking around quickly to see if anyone might have overheard. I leaned in closer and added in a low voice, 'That might happen sooner than you think.'

'Kat, Blake, good to see you both,' said Leo, suddenly

appearing from behind an archway where he'd apparently been lurking.

I moved towards him, and experienced a moment of uncertainty when he neatly side-stepped so I couldn't give him the hug I'd been planning to. I knew he'd said we'd be undercover again, but everyone else around us was being affectionate in their greetings, even though most of them had probably never met before.

'We need to check in as pairs,' said Leo. 'Are you guys...?' He gestured between me and Blake.

'Oh no, absolutely not,' I said firmly.

Blake pouted in mock indignation. 'I would be insulted by your eagerness to be rid of me, if I didn't know my place. Besides, I'd hate to get in the way of true love. Don't worry about me. I've managed to rope one of my colleagues from the theatre into joining me. She's notoriously late, but I'm sure she'll be along in a minute. Have fun, you two.'

I felt my face grow hot, but thankfully Leo didn't seem to have picked up on Blake's mention of 'true love'. It would be extremely disappointing to have worked myself up to this point only for Blake to steal my thunder.

'I guess we'd better...' I said, gesturing at the queue.

'Sure,' said Leo. Although he would have looked relaxed to those around us, I could tell that he was on edge from the slight tension in his shoulders and the way he was watching the crowd so intently.

'Don't worry, he won't miss his own event,' I said quietly, answering his unspoken question about why there was no sign of Dom yet.

'It would be disappointing if your new friend had

tipped him off,' muttered Leo. 'The reason the police are having to arrest him here is that none of his registered addresses seem to be current. It wouldn't take much for him to disappear off the face of the planet, and then we'd be back to square one.'

'Blake hasn't said anything, I'm sure of it,' I said.

Right on cue, Dom himself appeared at the entrance to the garden. He climbed onto a stool and addressed the assembled crowd through a megaphone.

'Welcome one, welcome all to Date My Mate by SO Ox. Do you have a hot friend who simply can't find the right girl or guy? Now's your chance to help them become lucky in love. Once you've registered in pairs here at the gate, follow the signs to the Literary Garden, and then get mingling. This is your chance to tell the world why your friend is the most eligible one here. Are you ready to pimp your pal and find them their perfect partner?'

The hubbub grew louder as a few people indignantly realised the nature of the event they'd been dragged along to.

'See, I told you he'd keep quiet,' I said to Leo. 'Why would Dom turn up if he had the slightest inkling he was about to be taken in for questioning?'

'Hmm, I'll reserve judgement until we get past the check-in desk,' he responded. 'The man's arrogant enough to do anything, if you ask me.'

But Dom didn't even give us a second glance as we ticked our names off on the list, after waiting until we were at the end of the queue so that we could keep an eye on him. I had no idea if Leo knew when the police would descend, but I was glad we were taking no chances on him getting away.

Leo and I followed Dom to the Literary Garden and positioned ourselves in a shady spot where we could keep a close eye on him. He was playing the role of benevolent host, darting between pairs and directing as many people as possible towards a small stand selling drinks and cakes. But I noticed he kept glancing over in our direction.

'We need to start playing along, otherwise he'll get suspicious,' said Leo.

'I was hoping it wouldn't come to that,' I said.

Leo frowned. 'Sorry, I know I'm a hard sell. Unemployed, history of depression, and let's not forget my giraffe-like walking tendencies.'

I think it was this flash of insecurity that gave me the courage to open my mouth and say what I should probably have said long before this moment.

'You're not a hard sell at all, quite the opposite in fact. You're one of the kindest, funniest, and sexiest people I've ever been lucky enough to meet. You've supported me while I learnt to have confidence in myself, and you've helped me to trust again. I have a very selfish reason why I don't want to play along with the event and talk other people into dating you. And that's because I really want to date you myself. I don't know if that's something you'd be up for, what with Jill and so on, but I'm falling for you and I needed to let you know.'

I'd thought I'd feel nervous, but as the words spilled out, I realised I'd never felt so sure of what I was saying. Previous relationships and the experience of being targeted by a scammer had made me fearful of ever taking a risk again. But, although I had no guarantees that Leo was even in a position to reciprocate my feelings, I knew that his reaction to my statement would be sensitively delivered, and that I would never experience that kind of unsettling vulnerability at his hands.

'Kat, I—' But whatever it was that Leo had been about to say, I didn't get the chance to find out, because suddenly his voice changed. 'Watch out,' he yelled.

I whipped round, just in time to see Dom about to run past me towards the exit, my police liaison Laurie and a uniformed officer in hot pursuit. I couldn't let him get away. Without even thinking about it, I stuck my foot out, tripping Dom over and sending him flying. He landed face first in a rose bed which, judging by his groans of disgust, had recently had a layer of manure dug into the soil.

The uniformed officer quickly slapped a pair of cuffs on him, while Laurie read him his rights.

Once the procedural bit had been completed, the uniformed officer helped Dom to his feet.

'Nice one, you two,' said Laurie, coming over to us. 'Thanks for setting us onto this guy. We've been doing some digging over the last few days, and let's just say there are several fraudulent matters beyond his SO Ox activities that we believe he might be able to shed some light on. I'll keep you posted about any charging decisions, but if you ask me, we've got him bang to rights. You should re-join the force, Leo, and if you ever fancy a career in investigation, Kat, I'm sure you'd do well too. We'd never have got to this point if it hadn't been for your work.'

A dejected Dom was escorted to a waiting police car, and the chatter in the garden grew louder again as the Date My Mate attendees started eagerly discussing the unexpected turn of events. Without saying anything, Leo and I moved away from the crowd and followed a winding trail to a more peaceful part of the gardens.

'What do you think will happen now?' I kept my question deliberately open to interpretation. I'd said how I felt. How Leo chose to respond was up to him.

'Hopefully, Dom will go to prison and won't be allowed near a computer for a very long time,' said Leo lightly. Then his voice took on a more serious tone. 'Jill's an old colleague, by the way. I've been friends with her and her wife for years, but there's nothing more to it than that. She's still finding things tough after the trial, but she's getting there. In fact, she's finally managed to get some counselling appointments and I've been providing moral support, trying to help out with practical stuff in the garden and around the house so they don't have to worry about it.'

'I'm glad,' I said, my heart singing. 'Jill's lucky to have someone like you at her side through it all.'

'I'm lucky to be her friend,' he said simply. 'As to the other thing you said... Did you really mean it?'

'What, that I'd like to date you? Yes, I did mean it. I'm not sure how you feel about me, but you've been a perfect investigative partner, and I'd love it if our partnership could develop from the professional to the personal. It seems appropriate that I'm saying this in the Literary Garden, because I was hoping to start a new chapter – with you.'

'You're not sure how I feel about you?' He took hold of

my hands and looked at me so intensely I was glad he was holding me upright. 'Let me be quite clear, because I've obviously still not completely lost the old copper's curse of concealing my feelings. I've been falling for you since the first moment you marched up to me in the library and told me off for putting my boots on the chair. Your determination to do the right thing captivated me from the start, and nothing would make me happier than to date you and see our partnership growing into something infinitely more precious.'

I think he might have happily carried on talking now that the floodgates had opened, but as the writing technique books in the library recommended, I decided now was the time to show rather than tell him how I felt. I reached up, ran my fingers through his hair, and pulled him close to me. This time our kiss was for real, and I was going to savour every moment of it.

Epilogue

1st May, the following year

Leo and I were already awake before the alarm went off, but being otherwise engaged, it took a good few minutes before we registered the noise.

'Maybe we should—'

'Are you sure—'

Both of us spoke at once, far too comfortable tangled up together beneath my duvet to want to move. I traced a line of kisses along Leo's neck and shivered with delight as he responded with an exploration of his own.

The phone buzzed again, this time to signal a text had landed.

'We should probably check that,' I said reluctantly.

Leo rolled over, taking me with him, then quickly read the message.

'Gavin's nearly in his surveillance position at the other side of the bridge.'

'We'd better get going then.'

We dressed in a hurry and left our sanctuary to join the stream of people emerging from their houses, marching purposefully down the street, mingling with those dressed in their party clothes and still clutching last night's empty bottles of wine. May morning in Oxford brought everyone out. There was little traffic on the road, and as we neared the Magdalen roundabout, I started to hear the hubbub of the crowd. Somebody had set up a stall selling hot chestnuts near one of the bike stands and their smoky smell filled the air, mixing with the pungent scent of more illicit substances that a few very chilled-out individuals had clearly been indulging in.

A team of Morris dancers was gathering, multicoloured strips of fabric streaming from their shoulders, the bells around their ankles chirruping as they finished off each other's blue stripey make-up and tried a few experimental leaps. I checked my phone. It was nearly six o'clock.

Since that Saturday just over a year ago when Dom Markham, the man formerly known to me as Scammer Brian, had been arrested, the SO Ox app had been taken down and its founder sent to prison for a catalogue of fraudulent activities. The success of our detective work had given Leo the boost he needed to establish his own investigations agency aimed at helping those who might not otherwise get justice. The bank had been most impressed with the business plan he'd compiled with Doris's help, and mine, and although it was still early days, the agency was going places. I was enjoying continuing my sleuthing exploits in a consulting position alongside my library work and had already started jotting down some notes on our adventures so far, thinking that there might be a novel or two in them. After all, the Oxford Community Library could never have too many books, and it would be nice to have a few of my own on the shelves.

'Where do we think this dodgy tour guide is going to be, then?' I asked.

'According to my sources, he'll be targeting tourists as they gather at the bottom of Magdalen College Tower for the singing.'

'We'd better blend in with the crowd,' I said. 'We can't have him clocking us before we're ready to take him down.'

'How do you suggest we do that?' said Leo, with a sparkle in his eye.

'I've got a few ideas,' I said, looping my arm around his waist.

At six o'clock, the bells in the churches and colleges around Oxford started their slightly out of sync chorus of chimes, and the choir at the top of Magdalen Tower began their song. The centuries old tradition celebrated the start of a new season and new beginnings.

I scanned the crowd, searching for our target.

'We'd better track him down today,' I said. 'It's going to be more of a commute from tomorrow once I've properly moved into our new home.'

Leo's friend had eventually decided that he wasn't going to return to the UK. This afternoon Leo and I were heading to the solicitor's office to sign the final paperwork making the chocolate box cottage in the Oxfordshire countryside ours. Well, ours and the bank's.

'No regrets?' asked Leo.

'None whatsoever,' I said. 'Although ask me again when you interrupt me mid-chapter.'

He laughed, and pulled me closer to him, dropping a kiss on my forehead.

'I would never dream of committing so heinous a crime.'

He really was a hero worthy of a book, but thankfully for me, there was nothing fictional about him.

Acknowledgments

Thank you so much for choosing *Read Between the Lines*, I really hope you enjoyed it! I have loved spending time among the dreaming spires of Oxford with Kat and Leo. Many of the places they visit are real (I would definitely recommend the delicious ice cream at G&D's for example) but I have taken a few liberties here and there. The Oxford Community Library is a product of my imagination, but it is inspired by the many libraries I have known and loved. As Kat points out, libraries are very special places, giving everyone free access to knowledge, entertainment, community and so much else. It's more important than ever that we support them. I am full of gratitude to the wonderful librarians who have cheered me on in my writing endeavours and continue to champion my books.

Speaking of bookish supporters, thank you also to Jennie Rothwell and the rest of the fab One More Chapter team. I feel very lucky to work with such a talented bunch. And a huge thanks also to my lovely agent Amanda Preston for your brilliant insight, enthusiasm and encouragement.

And finally, as always, thank you to my family for nurturing my love of reading in the first place and indulging my writing-induced daydreaming. I am also grateful to Humphrey and Sidney for taking me on plot walks and fact-checking all canine behaviour. You're both very good boys.

One typo. Two complete strangers. Ten thousand miles between them…

Amy and Cameron have never met. But when Amy receives an email meant for Cameron, their lives entwine in ways they could never have imagined.

Cameron lives a life of adventure as he navigates an expedition around Antarctica whilst Amy's life is firmly on solid ground in Edinburgh.

As their connection grows, Amy finds herself asking; is it possible to fall in love with someone you've never met?

Available in paperback, ebook and audio now!

What happens on holiday doesn't always stay on holiday....

When Lydia wakes up after a wild night out in Kefalonia with a tattoo saying 'Awesome Andreas', she's mortified. She doesn't remember meeting anyone called Andreas. And after all, she's an accountant with a five-year plan. She's definitely *not* a party girl. The sensible thing to do would be to research how to get the tattoo removed and move on. But she's had enough of being predictable.

Instead, Lydia decides to track down the mysterious Andreas, but the path to true love is never simple. Perhaps Lydia is looking in the wrong places, and the right man for her is just next door, if only she'd take a chance on him . . .

Available in paperback and ebook now!

HER FIXER UPPER
Emily Kerr

Unable to afford their own homes, two friends decide to buy a renovation house together as a project. What could possibly go wrong…?

Freya dreams of owning her own home.

Charlie is struggling to get a mortgage.

When the two old friends bump into each other on a night out, Charlie jokes that buying together would solve all their problems. He doesn't expect Freya to say yes, let alone yes to a less-than-perfect fixer upper.

Nobody said renovating their dream home would be easy, but will Charlie and Freya fall out of love with the house, or in love with each other…

Available in paperback and ebook now!

A laugh-out-loud, feel good romantic comedy to curl up in bed with!

Young lawyer Alexa Humphries's one true love is her precious duvet, yet she is torn from its comforting embrace every morning while the foxes are still scavenging the bins outside and doesn't get back until long after most normal people are already asleep. Worn down by the endless demands of her suspicious boss and her competitive, high-flying housemate and fellow lawyer, Zara, Alexa barely recognises herself anymore. This wasn't how life was supposed to be.

But today is different. Today, Alexa just cannot get out of bed to face the world. Everyone deserves a duvet day, don't they?

Available in paperback and ebook now!

ONE MORE CHAPTER

YOUR NUMBER ONE STOP FOR PAGETURNING BOOKS

The author and One More Chapter would like to thank everyone who contributed to the publication of this story...

Analytics
James Brackin
Abigail Fryer

Audio
Fionnuala Barrett
Ciara Briggs

Contracts
Laura Amos
Laura Evans

Design
Lucy Bennett
Fiona Greenway
Liane Payne
Dean Russell

Digital Sales
Laura Daley
Lydia Grainge
Hannah Lismore

eCommerce
Laura Carpenter
Madeline ODonovan
Charlotte Stevens
Christina Storey
Jo Surman
Rachel Ward

Editorial
Kara Daniel
CJ Harter
Charlotte Ledger
Federica Leonardis
Victoria Oundjian
Ajebowale Roberts
Jennie Rothwell
Sofia Salazar Studer
Helen Williams

Harper360
Jennifer Dee
Emily Gerbner
Ariana Juarez
Jean Marie Kelly
emma sullivan
Sophia Wilhelm

International Sales
Peter Borcsok
Ruth Burrow
Colleen Simpson
Ben Wright

Inventory
Sarah Callaghan
Kirsty Norman

Marketing & Publicity
Chloe Cummings
Grace Edwards
Emma Petfield

Operations
Melissa Okusanya
Hannah Stamp

Production
Denis Manson
Simon Moore
Francesca Tuzzeo

Rights
Helena Font Brillas
Ashton Mucha
Zoe Shine
Aisling Smyth
Lucy Vanderbilt

Trade Marketing
Ben Hurd
Eleanor Slater

The HarperCollins Distribution Team

The HarperCollins Finance & Royalties Team

The HarperCollins Legal Team

The HarperCollins Technology Team

UK Sales
Isabel Coburn
Jay Cochrane
Sabina Lewis
Holly Martin
Harriet Williams
Leah Woods

And every other essential link in the chain from delivery drivers to booksellers to librarians and beyond!

ONE MORE CHAPTER
YOUR NUMBER ONE STOP FOR PAGETURNING BOOKS

One More Chapter is an award-winning global division of HarperCollins.

Subscribe to our newsletter to get our latest eBook deals and stay up to date with all our new releases!

signup.harpercollins.co.uk/join/signup-omc

Meet the team at
www.onemorechapter.com

Follow us!
- @OneMoreChapter_
- @onemorechapterhc
- @onemorechapterhc
- @onemorechapterhc

Do you write unputdownable fiction?
We love to hear from new voices.
Find out how to submit your novel at
www.onemorechapter.com/submissions